Finding Home

Shelly Johnson—Choong

Copyright 2002 © by Shelly Johnson–Choong
All rights reserved

This is a work of fiction. All characters are fictional and any resemblance to persons living or dead is purely coincidental.

No part of this book may be reproduced in any form whatsoever, whether by graphic, visual, electronic, filming, microfilming, tape recording, or any other means, without the written permission of the author, except in the case of brief passages embodied in critical reviews and articles where the title, author and ISBN accompany such review or article.

Published and Distributed by:

Granite Publishing and Distribution, LLC
868 North 1430 West
Orem, Utah 84057
(801) 229-9023 • Toll Free (800) 574-5779
Fax (801) 229-1924

Cover Design by: Tammie Ingram
Cover Art by: Tammie Ingram
Page Layout and Design by: Myrna Varga • The Office Connection • Orem, Utah

ISBN: 1-930980-51-5

Acknowledgments

There are many people who have helped bring this book to fruition. A few individuals probably don't even know of their influence.

In 1991 when I began writing this novel, my mother, Sharon Johnson, was very optimistic. She was able to see through all blunders and appreciate the heart of the story I was trying to create. Her encouragement helped me to believe in myself, and I continued writing.

Years later, after this manuscript had been gathering dust for a while, I had a particularly poignant e-mail conversation with Kristen Randall, a favorite author of mine. We didn't talk about writing skills or our projects, but rather we discussed her teenage children. Kristen understood the privilege of being in the presence of their youth, vitality, and loveliness. After that exchange, I pulled this piece from its hiding place and began rewriting it. Kristen probably doesn't even recall the discussion, but I will never forget it.

Another author, Scott Parkin also deserves my gratitude. After I had rewritten the manuscript, he graciously took it in, and gave me an honest, thorough, and incredibly helpful critique that went far beyond these pages. He taught me a thing or two about writing.

I also need to thank two preliminary editors, Lavina Fielding Anderson, who looked at this piece when it was first born, and then again ten years later. Lavina edits with the skill of a fine surgeon. Her comments allow me to step back, and look at my characters with a more objective eye. Dan Hogan came on board later. With his sensitive approach to his craft, he has helped the characters who populate this novel reach their full potential.

I would also like to pay tribute to Larry, my husband. He is the most important part of my equation. His quiet support encourages me daily, and his confidence in me is so appreciated. I just don't love my husband … I like him a lot! He is my truest and best friend.

Dedication

For Christy ... because it was her idea
in the first place.

Chapter One

Tye walked into the quiet barn and smelled the sweet alfalfa. In all of the ten years that she had been riding, she never tired of the unique barn smell —warm horses, sawdust bedding and hay were familiar earthy odors that comforted Tye, even on this cold January morning.

A soft nicker caught her attention. Passing her own horse's stall, she moved quickly to Jade. The young chestnut mare was pregnant with her first foal. Jade's head was hanging down, her front legs splayed. When had her labor begun? How long had she been straining? She looked tired and feeble.

Hurrying down the aisle, Tye rang the vet. It was Saturday, so his answering service took the call and said they would page him immediately. Tye felt a stab of anxiety. "Tell him to hurry," she reiterated. "I don't know how long she's been working at this."

Walking back to Jade's stall, Tye glanced at her own horse, Trapper. His ears pricked forward as he watched with interest.

Once inside Jade's stall, Tye ran her hand over the mare's body. She could feel the muscles ripple as another contraction seized her fatigued body. Jade seemed to grimace. She shook her head as if to throw off some of this unfamiliar pain.

A couple of minutes later, Tye heard footsteps down the cement aisle way. She breathed a sigh of relief. "Oh, Dr. Robin—," she started, but it wasn't the vet. Instead, Kyle Jensen stood outside the stall. His face was lined with concern. "How is she?" he asked.

Usually Tye had Saturday mornings at the barn to herself, but she didn't bother to ask why Kyle was here. "She's not good," Tye replied quietly. She heard the tension in her own voice. "I phoned the vet. His answering service said they would page him."

"How long have you been here?"

"Fifteen minutes at the most."

Jade began to sway.

Tye jerked the lead rope that was attached to the halter. "C'mon girl. No going down," she said in a loud voice to keep the horse's attention.

Kyle opened the stall door, and Tye led the exhausted mare into the arena. "I'll get a lunge whip," Kyle said.

Tye could hear him hurrying to the tack room as she led the mare at a walk. Jade desperately wanted to stop, but Tye knew if she went down and tried to roll to ease her pain, she could easily twist her gut or in her pregnant state, rip the placenta or her intestines. Jade needed to stay on her feet. Within seconds, Kyle returned with the whip and stayed behind the pair. He wouldn't use it unless the mare refused to be coaxed into a walk, and even then it would just be with a quiet flick on the hindquarters to keep her moving. Jade seemed to understand the need to walk though, and continued to plod beside Tye.

Tye appreciated Kyle's quiet demeanor. He didn't get overly excited, which helped keep Jade calm. She also appreciated the way he allowed her to take the lead rope and work with Jade. He was a senior and one of the most experienced riders on the competition team. Tye was only a sophomore and still had eighteen months before she would be in Kyle's position. He could have easily taken command of the situation. Instead he seemed to realize that Tye had everything under control.

Tye continued to walk the mare. Kyle kept pace several paces behind.

"What are you doing here so early?" Tye asked, thinking that quiet tones of conversation might ease Jade's anxiety.

"My horse cut himself yesterday. We were crossing the creek when he over-stepped and scraped the skin off of his left foreleg. I'm just here to clean it out and make sure he doesn't get too stiff. How about you?"

"I always ride on Saturday mornings. It gives me and Trapper an opportunity to be together without worrying about the rigors of practicing our dressage or show-jumping." Pushing her honey blonde hair out of her eyes, Tye changed the subject, "I hope Ben isn't lame."

"He'll probably be a little stiff," Kyle said. "It's nothing serious though." He continued, "Maybe I could come with you on your morning walk sometime, if that's okay. Ben shouldn't be down for more than a few days. A quiet workout would be good for him by next Saturday."

"Trapper and I would like that," Tye said gently in spite of her racing heart. Kyle was the best rider on the competition team. He was the captain. She had always admired him. He stood close to six feet with black curly hair and deep brown eyes. He was athletic and agile due to many years in the saddle.

The conversation died as footsteps were heard in the aisle. Tye threw Kyle an anxious look.

"I'll get him," Kyle said

Kyle handed Tye the whip and hurriedly left the arena. Tye could hear the words being exchanged, but she didn't concentrate on the conversation until she heard the arena gate swing open. She looked to see Kyle standing beside Dr. Robinson. He was a lean, middle-aged man with a weathered look.

"How's our patient?" he asked softly as he approached Jade and Tye.

"She's exhausted and wants to go down."

"I'm glad you kept walking her. Let's get her back in her stall."

Tye gave Jade a reassuring pat as she led her to her stall.

Dr. Robinson began giving quiet orders. "Kyle, could you please bring a wheelbarrow full of shavings. She's going to need fresh bedding after the birth. Tye, I'd appreciate it if you would hold her head while I feel inside of her so I can determine the problem."

Tye cradled Jade's head and began crooning softly. She stroked her warm neck and couldn't help but see the fear in the mare's trusting brown eyes. *Poor thing*, Tye thought. *She doesn't know what's happening.*

Dr. Robinson hurriedly put on a long latex glove that ran to his shoulder. Then he inserted his hand and arm into the horse. Jade gave a little start, but Tye had been expecting that and held the mare still. "You're going to be all right," she whispered. Jade settled down.

"I think I know what's troubling our girl," Dr. Robinson said. "Her foal has one leg bent underneath its own sternum. Both legs should be forward. I just need to bring that leg and hoof forward …" He spoke as he worked inside the mare.

Kyle returned with the wheelbarrow of fresh shavings. He waited outside the stall.

Tye closed her eyes for a brief moment. It was hard to believe that she was actually assisting the vet as he worked with Jade. Ever since she was a child she had loved working with horses, but she had never planned on helping a mare with a birth. It was scary and thrilling at the same time. She looked at Kyle. He gave her a reassuring smile. Warmth began to replace the earlier anxiety. Anxiety trickled from Tye and was replaced with warmth for her older teammate.

"It looks like we have it," Dr. Robinson said.

Jade seemed to understand that things had improved. Even though she was fatigued, she worked with the contractions that gripped her body and within a few minutes the foal's hooves appeared.

Dr. Robinson snapped off the glove. "Kyle, we could use some fresh straw. Jade is going to need some help cleaning this little one."

Within a few minutes, Kyle came back with a bale of straw. He cut the twine and handed some to Tye and the doctor before taking some for himself and entering the stall.

The three stood, watching as Jade's labor progressed. Soon, the long legs of the new foal were beginning to show. Tye's anxiety was replaced with excitement. She had never witnessed the birth of a foal. Most mares gave birth in the middle of the night. It was a way they would protect their foal in the wild. She was witnessing a glorious and awe-inspiring moment—filled with the sweetness of new life.

Dr. Robinson patted Jade's hindquarters. "C'mon girl," he said quietly. "One more push and we'll have the head and shoulders. That'll be the worst of it."

As if listening, Jade gave a quiet heave and the foal came wriggling free.

Tye gave a little cry as she rushed to the newborn foal. Dr. Robinson began clearing the sack and birthing fluid away from the nostrils. The musky smell of the birth filled the stall. Jade turned around and nosed her way through the crowd in order to get a look at her new baby. She began licking her little one with enthusiasm—her large, warm tongue rubbing life into the little body as it struggled to get on all four legs.

With handfuls of straw, Kyle and Tye rubbed the foal where Jade missed. Within a few minutes, the baby was clean and on wobbly legs standing near Jade, searching for its first meal.

"We have a little filly," Dr. Robinson said.

Tye wanted to cry with excitement and her own exhaustion. Even though she had only been working with Jade for the last hour, she felt as if the morning's events had ebbed her strength. She was thoroughly worn out. Quietly, she leaned against the wall of Jade's cozy home and watched as mother and baby became acquainted.

Dr. Robinson wiped his hands on a towel. "What a way to start a morning!" he exclaimed. "I never get tired of bringing babies into the world." He turned to Tye and Kyle, who were leaning against the wall. "It's very possible that the two of you saved this mare and foal," he said. "We could have lost her if she had rolled. That would have been a real tragedy. She's a fine mare. I know Katie is thrilled with her. Has anyone thought to call Katie?"

Katie was the riding instructor at OSU and Jade's owner. Kyle and Tye looked at each other. Tye shook her head. "No."

"Well, I'll give her a call. She'll be pleased to hear that she has a new little filly. I'll wash up and find my own way out after I use the phone."

Tye sank down into the new shavings Kyle had dumped into the corner. Her legs felt as weak as the new filly's.

Dr. Robinson opened the stall door. Tye listened to his footsteps fade in the aisle. Settling back against the wall, she shivered, suddenly feeling a bit shaky and more than a little chilled.

Quietly, Kyle took off his jacket and wrapped it around Tye's shoulders. She pulled the warmth close as she pushed her arms through the sleeves. "Thanks."

"It's really something to witness, isn't it?"

"I've never seen a birth before."

"It never gets old. This is the third time I've been involved in the birth of a foal and the first birth where the mare needed help. Most of the time they're capable of handling it themselves."

"I'm sure glad we were here."

"I'm glad *you* were here. It might have been too late by the time I arrived," Kyle said.

Tye felt tears gathering. It was almost unbearable to think of losing this sweet, fine mare or this new precious filly.

Kyle stood and held out his hand to help Tye follow suit. "Are you still going to ride this morning?"

Tye shook her head. "No. I don't think I should. This completely exhausted me."

"Trapper won't mind the day off."

"I'll help you clean this stall though," Tye volunteered.

Kyle smiled. "I was hoping you would say that," he said as he handed Tye a shovel.

Between the two of them the work only took fifteen minutes. Jade completely ignored them now as she continued to tend her new baby.

After they were finished cleaning, Tye straightened up and took a deep breath. Standing next to Kyle, she allowed the warmth and satisfaction to surround her. She had helped to bring a new life into the world. She drew Kyle's coat around her. She didn't want to give up this moment. She didn't want to let the warmth escape into the cold January morning. She looked down at the fresh shavings and reluctantly began removing the jacket.

"Keep it on for a few more minutes. Your hands are still blue," Kyle rubbed Tye's fingers in his own roughened and warm palm. She gave in to his touch and could feel the heat coming back into her numb fingers and tired body. Whether it was just from Kyle's touch or from the excitement of the morning, Tye didn't know. She welcomed Kyle's warm fingers entwined with hers.

Tye looked at Kyle. Maybe he was feeling hesitant too. Maybe he didn't want to leave this moment behind either.

Finally Kyle said, "I bet you'd like to check on Trapper."

"He probably wonders what's going on."

Slowly, they let themselves out of Jade's stall. The mare looked up. Her eyes were soft and full of life and light.

"She looks like a different animal," Tye commented.

"The mothering instinct is strong," Kyle said. "Most animals can come from the brink of death to look after their little ones. She'll be fine."

Walking down the aisle, Tye stopped at Trapper's stall. Her heart warmed as she looked at him. He was the perfect picture of equine health with his shiny bay coat and soft brown eyes. At sixteen hands he was big and well-muscled from years of strenuous activity.

"He must be wondering what's causing all the fuss," Kyle said.

Tye let herself in, and immediately Trapper placed his nose on her sleeve. Tye laughed. "I smell different. He probably doesn't know what to make of it." She unzipped Kyle's jacket and pulled out an apple from the pocket of her own coat. "Or, he could be looking for this." She grinned as she fed Trapper his treat.

Giving him one last pat on the neck, she joined Kyle once again and walked to her truck. "Will you be staying long?" she asked.

"No. I'll only look after Ben's wound and then I'll go."

"If you see Katie tell her congratulations for me."

"I'll also tell her how you knew just what to do while we waited for the vet," Kyle replied.

"I wasn't alone. You helped."

"Yes, but you could've done it alone."

In spite of her fatigue, Tye wanted to linger in Kyle's company. This was the first opportunity to visit with Kyle since her arrival at Oregon State. Still, there was no reason to stay. Jade was out of danger, and Trapper was fine. She unzipped his jacket and handed it to him. "Thanks," she said. "I was cold."

"Adrenaline can do that. After the initial rush, it seems to sap the body of all its energy and heat. I sometimes feel that way after a competition." He grinned as he put on his coat.

"Are you looking forward to this competition season?"

Kyle furrowed his brow and slowly nodded. "This is the year that I can really prove myself and Ben. It's important that we have a successful year."

Tye opened the door and stepped into the cab of her truck. "You'll do well," she said. "You've been doing well since I've come on board."

Kyle smiled. "Thanks for the confident vote. I'll think about that when we have a rough day."

Tye wanted to laugh. Riding looked effortless when Kyle was working with Ben. But that didn't mean it didn't take work. Making it look effortless was part of the difficulty. With a final wave, she pulled out of the driveway. When she checked the rearview mirror, Kyle was gone.

Tye drove the familiar road with the warmth of the moment wrapped around her, feeling very much like Kyle's jacket. What did the future hold for Jade's little filly? Had Katie chosen a name? What would it be like to spend time with Kyle? Tye was surprised at how the thought distracted her from the horses. It popped into her head with no warning. Usually, nothing distracted Tye from riding —especially men. Tye didn't date much and she liked it that way. Men were confusing and Tye couldn't afford the complication. She had her hands full, just trying to keep her grades high, attend her church and institute meetings, and look after Trapper. Still, part of her longed for a man who would understand her desire to ride and her dedication to her sport and her horse.

Settling deeper into the driver's seat, Tye basked in the lingering glow of the experience. She loved horses. It pleased her to know that she had brought a new filly into the world. To share that moment with Kyle seemed right.

Tye brought the truck into third gear as she slowed for the vehicle ahead. What would Trapper think of the newest addition to the stable? Tye smiled. How she loved Trapper. Their years together had forged a strong partnership, a partnership that had led her to Oregon State University's equine program. The scholarship she received to ride for the equestrian team had clinched her decision to attend OSU.

The car in front of her turned and Tye moved the truck into fifth gear. What a morning! Jade had a new filly. Could it be possible that she had a new friend?

Chapter Two

Tye entered the apartment she shared with her best friend, Meggie. The warm aroma of fruit and cinnamon coming from the kitchen told Tye that Meggie was baking again. She threw her coat on the couch and grinned at her roommate from across the breakfast bar. "What are you making this time?"

"Blueberry muffins," Meggie said. "I saw this recipe in the paper and I had to try it. I ended up using the leftover berries that were in the freezer though, so I hope they turn out. Hey, aren't you home early?"

Tye grew serious. "I didn't ride."

"Why not?"

"Jade went into labor and delivered a little filly."

Meggie's eyes widened. "What wonderful news! A little girl. And you watched the whole thing? Tye, that's wonderful."

"I didn't just watch. I had to help. She was having a hard time when I got there." Tye told Meggie about her morning with Jade.

"My goodness. What an event! Who is Kyle Jensen?"

"He's a member of the competition team," Tye said. The

memory of her hand in his surfaced. "I've always admired his riding ability. I think he's the best rider on the team. I'm not the only one who thinks so, either. Katie groomed him to be the captain of the team from his junior year."

"You like him?"

Tye hesitated. "I would like to know him better."

"Why was he at the barn this morning? Is he Jade's owner?"

Tye shook her head. "His horse had hurt himself so he came in today to clean out the wound. It's nothing serious." Tye became thoughtful. "Because of all the activity around the barn, this is the first time I've ever had a private moment with him. It was nice."

Meggie grinned. "I can tell by the light in your eyes."

"He said he'd like to go riding with me when his horse is healed. Maybe he'll give me some pointers and let me in on his riding secret."

"I don't see any secret to riding," Meggie said. "It all looks like a lot of hard work and smelly sweat to me." She wrinkled her nose.

Tye grinned. "That's only about ninety-five percent of it. The other five percent is a secret." She grinned before changing the subject. "Meg, these muffins smell wonderful. They're so fragrant. It makes the apartment feel so cozy on this cold wintry day." She moved to the sink to wash her hands.

"Well, I hope you like them, because the recipe made twelve."

"Aren't you going to give any of them away to the starving young men in our ward?"

Meggie laughed, then grew melodramatic. "How I'd love to be loved for my looks instead of my cheesecake."

Tye giggled. "There's nothing the matter with your looks and you know it. Besides, cheesecake will get you farther than a pretty face any day of the week."

Meggie threw her a mischievous grin as the timer went off. "Get your butter knife ready," she said. "Hot muffins coming up."

Tye grabbed the butter, two knives and plates and set them on the table. Then she took the milk out of the refrigerator and poured two small glasses.

Soon Meggie was placing two piping hot muffins on her plate. Steam drifted to proclaim perfection. "Let them cool for a minute. You don't want to burn yourself."

Tye smiled. Meggie—always mothering.

Meggie settled at the table.

"I'm probably the luckiest girl on campus," Tye remarked. "Most folks hate to cook and they do it only because it's a necessity. You do it because you love it, and I get to sample all your creations."

Meggie flashed Tye a grin. "Don't you have any desire to cook?"

"No."

"But it's so—" she searched for the right word. "Satisfying. I love taking these ingredients that don't stand for much alone, but when put together they make something wonderful. It's kind of like painting. The color blue is beautiful, but I wouldn't want a whole canvas of it. But when it's mixed with yellows, reds, and purples, you've got a painting."

"You really should be taking some culinary classes."

Meggie sighed as she buttered her muffin. "No. As much as I love cooking, it can really only be a hobby. Accounting is a much more stable field. Besides, my folks are counting on me to take over the accounting firm when they retire. You know the history." Meggie sighed as she retold the tired story. "Grandpa Stewart started the firm fifty years ago, and he hired Grandpa Carter. My dad and mom both worked in the firm as teenagers and then went to school to become accountants. Then when my dad came home from his mission, they fell in love and got married. The firm isn't just a business. It's a part of the family. And you know my grandfather. He'd probably go into cardiac arrest if I decided to do something else. It's a family tradition. Stewarts are accountants."

"But you don't even like math."

"It's tolerable. And I can always have an income with it. Cooking is such a difficult field. Good positions are really limited and I don't want to end up as a short-order cook serving up pre-frozen hamburgers."

Tye bit into her muffin and her eyes widened. "Meggie," she mumbled with her mouth full. "These are the best blueberry muffins I've ever tasted. They're so light and delicate."

Meggie grinned. "I'm glad you like them. I added some cinnamon and an extra egg. It wasn't in the recipe, but it sounded like a good idea. Do you think it worked?"

Tye nodded vigorously as she swallowed. "I think they're marvelous. The cinnamon adds a nice depth to the flavor."

"Maybe I should take some over to Michael and Steve."

"Don't you dare!" Tye said. Then she giggled. "Listen to me—getting possessive over your blueberry muffins. Of course you should share them with the boys. You know they'll love them."

"And they'll chomp on them without tasting. They always say it's good, but sometimes I wonder how they can tell. They eat like a pack of ravenous wolves. Sometimes I think I could open a can of dog food and get the same reaction. I wish I could find someone who really appreciates my cooking."

"I appreciate it."

"I mean someone of the opposite gender."

"Can't help you there." Tye rose from the table and rinsed her plate, half-eyeing the remaining eight muffins. "Thanks for sharing them with me, Meggie. They're the best."

Meg beamed. "I'm glad you like them. I'll take a few over to the boys." She rose from the table. "After I deliver these muffins, I'm going to go grocery shopping," she said.

"I'm getting in the shower. Tell Michael and Steven hello for me."

After wrapping the muffins in a towel, Meggie walked down the hallway to the apartment three doors down and knocked. She could hear loud music for a moment, then someone turned down the stereo.

The door opened and Meggie was greeted by a mop of brown hair sitting atop a five o'clock shadow, worn T-shirt and sweat pants. Mornings were not always kind to Steve. He pushed his hair out of his eyes. "Hey, Meggie! What's that wrapped in the towel? A little Saturday snack?"

Meggie moved past Steve. "Not that you deserve it," she said with a grin. "But I made some muffins this morning and thought I'd share."

Michael came in from the hall. "Did I hear someone say muffins?"

"You look ready for church, where are you going?" Meggie asked.

"I have a job interview at Hothouse Flowers. They need a driver for their deliveries. Can you imagine scheduling an interview on Saturday?"

"Well, you look up to the task," Meggie replied. "When do you leave?"

"Oh, I've got time to eat whatever you brought over this morning," he said.

Meggie looked around the room and found a young man sitting on the sofa. He looked familiar with his curly blond hair and dark blue eyes. She knew he was from the student ward, but she wasn't sure of his name.

Michael made the introductions. "You know Neil. He transferred from BYU last semester."

Meggie noticed a look of sorrow briefly flit across his face, but she dismissed it. She hardly knew Neil. "We've never met formally," Meggie said. In fact she had never seen Neil up close. They always seemed to sit on the opposite side of the chapel.

"Neil returned from a mission in England a couple of years ago, and since Steve's call is for England, Neil offered to give him some tips," Michael said.

Meggie was grateful she had brought four muffins, instead of two. She handed the boys the still warm treat.

Steve and Michael ate their warm muffins in two bites.

"Got any more?" Steve asked.

"I'm not telling," Meggie said. "Not that it matters. You didn't even taste it. I don't know why I bother."

"This is delicious," Neil said.

Meggie turned. Neil had taken two bites and his muffin was only half-eaten.

"You like it?"

He took another bite. "This is better than those mega-muffins you get at the store," he said. Steve and Michael just looked at him. "You know, those muffins that are so big they're practically a meal. I always thought their blueberry muffins were the best I'd ever tasted, but these are better." He took another bite. "They're better than better. This muffin is incredible."

Steve shrugged. "Muffins are muffins." He looked puzzled. "Aren't they?"

"Oh, no," Neil said. "That's like saying all pasta is created equal. I love ravioli, but I hate that stuff that comes in a can."

"I know exactly what you mean," Meggie said.

"You don't make fresh pasta too, do you?" Neil asked.

Meggie shook her head. "No. I've thought about getting a pasta maker, but it's not exactly a priority when I have to pay for school books."

Neil nodded his understanding. "Listen, I was just finishing up with these guys. Would you mind sharing your secrets?" he asked. "I'd love to hear how you made these muffins."

"Are you a cook?" she asked,

"No. I've had a few mishaps and lost my courage. One time I made a chocolate cake that could've been used as a door stop. Does that count?"

Meggie grinned. "Sure. Chocolate cake can be a pretty ambitious undertaking."

"That's not true," Michael said. "Just buy the mix, add a couple eggs and presto! You've got a chocolate cake."

Meggie gave him a tired look before turning back to Neil. "You probably just forgot to put in the baking powder. I could teach you."

"I'd like that, but I don't want to interrupt your afternoon plans."

Meggie shook her head. "I was just going to go grocery shopping. I try to put one new recipe together every week, along with the regular menu. This week I was going to try vegetable lasagna."

"Oh, that sounds good," Neil said.

"Would you like to go to the store with me?"

"Sure, if you wouldn't mind the company," Neil said.

"No. It'd be fun to have you along."

Steve moved into the conversation. "I'd sure like some vegetable lasagna for dinner one night this week," he said.

"I'll bring over the recipe," Meggie said.

"We wouldn't know how to make it," Michael said.

Meggie smiled sweetly as she walked out the door with Neil. "Just buy the mix and add a couple of eggs."

Later that morning, Tye was sitting at the dining room table studying equine anatomy when Meggie breathlessly rushed into the apartment.

"Where have you been all this time?" Tye asked. "I was thinking about calling the National Guard."

"I've just met the nicest man," Meggie sank onto the sofa.

Tye's eyebrows rose expressively. "At the grocery store?"

Meggie shook her head. "No. I didn't meet him there, but we went shopping together. His name is Neil McCrorie. He was visiting with Michael and Steve when I walked in. Oh, Tye, he's so nice. We spent ninety minutes at the grocery store."

Tye knitted her brows as she repeated the name. "Oh, I know why that name sounds familiar. Michael was telling me that he actually transferred *from* BYU but couldn't get the reason out of him. Apparently he's not real comfortable talking about his time in Provo."

"Steve and Michael can be pretty nosy. Maybe he's just very private."

Tye shrugged. "Could be." She paused, then grinned. "I'm curious about what there is to do at the grocery store for ninety minutes."

"I taught him about picking out produce. I showed him the best cuts of meat. We just wandered around the aisles and talked."

"I hope the ice cream didn't melt."

Meggie hopped up from the couch. "I left the groceries in the car."

Tye rose from the dining room table. "I'll help you bring them in."

It took a couple of trips to the car with all the groceries Meg had gotten. At least the monthly chore was finished.

Tye began putting the items away.

"Thanks so much for doing the grocery shopping, Meg. I really appreciate you taking care of this side of business."

"I like shopping for groceries. It's no problem." She grabbed the receipt and after doing some quick subtraction showed Tye the amount she owed.

Tye wrote a check and handed it to Meggie, who put it in her purse.

"So, tell me about Neil," Tye said.

"He's a listener," Meg said. "He showed an interest in everything I said. I must've babbled on for forty-five minutes about the importance of choosing fresh meat and produce." She giggled. "We didn't talk just about food. He told me about his mission to England and his family. He's from Spokane, Washington. We talked about skiing. We both love it, and miss the slopes. He didn't mention his time at BYU though. He's coming over for dinner tomorrow night."

"Oh. Maybe I'd better disappear for a while then."

"Would you mind?"

"No. I'll just hang out at Steve and Michael's for a couple of hours."

"What are you going to make?"

"Vegetable lasagna."

"Will you save me a piece?"

"Absolutely. In fact I hope you won't stay away too long. I'd like you to meet him."

Tye raised her eyebrows. "Maybe Neil has other plans."

Meggie smiled. "It's too early to tell about that."

"How long has he been home from his mission?"

"Two years."

Tye grinned. "He's got other plans."

"Don't stay away too long. I really do want you to meet him," Meggie said as she put away the last of the groceries.

Later that evening, Tye stood before a sink full of soapy water. Meggie was the cook and Tye cleaned. It was a routine that worked well for the girls. Meggie had always enjoyed cooking. Tye thought of the many weekends she had spent at the Stewart household with Meggie putting some fancy dessert together and Tye cleaning after her. It made perfect sense that they would continue that pattern through college as roommates.

Tye dipped her hands in the hot soapy water, pulled out several pieces of silverware, and began washing them in earnest. She thought back to the morning's activities and wondered about Jade and her new little filly. Then her thoughts drifted easily over Kyle, and she let go of the silverware as she remembered his warm fingers entwining hers. The touch had seemed so natural and right. Tye smiled. She wasn't used to the sudden invasion of such a pleasant memory of a man. She tried not to put too much emphasis on it. For all she knew Kyle had completely forgotten about her by now. Maybe he would even take full credit for seeing Jade and her new filly to safety.

Tye placed her hands back in the soapy water and worked on a plate. No, she hoped that wouldn't happen. It didn't sound like something Kyle would do. But she had to admit that she didn't know him.

Deep in thought, Tye turned on the hot water and began rinsing the dishes. Somewhere between the plates and the spoons she decided she would find a way to learn more about Kyle Jensen.

Chapter Three

Meggie peeked through the glass on the oven door. The lasagna was bubbling, so she pulled it gently from the oven. The whole apartment smelled of melting cheese, bubbling tomato sauce, and a cornucopia of vegetables. The pungent aroma of garlic rose throughout the apartment as Meggie placed garlic bread in the oven. Meggie was starving. She glanced at her watch. Neil should be arriving in twenty minutes. Perfect timing. The lasagna could cool for a few minutes before she cut into it.

Earlier in the afternoon, during church, Meggie had sat next to Neil. Now he was coming to dinner and they were going to share a quiet evening.

Tye came from the bedroom and looked longingly at the oven.

"Don't worry," Meggie said. "The recipe made enough to serve an army. There will be plenty of leftovers."

"When do you want me to come home? Do you want to call me?"

"No. Just come on back about eight-thirty or so."

A knock on the door startled Meggie and she hurried to answer it. She looked through the peephole. It was Neil. He was early. Pulling the door open, she invited him in.

Quick introductions were made before Tye hurried through the door, shutting it gently.

Neil walked in and smiled. "It smells great," he said. "In fact, I could smell it out in the breezeway."

"It's almost finished. Come in and have a seat. What's in the sack?"

"I brought some ice cream for dessert."

"That will be a nice ending to the meal," she said as she moved into the kitchen. Neil followed her, placing the ice cream in the freezer.

Meggie checked the lasagna. It was just about ready to cut. She pulled the garlic bread out of the oven and gave the salad one last toss before dishing everything on plates and setting them on the table.

Neil held Meggie's chair as she sat down before sitting across from her. She asked him to offer the prayer, then they gave their attention to the meal.

"It's almost too good to eat," Neil said. "But that won't stop me." He grinned.

Meggie smiled and studied the man across the table. He was older than she was by a year or so, but the age didn't make a difference. Maybe that was why he acted more mature than Steve or Michael. Michael was a returned missionary also, but sometimes he acted as if he was twelve. She liked Steve and Michael, but she would never invite them over for dinner or agree to go out with them on a real date. No, this was different. Neil was quiet, gentle, and perceptive.

"This is marvelous," he said as he took a bite. "Really, Meg, you should consider opening your own restaurant or something. You know so much about food."

"The restaurant business is too risky," she said. "It's hard to make a living."

"That sounded rehearsed. Have you given it some thought?"

"Not serious thought. The northwest is full of good restaurants, and a lot of them don't make it."

"It seems a shame that the world at large won't be able to taste this lasagna."

Meggie blushed. "Thank you."

"What about your folks? Are they gourmet chefs?"

Meg shook her head. "No. They're accountants."

"I bet you did a lot of cooking at home, didn't you?"

Meggie shook her head. "Not really. We hired a cook. Both my mom and dad worked. They own an accounting firm and they both put in long hours, so we had someone come in three times a week and do most of the cooking and cleaning. Her name was Marsha. I loved to come home from school when she was working. She'd be in the kitchen and it would smell so cozy and inviting. I'd sit and keep her company. After a while I started to help her. She taught me things. Then my mom found out and told me to stay out of the kitchen. She paid Marsha by the hour, so she didn't want me in there gabbing and encouraging her to stay longer than necessary."

Neil continued to eat, but his eyes held Meggie. She could feel his attention as she turned her gaze to her plate. A little shiver raced down her neck. When she looked up, Neil was eating with gusto. She studied Neil carefully. His jaw was strong and his blond hair was full with a bit of curl. His green eyes were framed in heavy lashes and thick blond eyebrows. She had seen him in church on a number of occasions, and although she always considered him attractive, she didn't realize how handsome he truly was until this minute.

"Did she do the shopping also?"

Neil's question jerked Meggie out of her thoughts. "Marsha?

Yeah. Until I got my driver's license. Then I asked my mom if I could start doing the family shopping. It would save them money because they wouldn't have to pay Marsha to do it. Marsha came with me the first few times. She's the one who taught me how to pick ripe melons and fresh lettuce. What to look for when choosing beef and how the different cuts could be used. She cooked both fresh and frozen poultry and showed me the subtle difference between the two. She also taught me the difference between fresh and previously frozen fish. Now I can look at a fish and practically tell you how long it's been out of the water. I began doing some of the baking too during my senior year in high school. I would make the desserts and pastries, and Marsha would make the main courses."

"Do your folks still have her come in and cook and clean?"

"Only during the school year. I do the cooking during the summer. My older brother and sister are both married, so that makes the job a little easier."

Meggie became uncomfortable with the focus of conversation. She changed the subject. "Did your family have any cooking traditions?" she asked.

"No, but we had family vacation traditions. Every January we went skiing. My folks put me on skis when I was just a little tyke. It's as natural to me as walking."

"We have the same tradition. We spend a good part of our Christmas vacation at Mt. Bachelor."

"Have you ever been hurt?" Neil asked.

"No, but I'm a careful skier," she replied. "How about you?"

He shook his head. "We were taught from a very early age to be responsible. If our parents caught us hot-dogging or fooling around in a way that could hurt someone, that was the end of our ski vacation. We had to wait in the lodge while the rest of the family was out on the slopes."

Meggie smiled. "Are you speaking from experience?"

Neil returned her smile. "It only happened once, but it taught me a good lesson. My brother, Scott, and I, were racing around these people to see how close we could get to a moving target. I wasn't much older than eleven. My brother was probably thirteen going on ten. It was a stupid thing to do and Dad caught us in the act. It was just Monday, but we had to stay inside the rest of the week."

"Sounds like you deserved it. Terrorizing people that way."

"Something else too. It wasn't until I got older that I realized the sacrifice my folks made to follow through on their threat. At the time I could only think of how unfair it all seemed. Now that I'm older I realize that one of them had to stay off the slopes in order to watch us. They traded days, which meant they couldn't ski together—and they love to ski together. It must've been just as hard on them as it was on us." Neil smiled. "It never happened again."

"I'm glad to hear it. I wouldn't have pegged you as a slow learner."

Neil laughed. "You wouldn't say that if you saw my last cake."

Meggie laughed. "When do you want to try again?"

Neil became thoughtful. "I don't know. You might not let me visit you anymore after you've witnessed my lack of kitchen skills. Besides, how could I pay you back?"

Meggie shrugged. "You don't have to pay me back. It would be fun." She paused. "Maybe someday I could catch a ride with you to the slopes. I don't have a car, so the only ski time I've had was during the Christmas break. I've been going through withdrawals." She rose from the table, holding her plate. "I bet it was hard to leave BYU and Utah with all that great powder."

A long thoughtful silence followed. A trace of emotion came into Neil's face. Then he stood and helped Meggie clear the table. "Taking you to the slopes would be fun, but let's not wait until we can go skiing to get together. Can we try the cake first? Are you free Tuesday evening?"

Meggie grinned. "Not anymore. I think I'll be baking a chocolate cake."

Neil grinned as he stacked the dishes in the sink and began running the warm water. "How about if I wash and you dry?"

Meggie stood next to Neil. They worked silently for several minutes, touching hands briefly as they handed plates and silverware to each other.

Several minutes later a soft knock sounded at the door interrupting the quiet spell. Tye slowly opened the door and peeked in. "Is it safe?" she asked. "Can I come home now?"

Neil was scrubbing the sink as Meggie moved to wipe the table.

"Sure, we're just finishing," Meggie said. "You're just in time for dessert. Neil brought over some ice cream."

"I think I'd like some lasagna first," Tye replied. She moved into the kitchen and fixed herself a plate. "The boys are starting to regret the fact that they introduced the two of you," Tye said as she forked her lasagna. "They're worried that the good stuff is going to come to an end." She giggled. "They can smell the lasagna in the breezeway. It's driving them crazy."

Meggie spooned up her ice cream. "You can take them some lasagna after you're finished."

After Tye had gone back down the hall, Meggie and Neil said a lingering goodbye at the door. He took her hand. "I'm looking forward to Tuesday," he said.

"Me too."

"I'll call you tomorrow so you can give me a list of ingredients I need to buy."

Meggie nodded.

Neil stepped back. "Tuesday," he said. Then with a quiet goodbye and a soft caress to Meggie's face, he opened the door and was gone.

His touch on Meggie's skin still lingered. She put her hand to her cheek. Could it be that Neil was an answer to an unborn prayer? She thought back to the day before she met Neil and how she had wished for someone who would appreciate her. She was being silly at the time, but the wish was truly a fervent one.

Later that evening Meggie sat at her desk and stared at an unrelenting column of numbers on her computer screen. But her mind was on Neil and the wonderful evening they shared.

Neil made Meggie curious. She wondered why he had chosen to leave Utah if he loved skiing so much. Did he simply miss the Northwest? What was he studying? They hadn't even talked about his classes.

Meggie leaned back in her chair and closed her eyes against the unblinking numbers. Her impressions of Neil went beyond curiosity. There were other things that she appreciated. His gentle voice and ability to give her his full attention beckoned her. He took a genuine interest in her cooking. That was more than she could say for her family.

Meggie thought about her parents. She remembered the first time she had approached them about going to a culinary institute. They did everything to discourage her except forbid it. She needed a reliable source of income, they said—something she could count on. Her grandfathers had been accountants. Her parents were accountants. When they retired, they wanted to turn the firm over to Meggie.

Meggie's older brother, Justin, had gone against all tradition to become an auto mechanic. Her older sister, Madeline, had started her education in accounting, but she had met a Californian during her first year at BYU, and now she was married and living in the San Jose valley with two little children. All of her parents' hopes were pinned on Meggie.

Meggie sighed. She didn't want their hopes. She had her own, and they had nothing to do with ledgers, computer programs, and rows of numbers.

The pain in the back of her eyes began to throb. Could she take a chance on cooking? What if she failed? The thought was not new. It had nagged at Meg for a good part of her college education, but Neil's gentle and probing questions brought the conflict to the surface once again. The idea of failing at something that meant so much was frightening. Accounting offered a steady if not plodding path, and she had the best the accounting world could offer. She would be stepping into a business that most accounting majors would have to work a lifetime to own. She should be grateful.

Closing her eyes, Meggie tried to push away the fatigue and concentrate. Yes, she was grateful. Accounting had given her and her family a good life.

Opening her eyes, she stared at the monitor once again. She needed to remember that and put away the foolish notion that she could earn a living from cooking. Digging another pencil out from her desk drawer, she focused on the computer screen once again and began her assignment in statistics.

Chapter Four

The following Saturday, Tye sat astride Trapper, wishing she had taken more care with her hair. She hadn't even bothered to brush it. Instead, she had simply tied it back in a disarrayed ponytail, pushing stray hairs out of her face with her fingers. The result was a matted mess.

She watched Kyle mount Ben and mashed her riding helmet down. All week long she had hoped for the chance to talk again with Kyle, but with the rush of training and caring for the horses, she didn't get the opportunity. If it weren't for Jade's little filly, meeting Kyle and helping Jade would seem like a dream. Throughout the long week Tye had simply convinced herself that Kyle had just been making small talk to help quiet Jade when he mentioned the possibility of riding together. He had never called to confirm their riding appointment, and it had been easier to assume that he had forgotten about the whole thing. Now Kyle was sitting in the saddle, ready to move.

"Lead the way," he grinned.

Tye gave one last thought to her ratty ponytail and nudged Trapper forward. She led Trapper down the familiar, narrow path that led to the meadow. He sloshed through a small creek before pulling himself up the bank and into the meadow. Ben and Kyle were right behind her and soon they were standing side by side, looking into the green and gray expanse of the rolling fields. A silent fog obscured the meadow, shrouding everything in a light gray mist. Fence posts and trees looked like disappearing sentinels as Tye gazed into the silent morning.

"I can't believe I've never been here," Kyle said. "I guess I'm not used to taking Ben out on long walks. You've made me feel neglectful, Tye." He grinned at her.

She grinned back. His presence was a ray of sunshine in an otherwise dismal dawn. "You're hardly neglectful, Kyle. All of these horses get plenty of exercise. But I think this is good for Trapper's mind." She reached down and stroked Trapper's neck.

Tye nudged Trapper with her leg and the horse moved forward, sinking hoof deep into the soft ground.

"How long have you been riding?" Kyle asked.

"I started riding horses at age seven. By sixteen I had saved a wad of cash from birthdays and Christmas so I could buy a horse. Trapper was that horse. I've had him five years."

"How did you keep him in oats?"

"I got a job as a courtesy clerk in a grocery store." Tye giggled at the memory. "I started at fourteen so I could continue to save for a horse. I was desperate for a job and my folks gave me permission to work as long as my homework didn't suffer. Every week my mom would drive me to this store and I would talk to the same manager and ask if he had any openings. Every week he said no. One day I wanted to give up and my mom said that if I kept at it, one day he'd give me a job just to get me off his back." Tye laughed. "That's exactly what happened. It got to the point where all of the checkers knew me and would give me this knowing smile. Then one day, the manager threw his hands in the air and said he'd hire me just so that he didn't have to see me come in his office. He scheduled me on his days off."

Kyle laughed. "You can be persistent."

Tye sobered. "I had to be. I would imagine you know what that's all about—this sport requires it."

"Yes, I know what you mean. We have something in common," Kyle said. "I also had to work to keep my horse. I worked in a pizza joint during high school." He laughed. "No proms for this barn rat. All my money went to horses, tack, lessons—you know," Kyle shrugged. "But I wouldn't change a minute of it." He continued, "I found Ben at the race course in Portland. After the season is over, they sell the horses that didn't do well. I was able to pick him up for around three hundred dollars. But he needed a lot of work. For one thing, he was too thin. We tried all kinds of things to help him gain weight but keep him mellow. He was pretty high strung when we got him so he didn't need a lot of the sweet grains that can make a horse uptight and hot. Finally we found that he liked oats and oat straw."

"I bet that was only one of your problems though. When a horse comes from the track they have only one speed—fast."

"Exactly," Kyle replied. "We had to go about helping him unlearn everything he learned at the track. We spent hours trotting and walking him in large and small circles so that he would understand that speed didn't matter. He wasn't going anywhere until I told him to go. Racehorses always prefer the left lead, so he was very stiff to the right. The circles helped loosen him up too. My trainer was great. She's from England. They have a great riding tradition there. She taught me to be patient." He paused. "I don't know about Ben, but I got sick of circles. Finally, he began to understand and he started to relax. That was a great triumph for us."

Tye smiled. She loved hearing horse stories from other owners. It helped her feel connected to Trapper.

"So you don't regret any of it?" Tye asked.

Kyle became thoughtful. "No. I never have. I admit though, it's not for everyone. I've always had big goals for my riding, and I've been willing to put it first."

"What are your goals?"

"To ride professionally," he answered without hesitation. "I want to compete on the national and international circuit, to be a real contender. And I would like to be on the Olympic team someday."

Tye wasn't surprised by Kyle's desire. His professionalism showed in his hard work. She was aware that she had a promising career in the horse business—as a teacher. But to become a real contender would require a move to the East Coast. That was more than Tye was willing to give.

"I think the horses are enjoying being together," she remarked.

"It's nice for me too," Kyle said quietly.

They walked for three hours and watched the countryside transform into green hills and blue sky as the fog began to lift. The conversation flowed at the same easy pace that they encouraged in their horses. They talked about college life and high school, but the conversation always drifted back to horses. They spoke of the many competitions each of them had endured as teenagers. They discussed the upcoming season and the hope that the team would be able to maintain their number one ranking.

It was obvious that the team placement concerned Kyle. He was hoping that the team's glowing record would help him land a job in a prestigious barn.

As their ride continued, Tye's earlier anxiety was replaced with the same warmth and interest she had experienced during Jade's crisis. She felt at home with Kyle's deep voice. He belonged in the woods with her. He didn't disturb the surroundings with loud or silly conversation. It was obvious that he respected their environment with the same reverent awe that was such a big part of her life. Never before had she met someone who loved horses as she did. Tye drank in his conversation and presence.

As they arrived back at the barn, she was almost sorry. Even though it had been one of the longer walks she and Trapper had taken together, Tye wished it could have continued.

After they dismounted, they lingered. Several familiar cars were in the parking lot, indicating that they would not be alone once they led their horses inside. Tye was reluctant to give up the morning. But Trapper needed to be unsaddled. He was probably thirsty.

"Well, we should look after our boys," she said, referring to the horses.

"I'll meet you here after we're finished," Kyle said.

Tye was delighted. "Okay," she said.

Leading Trapper in the barn, Tye noticed that the cross-ties were full. Other riders were preparing their horses for riding. She smiled and said hello to CarrieAnne Smithers and Jim Kendall—both were riders for the junior team. Bringing Trapper to his stall, Tye grabbed his lead rope and halter. Once inside his stall, she quickly removed his bridle, replacing it with the halter. Methodically, she removed the saddle, placing it on the bar on the outside of Trapper's stall door before beginning to brush him. Slowly, she ran the brush over his body, talking in a soothing voice as he slurped his water.

"So, what do you think of Kyle?" she whispered softly. Tye didn't expect an answer, but it helped to voice her own questions.

She ran the brush over his shoulder. "You and Ben sure seem to get along," she continued. "The two of you make a handsome pair." She thought about Kyle's horse, Ben, who was a dappled gray with a full, deep gray mane and tail. He stood out against Trapper's bay coat and black mane and tail. Both horses were beautifully built.

Trapper turned his head and began to sniff. He was looking for the apple.

She rubbed his nose. "Not yet, you silly boy." She brushed his face, and Trapper tolerated it well. Then she handed him the apple. He bit it in half.

Tye was so involved in her thoughts as she fed Trapper that she didn't hear the footsteps that came to the stall. It wasn't until the woman's voice broke into her thoughts that she even realized someone was there. "Tye?"

Tye looked through the bars of the stall and noticed her trainer, Katie. "Yes?"

"Can I see you in my office after you're finished?"

"Sure." Tye hurriedly placed Trapper's blanket on, fed him the rest of his apple, and with one last pat on the neck, hurried to Katie's office.

Katie looked up from an old desk that had one leg missing. Several two-by-fours propped up one corner to keep it level. It was littered with papers. Applications from hopeful riders, entry forms for various horse shows, and the personal files of each horse and rider were scattered in an disheveled heap. Tye noticed that her file was on top. "Sit down," Katie invited.

Obediently Tye sat as Katie began pushing papers into a manila envelope. After she was finished she looked at Tye and smiled. "I just wanted to thank you for looking after Jade in her hour of need. That mare means a lot to me, and she's got a pretty little filly thanks to you."

Tye beamed. "She is a sweet little thing, isn't she? Dr. Robinson was very pleased."

Katie smiled. "I know. He called me and I came right over, but by the time I arrived you had left. I've named the little filly Gypsy, and she has all the fine makings of a nice animal. Her legs are perfect; straight and even. Her neck is well formed, and she's not going to be too short or long in the back. I couldn't be happier." Katie leaned back in her chair. "But this isn't really why I called you in here. I've been thinking of the alternate position and I was hoping you'd take it."

Tye blinked. "You mean, alternate to the competition squad?"

"Yes. You wouldn't have to go to any show where you weren't required to ride, but if one of the horses or riders couldn't compete, you'd be next in line."

"That position usually goes to a junior."

"I know." Katie showed some concern. "And there's going to be some unhappy people when the decision is announced, but no one can deny that you're the best rider for the job. Actually, I'm hoping to have two alternates. I'll choose a junior so that she can be groomed to be the captain of next year's team. She'll go to every competition and learn the ropes. But you would ride if we had notice that the team needed another horse and rider pair. Will you take the position?"

"I'm honored," Tye stammered. "I don't see how I can say no."

Katie smiled easily. "I was hoping you'd say that. I'll make the announcement on Monday. If anyone gives you any trouble, tell them to come to me."

Tye nodded.

The phone on Katie's desk rang. The loud jangling made Tye jump.

Katie spoke above the noise. "If you have any questions, call me and we'll talk."

Tye heard the dismissal in her trainer's voice and she stood. She walked out into the parking lot in a daze.

Kyle was leaning against his car.

"You're not going to believe this," she said. Then she wondered if she should say anything. Katie said she would make the announcement on Monday. Then the full realization of what she had been offered flowered inside and she couldn't contain her excitement. She looked at Kyle. "You're not going to believe this," she repeated.

"I've just been asked to be the alternate to the competition squad."

"Yes, I know."

Tye looked at Kyle incredulously. "How?" she asked.

"Because I'm the captain of the competition squad, Katie asked my opinion. I told her I'd like to see you on board."

Tye wanted to throw her arms around Kyle, but instead, she stood and stared at him.

"Katie thinks you've got a lot of potential, Tye. She would like to see you come out of this program as one of the top young riders in the country."

Tye shook her head. "I know Trapper and I make a good team. We work hard, but I had no idea …"

"Congratulations!" Kyle said. He reached out his hand.

Tye placed her hand in his, but she wanted more. She wanted him to pull her close. The electricity in their touch drew her to him and soon, she was in his arms for a congratulatory hug. The strength of his embrace was warm and inviting.

Reluctantly, she pulled away from him. It wouldn't do if other team members saw them together. She could tell that Kyle was thinking the same thing as they drew apart.

"I'd like to see you again," he said softly.

"That would be nice."

"How about tomorrow?"

"Sundays aren't good for me," she replied. "I have church and I try to relax. I don't ride and I try to have my homework finished."

"A day of rest, huh? Not a bad idea."

"Maybe you ought to try it," she teased.

"How do you feel about riding early during the week?"

"We could go out on Thursday morning," Tye suggested.

"All right."

"Can you be ready by six-forty-five? I have a nine-thirty-five class."

Kyle grinned. "It'll be a struggle, but I'll be here."

He opened her car door for her and waved her out of the driveway.

Chapter Five

Tye sat in the bishop's office and waited for Brother Farrell, the high councilor from the stake. She had been surprised when he called before church and asked if she could meet him prior to sacrament meeting.

When Brother Farrell arrived, Tye stood and they shook hands.

Settling into the chair across from Tye, Brother Farrell said, "I bet you're wondering why I've called you in here."

Tye nodded.

"Well, I'll get right to the point," he said. "We have a new calling for you."

Tye felt her heart drop into her stomach. She loved her calling on the Relief Society board. She wanted to protest but couldn't find the words.

Brother Farrell continued, "We'd like to call you to be a stake missionary. Sister missionaries just arrived in this stake, and we need to call sisters to go out on splits with them. I know you've got a busy school schedule, but we're hoping you'd be willing and able to be flexible and allow some time for splits with the missionaries."

Tye bit her lip. "I'd have to be released from my Relief Society calling, wouldn't I." It was more a statement than a question.

"Yes, I'm afraid so. I hear you're an excellent teacher."

Tye took a deep breath. She didn't want to be a stake missionary. It didn't make any sense for her to be a missionary. She and Meggie had been in the Relief Society since the beginning of their freshman year. Besides, her mother wasn't a member. If Tye was so good at teaching the gospel, why couldn't she teach her mother? She stalled. "Are you sure you don't have me mixed up with someone else?"

Brother Farrell smiled. He had obviously heard that line. "No, I don't believe we've made a mistake."

Tye thought for a moment. Relief Society was so rewarding. She enjoyed tackling the monthly lessons and presenting them to the sisters in her ward.

"Preaching to the converted is always comfortable," Brother Farrell said. "It's when we're asked to share the gospel with the unconverted that things become interesting."

Tye thought about her mother. "Yes, I know," she said dryly. For all of Tye's desire to say no, she couldn't muster up any solid argument. But something nagged at her. Something familiar. "Can I think about it for a few days?" she asked.

Brother Farrell nodded. "Yes, of course. I think that's a good idea. Do you want to call me when you're ready?"

Tye accepted Brother Farrell's phone number.

"I'd like to sit here for a few minutes," Tye said quietly.

Brother Farrell rose and shook Tye's hand. "We'll be in touch," he said before leaving the room.

Tye sank back into her chair. She had never turned down a calling. But was this really right? She thought about her mother and closed her eyes, willing that concern away. This was not the time to worry herself with the past. She had the future to think about. What about her new position on the competition team? The nagging feeling grew stronger. It was familiar to Tye, but she was sure that yesterday's promotion would have squelched that. Instead, she found it pulsing inside of her like giant thunderheads. She had never shared the restless desire with anyone. It was too vague and too difficult to explain even though it had been around for years. Sometimes it came with spring and the fresh awakening of the land. Now, even though the land lay dormant, it churned inside of her like a tumultuous sea. She began to pace. Was this calling an answer? She didn't want it to be. It would be so much simpler if she could just continue to teach Relief Society and compete on the squad. Relief Society was familiar and safe. The turmoil did not subside.

When she left the office, she gave Meggie an intense look.

"What is it?" Meggie asked. "I was beginning to worry about you. We're almost late for sacrament."

"I've been asked to take a new calling as a stake missionary."

"I wonder if Karla knows," Meggie said, referring to the Relief Society president.

"I don't know."

"Cheer up!" Meggie said. "It'll be fun and exciting. Just think of all the new people that you'll be able to meet and introduce to the gospel. I know it'll be hard, but I'm sure the Lord must feel you're capable or you wouldn't be given this calling."

"I haven't said yes."

Meggie stopped. "Why not?"

"If I'm so capable why does my mom still have a smoking habit?" The question popped out before Tye could capture the words.

Meggie looked down, then back up at Tye. "You're not responsible for your mother's smoking habit, Tye. You know that."

"I know. But I wish I could be. She would've quit long ago if it was up to me," Tye said miserably.

"But it's not up to you." Both girls settled into a pew. "Has your mom ever given any indication that she's interested in the gospel?" Meggie asked.

Tye shook her head. "You know the story. We've had the missionaries in our home since I was six. Sometimes I think she just has them for dinner and a lesson so she won't hurt their feelings. Whenever anyone mentions that she should quit smoking, she nods her head in agreement." Tye paused. "It's so frustrating," she said. "How can you argue with someone who agrees with you?"

"Maybe you shouldn't be arguing with her," Meggie said. "It's common knowledge that smoking is bad for the lungs. You can't force her to quit. Just like you can't force her to come to the gospel. Arguing just irritates everyone."

"I don't know how Dad stands it."

"That's easy," Meggie replied. "He loves your mom. It's so obvious by the way they treat each other. I've always envied that about your parents."

Tye had to agree with Meggie. Her parents did love each other. But was love enough? It wasn't for Tye. She wanted more. She wanted to be sealed to her family. All through her childhood, Tye had felt different from the other children in her church classes. Their mothers went to Relief Society or they taught Primary. Tye's mother stayed home and smoked cigarettes. Tye's most hated moments came during the ward's annual mother and daughter dinner. Every year Trudy would attend the event with Tye, but they never went alone. Cigarette smoke hovered around them like an unwanted traveling companion. It clung to her mother's clothes, hair and skin. When Tye went to church with her father, it wasn't so bad, because she could wash and air everything right before church. But when her mother was with her, the odor clung to them like spider webs. During the mother and daughter dinner Tye would look for a table in the corner, away from most of the activity, but it never mattered. Sisters from the ward always came to greet and welcome Trudy while Tye would fold into her seat, hoping not to be noticed.

Why couldn't her mom see the truth of the gospel? Didn't she want to be sealed to her family? More than anything Tye wanted to be sealed to her parents. On Sunday, she would sit with her father and look at all the Mormon families. Tye was sure every one of them had been sealed in the temple. Tears of unfulfilled yearning would come to her eyes, and she would be forced to blink them back so her father wouldn't see.

Meggie handed Tye a hymnal. Tye focused on the page and began to sing. Her strong soprano mixed comfortably with Meggie's alto. Still, she continued to think of her parents. What would her folks think of her new calling? Her dad would be proud of her. What about her mother? She understood missionary work—probably better than most members.

Tye thought back to the scores of missionaries who had traveled to the Jorgenson home. She had always admired them and their willingness to put their lives on hold to teach the gospel. At one point she decided she wanted to be just like them and convert her mother. But after Trudy continued to refuse the gospel, Tye became irritated with her mother and even with the missionaries. Wasn't it their job to convert people to the gospel? A hollow feeling began to open up inside of Tye as her frustration grew. How could the Lord expect her to teach and convert strangers to the gospel if she couldn't even convert her own mother? It made no sense.

Once again, she considered turning the calling down, but the restlessness came alive like warring shadows. She closed her eyes and bowed her head as the opening prayer was spoken, offering a little prayer of her own.

The program was announced. The sister missionaries would be speaking. *Great*, Tye thought. *A guilt trip is just what I need.* She folded her arms and pushed herself down into the pew.

It wasn't until the second sister missionary on the program began her talk that Tye found herself concentrating. Her name was Sister Sutton. In spite of all of Tye's misgivings, she had to admit that she was enthralled with Sister Sutton's enthusiasm for the gospel and her work. Tye wished now that she had paid more attention to the first sister missionary, Sister Kohler. She did remember that Sister Kohler was from Houston and would be going home in six months. Sister Sutton would be going home to New Mexico in eight months. She spoke of her reluctance to leave her mission behind. There was so much work to do, she said, and she was sure it would never be completed before she needed to go home. Sister Sutton's words stung Tye. She knew exactly how Sister Sutton felt. But how? How could she know how Sister Sutton felt? She had never been on a mission. She hadn't even really considered a mission. Horses were her mission. Did her new calling have something to do with the vague desire? Were her feelings based on an urgency to do more? Was that at the heart of the restlessness? No, that couldn't be it. Tye had always done all she could when it came to fulfilling her callings. With all her will, she pushed the feeling aside. She needed to be paying attention to Sister Sutton's talk.

After the meeting was over, she waited in the foyer for the two sisters. Meggie had gone to Sunday School, promising to save Tye a seat. When the sisters appeared, Tye walked up to them and introduced herself.

Both sisters were happy to meet Tye. "I just wanted to tell you that I really enjoyed your talks. You both did a very good job. It must be hard to get up in front of so many people. I haven't given a talk in sacrament meeting since I was fourteen and it only lasted two minutes," Tye said.

Sister Sutton shrugged. "You get used to it," she said. "When I first came out, I thought I'd never be able to knock on doors and ask strangers if they'd be interested in hearing about the gospel, but now it's second nature to me. It's not my favorite part of missionary work. I'd rather be teaching. But giving a talk in sacrament meeting is a piece of cake. It gives us a chance to preach to the converted." She grinned.

"I think the Lord blesses us while we're in his service," Sister Kohler said. "He helps us choke down our fear and face people because this is His message. We're only the messengers."

As they chatted about their work, Tye's doubts began to fade as the shadows began to recede. Getting to know these two lovely sisters seemed more like an opportunity than drudgery. Maybe missionary work could be the same. There wasn't any doubt over the two missionaries' feelings. She knew she should congratulate the sisters once again on a good job and then move on to Sunday School, but something kept her riveted in her spot. Sister Sutton and Sister Kohler both had such an inviting spirit about them that she found it difficult to leave.

Sister Sutton seemed to read her mind. "You know, we're always looking for sisters to go on splits with us. Would you be willing to help us with that?"

Tye wanted to, but she wondered if she should wait until she was properly called. "Let me think about that," she said.

Sister Kohler and Sister Sutton looked disappointed for a moment. Then Sister Kohler pulled a program out from her scriptures. "Our number is on the back," she said. "Give us a call if it works out."

Tye felt heartened, but she couldn't say why. She took the program. "Thanks," she said. "I'll do that."

"Well, we really need to get going. We've got to teach a gospel principles class in a ward across town," Sister Kohler said. "It was good to meet you."

Tye shook hands with the two sisters before waving goodbye. Quietly, she moved through the hallway towards Sunday School.

"Did you talk with the sisters?" Meggie asked as Tye settled into her seat.

Tye smiled as she nodded.

Meggie returned her smile. "It'll be okay," she said.

Opening her scriptures, Tye tried to concentrate on the gospel doctrine lesson. They were studying the Book of Mormon and most of the time the lessons held her interest, but today she found herself wondering what it would be like to go on missionary splits. She knew that returned missionaries often went with the missionaries. She wished she could talk to someone and ask what would be required of her. She thought back to all the missionary discussions she had heard while living at home and her childhood desire to become like the missionaries. That seemed so long ago.

Maybe she should just relax. It wouldn't hurt to pray about it though. Maybe when she was set apart she would feel calmer. The thought surprised her. Just a couple of hours ago, she was wondering if she should even be receiving this calling, and now she was thinking about being set apart. She closed her eyes. The restlessness had retreated a little. It had left a dull headache, but it no longer rumbled. It ebbed away as she took a deep breath.

Chapter Six

Meggie and Neil stood in the kitchen and waited for the mixture on the stove to cook. The apartment held the rich aroma of warm chocolate.

"I've never seen a frosting that needed to be cooked," Neil said.

"This is so good," Meggie said as she stirred the bubbling full-flavored confection. "After the frosting is done, we'll pour it over the cake while it is still warm from the oven. It seals in the moisture so it will never dry out. This will be the best chocolate cake you have ever eaten."

Neil grinned.

"What's so funny?" Meg asked.

"Nothing. I just enjoy watching you work, that's all. Your eyes sparkle."

"You might not be so amused when you have to clean up," Meggie grinned back.

Neil leaned against the counter. "That was convenient of Tye to take off right after dinner. She won't even be around to help me."

"Convenience has nothing to do with it. The sister missionaries needed someone to go out on splits. You wouldn't want to keep her from doing her duty, would you?"

"Of course not," Neil said. "Besides, I can tell that you don't make much of a mess."

"I might just surprise you."

Neil continued to grin. "Don't do me any favors," he replied as he pushed himself away from the counter. He moved beside Meggie and stuck his finger in the warming frosting, then licked the sweet chocolate.

Meggie made a face. "Don't do that!"

Neil laughed. "You are particular, aren't you?"

"Fingers have to stay out of the food or it can't be served. Too many germs."

Neil turned serious. "Okay. I promise I won't do it again," he said. "I wouldn't want to upset the cook. I might get poisoned."

"Only from your own germs," Meggie giggled. She turned to the stove and stirred the frosting in earnest. "Okay, bring the cake over here."

Neil picked up the potholders that surrounded the warm pan and carried the cake to the stove.

Meggie slowly drizzled the frosting over the cake until it was covered.

"How do you know the frosting is ready?" Neil asked.

"See how smooth it is? That means all the ingredients have blended together. You can smell it, too."

Neil sniffed. "What do you mean?"

"It takes practice. When I smell this pan of frosting, I don't smell chocolate, sugar, heat or vanilla. I smell a blend of ingredients that produce frosting. But you can also tell just by looking at it. Good cooks employ all their senses."

Neil nodded.

Meggie finished with the cake and placed it on a rack.

"How long does it have to cool before we can eat it?"

"About an hour. We can take some over to Michael and Steve when it's ready."

"If they don't find us first. I'm sure they will follow their noses right to this very spot. They won't smell sugar, chocolate, heat and vanilla either. They will smell chocolate cake. Maybe you should teach them to cook. They already seem to have the smell part down," Neil said.

Meggie smiled. "Can I get you something to drink while we wait?"

"Hot chocolate sounds good."

Meggie began to warm milk on the stove. After she was finished, she handed Neil his mug and settled onto the couch. He sat next to her.

"Tell me about BYU," Meggie said. "What made you decide to transfer? Most folks are trying to transfer to the Y."

Neil sucked in a breath and stood.

"I'm sorry," Meggie said quietly. "I didn't mean to pry."

"No. It's not your fault. There's no way you would be able to know." He began to pace. "You see, I was engaged last year." He paused. "Maybe I'd better start at the beginning."

Meggie shook her head. "Don't feel like you have to explain, Neil."

"No. I want to explain. Maybe for the first time, I want to talk about it."

"All right."

"After my mission I came home and went directly to BYU. That's where I met Samantha. Everyone called her Sammi Rae. She was from Orange County, California. Her folks owned several florist shops. She was everything Californian—warm, bright, active and sunny. Just being in her presence made me feel like I was holding a sunbeam. We did everything together. She was an avid outdoors lover. She would ski in the winter and backpack in the summer. I was in the pre-law program there, and she was a year ahead of me in the physical education program. She wanted to teach kids about the joys of physical activity. It just all seemed so right. Nine months later I asked her to marry me and she said yes. We were going to get married in the San Diego Temple on May twenty-eighth."

Neil became quiet and shook his head to dispel the memories. "Then on April third I found her with someone else. It was pure fate. I was fifteen minutes late for class one day so I took a shortcut through one of the buildings on campus. She was with some guy from her exercise physiology class. They had been thrown together to work on a project and became closer as the semester moved along. I had no idea. When I found them, they were *very* close."

Meggie's heart ached for Neil. "Oh, I see," she whispered.

Neil grew quiet. "I think it all boiled down to the fact that Sam just wasn't ready to get married."

"Did you confront her right there?"

He shook his head. "No. I was so shocked, I just slunk off. I didn't even go to class. I went home instead and tried to find some clue in our relationship that I missed. Something that would make it all clear. When I saw her later that evening I talked to her about it. She was very remorseful. She cried and told me how sorry she was. She promised it would never happen again." Neil's voice became sad. "I wanted to believe her. But I just couldn't. She was wearing my ring. To me that's a promise and she broke that promise. How could I ever trust her? In the long run I felt like I was doing her a favor too. I mean, if she had really been ready to get married, this never would've happened."

"Do you ever hear from her?"

"No, not anymore." Neil began talking as if sharing random thoughts for the first time. "I told her I thought it would be best if we never saw each other again. She wanted to start over and forget this guy, but I think I became part of the walking wounded—all I wanted to do was purge myself of this awful pain, and at the time that meant purging myself of everything Sammie Rae touched." He grew thoughtful. "But sometimes I think I was just reacting out of shock. I lay awake at night and wonder what would've happened if I would've given her another chance. Could we have made it work? Was I too hasty in the decisions I made? After all, I had made a promise too." Neil stopped pacing and ran his fingers through his hair. "After that, I couldn't stay on campus. Everything reminded me of her. The snowfall. The mountains. Everything." He turned toward Meggie. "So, I applied here at OSU." Neil sighed. "It's been almost a year and yet sometimes it's still so fresh and vivid it feels like yesterday."

Meggie resisted the urge to go to Neil and pull him close. "I'm so sorry," she whispered.

"Yes, well. These things happen."

"Yes, I suppose," Meggie said. "But that doesn't make it any easier. A broken promise always hurts." She paused. "She should've talked with you, Neil, if she was having second thoughts, or feelings for someone else. It would only be fair."

Neil nodded. "You're right. I know. I'll heal from this. It's not that big of a deal, really. That's what I'm told anyway. But some stubborn part of me refuses to let go—and I don't think I can heal until I completely give it up."

Meggie nodded. "Well, I don't think you're going to help yourself heal by claiming that it isn't a big deal. You were betrayed by someone you loved and trusted. That's always a big deal."

Neil moved to the couch and sat down. "You probably think I'm a real creep not to give her a second chance. I mean if I really loved her, wouldn't I be willing to try to make it work? I bet you won't want to see me anymore now that I've told you about this."

Meggie faced Neil and stroked the back of his hand. His fingers were cold. "You couldn't be more wrong about what I think, Neil. But what do you think? Do you believe you were a creep for refusing to give her a second chance?"

"Sometimes I wish I hadn't been so harsh with her. I wish I would've thought things through before I called everything off."

"Do you regret calling off the wedding?"

Neil paused. "I wouldn't call it regret," he said slowly. "I guess I just wonder. I wonder what my life would be like if I had been more forgiving and willing to work through it with her. Sometimes I think we should've just postponed everything instead of calling the whole thing off. But there's no use worrying about that now. It's over and finished. I'm sure she's moved on with her life and I'm trying to do the same. It just wasn't meant to be, I guess." Neil reached up and caressed Meggie's face. "Thanks for listening. I haven't told anyone about this. My family knows, of course, but that's it."

"I'm glad you feel like you can share it with me," Meggie said.

"It's nice that someone else knows. It seems to help with the burden."

Meggie smiled. "I'm glad."

A knock on the door interrupted them.

"Guess who?" Neil asked.

A voice from the other side of the door came through. "We know you're in there, hoarding chocolate cake!"

"That would be Michael. He always has such perfect timing," Meggie made a face. "I don't know what I ever did to make those two feel so comfortable."

Neil turned to Meggie and gently took her hand. "I do," he said quietly.

Meggie returned Neil's squeeze and smiled. "We'd better open the door before the manager comes up. Otherwise, we'll have to feed him too."

Neil laughed and moved to the door. The two boys entered and breathed deep.

"Okay. Where's the cake?" Michael asked.

"Did you smell it from your apartment?" Meggie asked.

"No. On Sunday, Neil told us he was coming over here to learn to bake a cake. We figured it would be finished about now. We did smell it in the breezeway."

Meggie shot Neil a withering glance.

"Hey, I'm sorry," Neil said. "I can tell I'm going to have to be careful about what I say."

"I should've warned you," Meggie said as she rose from the couch.

She turned to Michael and Steve. "I'll make a deal with you. If you go get a half-gallon of milk, we'll share the cake."

"Deal. We'll have to run to the store though. We don't have any milk at home."

"Well, you'd better hurry. The cake is cooling now."

Steve and Michael began to walk out the door. Michael stopped. "Hey, maybe one of us should stay and stand guard. We wouldn't want you disappearing with the goods."

Meggie gave Michael a push. "Get going. All this talk is wasting time."

Both boys walked out the door with a promise to be back within a few minutes.

Meggie turned to Neil. "Were you finished talking about your experience at BYU?"

"Yes. That's really the whole story," Neil said as he gently pulled her close. Meggie hesitated. Should she encourage this or would their relationship be served better by friendship? Could she help him heal from his wound? Or would she end up being a casualty of Sam as well? Slowly, she drew close to Neil. She could feel Neil's hand gently rubbing her arm. His fingers were cool. The desire to embrace him and pull him close swelled up inside of Meggie, but no, it wasn't right. It was too soon. They both needed time.

Neil pulled away. "I wonder how Tye is doing tonight?"

"I'm sure we'll hear all about it when she comes home. I know she was nervous."

"Missionary work can be the highest of highs and the lowest of lows."

"C'mon," Meggie said as she reached for Neil's hand. His fingers had warmed. "Let's check on our creation of a cake."

Neil followed Meggie to the kitchen.

"I appreciate you taking time to teach me how to cook a few simple meals," Neil said. "Being a starving bachelor has never appealed to me." He paused. "I think you should cook for a living. It seems to bring you such pleasure."

Meggie bit her lip. It did bring her pleasure. Nothing was more satisfying than creating tasty meals. She shook her head. "No, I'm an accountant."

"Maybe in your head. But your heart is a master chef."

Meggie sighed.

"What is it?" Neil asked.

Neil's warm fingers brought Meggie back to the present as he placed his hand over hers. She shook her head. "Nothing," she said quietly. She squeezed his fingers. But part of her wondered if she could ever reconcile her accounting mind with her creative heart.

Chapter Seven

Tye sat in the car as she watched the youth from another ward filter into the church building for their activity. In many ways she felt like she should be joining them. She wondered what they would be doing for their activity, but she didn't have time to dwell on it. The sister missionaries pulled up next to her car. They greeted each other and soon were joined by another woman from another ward. Sister Kohler made introductions, and then Tye was paired off with Sister Sutton, who settled into the passenger seat of Tye's car.

"We're so glad you called," Sister Sutton said. "We really needed to pair off tonight."

"Who are we teaching?" Tye asked.

"A college student. Actually, she's an inactive member. Her name is Toni Chandler. She lives in one of the new homes on Rock Rose drive. I guess her father bought it about five years ago, but he's never home."

"Is he a member?"

"No. I believe her mother was a member, but her folks are divorced and she chose to live with her dad when she was about twelve. That's when she stopped going to church."

"How did you meet her?"

"We were tracting one evening and she invited us in. I think she was lonely. She didn't talk much about the church. Then she said her boyfriend was going to come over and we'd have to go."

"She couldn't be too lonely if she has a boyfriend," Tye said.

Sister Sutton looked at Tye. "Sometimes it's our spirit that gets lonely."

Tye considered Sister Sutton's words. "Yes, I understand," she replied quietly. "So, what will we be teaching tonight? Do we have an appointment?"

"Well, we're going to try to teach her the first discussion—you know, the Joseph Smith story. You see, I think she's afraid to commit to anything. She says we're welcome to stop by but she won't set down a definite time. She's not real anxious to talk about the church, and when we brought it up last week she got kind of tense."

Tye withered inside. Great. Sometimes inactive members could be more hostile than non-members. "So, what do you want me to do?"

"Just follow my lead. We'll see if she's willing to take the first discussion, which is about Joseph Smith. If not, we'll talk about other things. Don't worry," Sister Sutton said softly. "It'll be fine."

Tye smiled with more confidence than she felt. Then she became agitated with herself. What was she worried about anyway? She had a testimony of the gospel. She knew the fundamentals of truth. Even if Toni Chandler didn't want to talk about the church, Tye could possibly talk about school. At the very least she could share her testimony or possibly invite her to attend Sunday meetings. It might be all she had, but it was important.

"Take a right at the next light," Sister Sutton said. "Then a left at the stop sign."

Tye followed Sister Sutton's directions, and soon she was easing the car into the driveway of a newer two-story home. The outdoor lighting showed a small but immaculately landscaped yard.

Tye followed Sister Sutton onto the porch, where she rang the doorbell. They heard footfalls inside the house. Then the door opened and Tye was facing her first contact as a possible stake missionary.

Sister Sutton smiled and said, "Hi, Sister Chandler. My companion and I split up this evening, so I brought someone from the student ward with me tonight." Introductions were made. "Can we come in?"

Toni Chandler stepped aside and opened the door wide. "Sure."

Toni led the way to a living room with white carpet and expensive furnishings. The fireplace was made of a deep green marble, and a matching vase stood on the mantle. The room looked more like a showcase than a place where people lived.

"You have a beautiful home. How many bedrooms?" Tye asked.

"Four," Toni said flatly before inviting Tye and Sister Sutton to sit down.

Tye noticed Toni's lack of enthusiasm. Was it because of their visit?

Once again, Tye tried to put away her nervous feelings. Sitting on the edge of the sofa, Tye hoped that her clothes were free from Trapper's hair. It wouldn't do to leave a hair ball on the furniture or carpet. She smoothed her dress down over her knees. She didn't know why she was worrying about Trapper's hair. It never migrated to her Sunday clothes.

"We thought you might like to hear a little bit about the student ward," Sister Sutton said.

Toni stiffly settled into one of the chairs. "I don't think so," she said. "I doubt I'd go." She turned to Tye, "What's your major in school?"

"Animal husbandry," Tye replied. "I'm on the equestrian team."

"That sounds interesting. Are you a sophomore?"

"Yes. How about you?"

"I'm a sophomore too," Toni said before explaining her major in business and the schedule that accompanied it.

After Toni had finished, Sister Sutton asked if she'd be willing to hear the first discussion. Tye watched as Toni's eyes darted to the green vase and then to the immaculate white carpet.

"Do you remember hearing about Joseph Smith?" Sister Sutton asked quietly.

Toni's head snapped up. "Yes. In Sunday School." She thought for a moment. "Or maybe it was Primary. He wrote the Book of Mormon—or something," her voice trailed off.

"He didn't exactly write it. He translated it from gold plates."

"Of course," Toni said. "Where are those gold plates now?"

"They've been taken up to heaven," Sister Sutton said.

"That's convenient," Toni quipped.

"Convenience has nothing to do with it. It's all about faith. How can we have faith in something we can see?" Sister Sutton asked in a soft patient tone that reminded Tye of Kyle. "Sometimes we have to leave the senses behind and let our spirit lead us."

Toni became silent.

Tye's respect for Sister Sutton grew.

"I hadn't thought of that," Toni said. "What is the Book of Mormon, anyway? A set of Mormon rules and regulations?"

Sister Sutton shook her head. "It's another testament of Jesus Christ."

Toni looked bored. "Oh."

"Do you remember being told about Joseph Smith's First Vision?" Sister Sutton asked.

Toni shook her head.

Sister Sutton explained the First Vision. In the process she asked Tye to read a couple of scriptures. Then she handed her scriptures to Toni and asked her to read.

Toni hesitantly took the leather-bound book and ran her finger down the page until she came to the correct verse. She read it quickly and handed the scriptures back to Sister Sutton, who finished the lesson.

Tye could tell that Toni was uncomfortable with the religious discussion. Why? Was she bored? Or was it something deeper? Sometimes she appeared bored and at other moments, she seemed to pull back into some personal space like a clam burrowing in the sand.

Sister Sutton rose. "Well, we'll leave you a copy of the Book of Mormon." She placed it on the glass coffee table. "I've also got some pamphlets you might enjoy reading." She placed those under the book.

Tye stood. She toyed with asking her own question as they walked toward the door. As she stepped outside of the house, she turned. "Are you sure you don't want to go to church on Sunday? I could come pick you up."

Toni shook her head. "Sunday's are pretty busy around here."

"Is that the day your father comes home?" Sister Sutton asked.

Tye noticed Toni's jaw tighten. "No," she said. She didn't give any further explanation.

"Could we come back this time next week?" Sister Sutton asked.

Slowly, Toni nodded.

Chapter Eight

Toni turned the lights off in the living room and wandered through the rooms in silence. It had always been more house than she or her father had ever needed. Toni had told him as much when they were looking, but Anthony had fallen in love with the newness of the house and had bought it, telling Toni it would be a good investment. Now it mostly stood empty.

Toni walked into the dining room, where her school books beckoned. With resolve she picked them up and walked to the computer in the family room. She had moved the computer from the den into the family room soon after her father had moved out. The den had been her father's room, and although he didn't sleep there he had spent most of his time working on the computer or on the phone with clients. The old leather chair was shaped to his body, and the big desk was full of his personal mementos. Toni didn't feel right moving things around. Some part of her fully expected her father to come home and catch her where she didn't belong. That didn't make any sense though. The den had never been off limits. But it was now. Strange and sad feelings had been so overpowering that she had moved the computer downstairs and shut the den. She didn't use the room anymore. It was as if it had been exorcised from the house and no longer existed.

Placing the books on the desk, Toni opened up her geometry, but she couldn't focus. The visit with the sisters seemed to have drained all of her energy. Or maybe it was the first line in the Book of Mormon she had read as soon as they left. "I, Nephi, having been born of goodly parents... ." What were "goodly parents" anyway? She guessed that if she'd had them she would know. At the age of eleven, her parents separated. Toni didn't know why and no one ever bothered to tell her.

She got up and began wandering again. The question nagged at her. Why had her folks divorced? What had caused such bitterness to grow between them until it festered into a deep and abiding hatred? They must have loved each other at one time.

As a child she remembered hearing pressed voices in angry dialogue at night, and she would know her parents were fighting. When the morning would dawn, her father would be gone and her mother would sit at the table with red-rimmed eyes and little interest in breakfast. Soon her father moved out permanently, but he started going to church. At first, Toni didn't understand his reasons. His attendance had always been sporadic, but after the separation he attended his meetings regularly. As the divorce dragged on, Toni came to realize that his only reason for attending church was to try to take away from her mother her only support. If he were in church, Toni's mother would not go—and she would not allow Toni to go either.

The Sabbath became a tense affair. Every Sunday, Toni and her mother would dress for church. After the meeting had started, they would pull into the parking lot and drive around, looking for the familiar black Mustang owned by Toni's father. If it wasn't in the parking lot, they would go inside. Anxiety would fill Toni as she scanned the congregation from behind, looking for her father. Part of her wished she would see him. She missed him, and her childlike hope was always wishing that her parents would somehow get back together. Then her pragmatic side would hope he was not sitting in the congregation. If Toni's mother saw him, she would leave and drag Toni with her. The chapel became the battleground. Toni was caught in the crossfire.

Toni rubbed her forehead in hopes of pushing out the dreadful humiliation that still washed over her. Even now, alone in the house, her face felt flush with shame. She fanned herself and then opened the French doors to the back deck, stepping out into the darkness. She took great gulps of air, but the thoughts kept coming.

After the divorce, Toni was given the choice of either living with her mom or moving out of Idaho with her father. Toni didn't choose her father so much as she chose the move. Too many times she had been humiliated by her mother's dramatic exits during church meetings. She wanted to go away and start over someplace where no one knew her name or her history. Corvallis, Oregon, became her destination.

The relationship with her mother never did recover. Toni was sure her mother saw her departure as a betrayal. Empty phone conversations and two weeks of dreaded summer vacation was all they shared. At least her mother didn't go to church anymore, so she was spared that humiliation whenever she was forced to go to Idaho.

Her father didn't go to church anymore either. For a while he stayed home on weekends and spent his free time with Toni. Then he began dating a lot of different women and spent fewer and fewer hours at home. Toni became stubbornly self-reliant. In high school she would brag to her friends about her unlimited freedom. Her friends hung on every word with envy. But deep down inside, where it counted, Toni envied them. They had parents.

Then just last week, two sister missionaries had come to her door, and Toni had felt a tug of the good—the days before her folks separated and she had been active in Primary and other church activities. She remembered the potluck dinners where people lined up for her mother's spaghetti. She thought about the Primary teacher who would spend extra time with her after class and gently French braid her long brown hair. That hair was bleached blonde with frazzled ends now.

Toni fiddled with the frizzy strands. Her hair color wasn't the only thing that had been damaged. She would never be able to go back to church. Too much had happened. Still, when Tye Jorgenson had offered to pick her up, Toni had been surprised at the rush of desire she felt to attend. Sundays were lonely in this big house with nothing but the television for company.

Shivering slightly, Toni walked into the house and moved towards the kitchen, where she fixed herself a snack of a bagel with cream cheese, and a glass of milk. She looked at the calendar and wondered when her father would come home for a visit. After Toni had graduated from high school, he had received a promotion and a new sales territory—Texas. Gloria, his new girlfriend, lived in Houston; between her and his job, he rarely made it home. Toni always thought that it was the kids who were supposed to leave home, but she never got the chance. Her father beat her to it.

"You've always been independent," he told her one evening on the phone. "You'll do just fine without me there."

On the outside, she was fine. She got up and made it to school on time—just like thousands of other students. But inside, she was as empty as this house.

Sitting on the couch, she flipped on the television, using the remote. The news reporter blared out headlines, but Toni didn't hear. What did it mean when Sister Sutton said that the Book of Mormon was another testament of Jesus Christ? Who really was Jesus anyway? She thought back to her Primary lessons and remembered being taught about Jesus being born in a manger or a stable. She remembered daydreaming about falling asleep on a haystack—like baby Jesus.

Finishing the last of her milk, Toni turned off the TV and walked to the staircase. She turned and looked into the living room. The silhouette of the Book of Mormon sitting on the coffee table stood out. The silence of the house screamed, and the emptiness that surrounded her swallowed her up and felt as vast as the Grand Canyon. Moving into the darkened living room, Toni picked up the book. Could this Book of Mormon fill the empty void that had been punched into her on the day her parents separated? No. Nothing could do that. But maybe it could offer another path. Maybe it could help her walk away from the teetering edge of loneliness and hurt.

Squeezing the book, Toni turned back to the stairs.

Chapter Nine

I Nephi, having been born of goodly parents ...

She scanned over that line now that she was prepared for it. Toni could remember a dim recollection of her parents playing with her on the lawn with the watering hose. It had been a sweltering day, and the water relieved the burdensome heat and crankiness. In thirty minutes everyone was soaking wet and giggling.

Holding the book close, Toni tried to put those thoughts away and think about Nephi. Who was he? She hesitated a moment before opening the book again. Skimming the first line, she began to read. As the story began to unfold Toni found herself caught up in Nephi's dilemma. He might have had great folks, but his older brothers gave him a horrible time—eventually causing Nephi to flee for his life. Toni drew her knees to her chest. Hadn't she fled for her life when she moved from Idaho? Or had she fled from her life? What would have happened had she stayed in Idaho? Toni had never allowed herself to think of what could have been. It was futile. And more than a bit frustrating.

Nephi had moved also. Toni felt a kinship with the prophet she had never met. His life jumped from the page and entered her heart.

She knew how it felt to be alone in a wilderness—to wander in a strange land. But as she read she noticed one difference between herself and Nephi. He had relied on the Lord. Toni didn't even know the Lord. That was her father's fault. He should've seen that she attended church. Toni sighed. He should have done a lot of things.

Shaking her head, Toni set the Book of Mormon on her nightstand. If this book was only going to remind her of unhappy things she shouldn't read it. She stared at the gold-embossed letters that shown in the light of the table lamp.

What would it be like to have goodly parents? Deep inside, Toni knew the feeling of love. She remembered her ninth birthday when her folks had taken her to Sun Valley for her first skiing lesson. She had been a gangly youngster—all arms and legs. Yet between the coaching from her dad and the encouragement from her mother, she had learned to ski.

She recalled the snowstorm that lasted three days and kept her from school. Even when the power went out, Toni wasn't afraid. Her dad kept the wood stove burning and her mother brought out the cast-iron skillet and Dutch oven, turning it into an indoor camping trip. Oh, the outdoor camping trips! Those were some of Toni's favorite memories. Packing the family truck and heading to unknown camping grounds where she would explore the hiking trails with her parents. The pungent sweet odor of pine and cool mountain air was intoxicating. One day they had stumbled upon a family of rabbits eating in the shady undergrowth of the forest. It had been a moment of discovery, a discovery she had painted in the eighth grade only to have her father give it a blank look and an uninterested, "Hmmm."

Frustration welled up inside as she remembered wondering why her father couldn't see the likeness. "Don't you remember Dad?" she had asked.

"Remember what, honey?" he had asked.

"The rabbits we saw when we went camping."

"Oh, right. The rabbits," he had answered absently.

Putting the book aside, Toni wondered where she had put that painting. She got up and opened the plastic bin under her bed that held her old school work. It wasn't there. She moved to her closet and then stopped.

Closing her eyes, Toni felt the hot tears spill onto her cheeks. It was hard to remember such things and realize that she really wasn't a part of either parent's life now. Her dad was happily going about his daily life in Texas with a woman Toni didn't even know. And her mother—well, it had been months since Toni had talked with her mom. She hadn't seen her since she graduated from high school. The compulsory yearly visits had ended when she turned eighteen, and Toni had breathed a sigh of relief.

Opening her eyes, Toni picked up the book. Nephi probably understood her heartache. He knew what it was like to leave family members behind and never see them again. At least her folks didn't despise her like Nephi's brothers despised him. She wondered what early memories Nephi carried with him. Did he go hunting with Laman and Lemuel? Did they play children's games together, only to turn on him when they grew into adults?

Almost against her will, Toni opened the book again.

Chapter Ten

Tye pulled into the parking lot of her apartment. Sister Sutton had asked if she could meet them again next Wednesday evening. Tye had agreed.

Now that she was home, emotions flooded through her, not the least of which was overwhelming relief. The evening was over and she had withstood it. Could it be that with the help of her Heavenly Father, she had even thrived? She couldn't let go of the moment of triumph she had felt when she had asked Toni to come to church. The answer had been no, but Tye couldn't deny the push she had felt to ask.

Tye got out of the car and stretched. The air was heavy with a rain shower that had just passed. The clean scent of the nearby fir trees carried itself on the cool breeze, refreshing her skin and awakening spirit. Her thoughts turned to her family and the many evenings they had spent with the missionaries. Her family—especially her mother—had always enjoyed the sister missionaries the most. They brought such a warm spirit into their home. Even Tye's mother couldn't deny it, and the whole family looked forward to the dinners and evenings spent with the young women who were teaching the gospel. But as Tye got older she became frustrated with sisters and elders alike. Why couldn't they convert her mom? Tye bit her lip. Was that a fair question? It had seemed fair until tonight. Now she wasn't sure.

Tye slowly walked the stairs, and let herself into her apartment. Meggie was sitting at the dining room table, but it was obvious she wasn't concentrating on her work. Tye became concerned. "Hey, are you okay?" she asked quietly.

Meggie turned away from the table to face her longtime friend. "I'm fine, thanks. You just missed Neil. I'm surprised you didn't run into him in the parking lot."

"Did you have a nice evening?" Tye probed.

Meggie nodded before closing her books. "Do you want a piece of cake?"

Tye's eyes lit up. "Since when do you have to ask?"

Meggie smiled, but Tye could tell she was distracted. Tye joined Meggie in the kitchen, cut herself a piece of cake, and started working on two mugs of hot chocolate. When the steaming chocolate was ready, Tye moved to the table and began nibbling at the cake, waiting patiently.

Several minutes went by before Meggie spoke. "Tye, can I ask you something?"

"Sure."

"What's it like to follow your dream?"

"You mean Trapper, don't you?"

Meg nodded.

"I don't know any other way, Meggie, so I can't compare." She sipped her chocolate. "Still, I sometimes wonder …"

Meggie looked at her.

"I wonder if there's more—or maybe something different. I don't know. Sometimes when I'm all alone and real quiet, I get this vague restless feeling that I can't name. Like I should be doing something different." She looked at Meggie. "I've never told anyone about that before because I don't know how to explain it."

Meggie was taken aback. "I didn't know," she said slowly. "When was the last time you felt that way?"

"Sunday."

"You mean just this last Sunday?"

"Yes."

"Do you think it has something to do with your new calling? Do you feel it now?"

Tye blinked and thought for a moment. No, she didn't feel it. She hadn't even thought of it. But that's how the feeling could be. Roaring in her ears one day and gone the next. "It's gone for now," she said. "What does this have to do with Neil?"

Meggie shook his head. "Nothing really, and yet everything. He said something tonight about how I should be a master chef."

"What happened?"

Meggie leaned back in her chair and sighed. "Did you know he was engaged before?"

"No."

Meggie nodded. "They called off the wedding because he found her on campus with someone else. That's the reason he transferred from the Y. The betrayal really hurt him."

Tye didn't see the connection between Neil's decision to transfer from BYU and following dreams. She took a bite of cake and waited.

Meggie was silent. Then she said, "To turn away from accounting would feel like a betrayal of everything my folks want for me and from me. To continue in a field that I have such little passion for feels like a betrayal of myself." She shook her head. "I know this isn't the same as what Neil has gone through. But still, it made me think. Betrayals come in all sizes—big ones and small ones."

"Don't you think it all comes down to being true to the Lord and ourselves?" Tye asked.

Meggie nodded thoughtfully.

"Have you talked to your folks?"

Meggie shook her head.

"What exactly did Neil say?"

Meggie repeated the conversation.

"I've told you that a thousand times. So have Steve and Michael. Why did it make such a difference tonight?"

"I don't know. I guess I just saw him living with the hurt of a betrayal and I had to ask myself. How am I going to feel in five years, when I'm working for my parents but I'd rather be cooking? Am I going to feel like I betrayed myself?"

"Maybe you're just struggling with some classes. Maybe school is harder than you thought it would be."

"It is hard," Meggie replied. "But only because I want to be doing something else. I want to cook."

Tye nodded.

"I started to think about you and how you work with Trapper. You're building a career in the field of your choice, even though it's dangerous and hard work."

"We've been together practically all our lives, Meg. It's not like you haven't seen Trapper and me working together. Neil is the new number in this equation."

"I just see this quiet determination in him to try to work through this hurtful thing. I see that same quiet determination in you too."

"And what do you see in yourself?"

"I'm just doing what's expected of me."

"Is that so bad?"

"I'm not sure. Tonight Neil asked me what made me decide to go into accounting, and the only answer I could give was my folks and their business." Meggie sighed.

"What are you going to do?"

Meggie sighed. "I don't know. My folks fully expect me to take over the business when they retire in ten years. I'm almost halfway through my schooling. What can I do?"

"Is there any way you could combine cooking and accounting?"

"I don't see how, unless I opened my own restaurant, and any accountant will tell you that's financial suicide. Competition is fierce and start-up costs are enormous."

"Yes. I can imagine."

"I'm sorry. I didn't mean to depress you. We don't have to solve this riddle tonight. Besides, I don't think there's really an answer. I can't just throw two years of schooling away for a dream. I've got to be practical."

"That's the accountant side of you talking."

"Well, I guess I've learned something in the last two years," Meggie said quietly. Then she changed the subject. "How did your missionary evening go?"

"I was so scared," she began before telling Meggie about her evening. Then she became thoughtful. "I guess I'm looking at the missionary process from the other side of the fence for the first time. In the past I was the part-member family who had missionaries come into the home to teach my mother. Now I'm the missionary. I can tell that I'm looking at things differently."

"How is that?" Meggie asked.

"I'm not sure exactly. I guess I'm beginning to feel more patient with the missionary process and realize that those who were teaching my mother were doing the best they could do. Tonight I asked the young woman we're teaching if she wanted to come to church with us, and she said no—just like Mom said no a thousand times."

Meggie sipped her chocolate. "Maybe that's just the Lord's way of blessing you for doing his work."

"Maybe so," Tye mused.

"You're braver than I am," Meggie said. "I think it takes courage to go out and talk to people about the church."

"You might not feel that way if your mom wasn't a member."

Meggie became thoughtful. "Maybe. By the way, have you talked to your folks about becoming a stake missionary?"

Tye shook her head.

"Why not? Knowing your folks, they'll think it's a great idea. It's not too late. Maybe you should call them tonight."

"I think I'm going to call Brother Farrell and accept the new calling first," she grinned. "Then I'll call my folks."

Tye finished her cake and moved into the kitchen to wash her dishes. She picked up the phone as the warm water ran into the sink. The conversation with Brother Farrell took only five minutes. She turned to Meggie. "It's done," she said.

"I bet it feels good to have that settled." Meggie yawned. "I'm going to get ready for bed. I've got an early class in the morning."

"Oh, and I'm meeting Kyle for an early ride. I almost forgot," Tye rose from the couch.

"Again? This is sounding serious," Meggie said.

Tye shook her head. ""His mind is so focused on horses," Tye said. "He hardly notices that I'm a girl. I think he's more interested in Trapper than he is in me," she giggled, then became serious. "Still, I have to admit, I like being with him. Saturday was wonderful."

"It sure is nice to spend time with Neil," Meggie said.

"Has he kissed you goodnight?" Tye asked.

Meggie shook her head. "I'm not sure we're ready for that under the circumstances."

"You mean because of what happened with his fiancée?"

"You mean, ex-fiancée," Meggie corrected, then asked, "Has Kyle kissed you?"

Tye grinned. "If Kyle kisses anyone, it'll be Trapper."

Both girls giggled before saying goodnight.

Once inside her room, Tye picked up the phone. She thought about her folks. Should she tell them about Kyle? It wasn't a serious relationship, but it was a new development.

Cradling the receiver to her ear, Tye dialed her home phone number.

Rex Jorgenson answered. "Hello?"

"Dad?"

"Tye! How are you?"

Tye smiled at the familiarity of her dad's voice. He never changed. "I'm fine, Dad. How are you?"

"We're all fine here. Your mom was just telling me about a magazine she bought for you. It's all about the Olympic three-day-event team. She thought you might like it."

"I'm sure I will. Speaking of horses, I've got lots of news."

"Wait a minute. Let me get your mom on the other line."

There was a brief pause before Trudy Jorgenson came on the line.

"Well, Tye. I was just thinking of you. I'm glad you called. What's this news you have to tell us?"

Suddenly, the excitement of the last few days overcame Tye and she wasn't sure where to start. "Well," she began slowly. "I've been named as the alternate to the competition team."

Her parents gasped in surprise. Her mother was the first to speak. "Tye, that's wonderful news! How did this happen? You're a sophomore. I thought you'd have to wait another year."

Tye filled them in on the details of her appointment.

"Oh, Tye, we are so proud of you. Aren't we, Rex?"

"Absolutely!"

"There's more. I went riding with the captain of the competition squad. His name is Kyle Jensen. I hope we see each other again."

The earlier enthusiasm turned cautious. "You've never shown much interest in boys, er, I mean, men," Rex said. Then he laughed. "And I've always been grateful." Then he sobered. "What makes Kyle different?"

"He understands my feelings about Trapper," Tye explained. "He's a wonderful rider. We have so much in common."

"Then he's a member of the church," Trudy said.

Tye was taken aback. "No," she said slowly. "Why would you think that?"

"Well, you said you have a lot in common. I just know how important the gospel is to you." Trudy began to stammer. "I-I-I thought you would want to see someone who's LDS."

The phone line became fraught with tension. "I just meant that we have horses in common. We've ridden together. That's all. It's not serious," Tye said quickly. "He's just a lot of fun."

"Of course," Trudy said. "Are you seeing anyone else? Someone from the ward?"

"No." Tye tried to laugh. "Like Dad said, I've never been all that interested in men." The effort fell flat.

Tye could feel her father's disappointment in his silence. She was shocked at their reaction. What right did her parents have to judge her? What did it matter to them if she dated a non-member?

"There's more too," she continued, hoping to break the tension. "I have a new calling. I'm a stake missionary."

She could feel her parents breathe with relief. "You've been in Relief Society since you started college," Rex said. "This must be quite an adjustment."

"It felt strange at first, but now that I'm initiated I think it's going to be okay."

"What do you mean by initiated?" Trudy asked.

"I went out with the sister missionaries for the first time tonight."

"You mean you go out and teach?" Trudy asked.

"Yes. I went out tonight."

"My goodness," Trudy said. "It's hard to believe that I have a daughter old enough to be a missionary. I always think that the elders and sisters who come to our home are so grown up."

Tye felt a sting of irritation. She wasn't a child any longer. "I'll turn twenty-one next month," Tye said.

"I know," Rex said solemnly. "It's hard to imagine our only child isn't a child anymore."

Tye's heart softened.

"We sure are looking forward to you coming home this summer," Trudy said. "We miss you, Tye."

"I miss you too," she said. "Well, I'd better let you go. I need to get to bed."

"You've probably got an early morning class tomorrow," Rex said.

"Yeah." Tye didn't tell them she was meeting Kyle.

After a quick goodbye, Tye hung up feeling strangely empty. Maybe she shouldn't have told her folks about Kyle. Their relationship wasn't serious. It certainly wasn't keeping her from the church or her duties. There was no point in them worrying about it. A pulsing irritation grew inside. Why would they be concerned about Kyle's non-member status? Mom wasn't a member, and they got along just fine. Tye sat on the bed and hugged her knees. Maybe the less said about Kyle, the better.

She couldn't deny that she was looking forward to their early morning ride. She dreamed about his soft, gentle voice and had thought about their one embrace so many times the memory was wearing thin.

Tye stood and walked to the window. Rain dashed against the glass. It was late and she had a busy day ahead. Hurriedly, she pushed away all negative thoughts about Kyle and began to concentrate fully on each task as she prepared for bed.

Chapter Eleven

The dawn drew itself onto the horizon painting new light and long shadows on to the morning sky and earth. Rich hues of green, gold, and misty purple awakened with the morning sun like colors splashed across a canvas. Tye breathed in the heavy air still filled with the freshness of dew. "What a gift," she murmured as the sunbeams caressed her face.

"Yes, I know," Kyle replied softly.

Quietly they rode through the morning as the world began to stir. The air began to be full of chatter. Birds, frogs, and other wildlife began to voice their joy over the day. Tye took it all in with gratitude and love. A heavy mist lay close to the ground, and in the distance she could see horses grazing in the next field.

Tye thought of the previous evening's conversation with Meggie. Meggie was right—she was living her dream. Nothing could compare to being with Trapper, and now with Kyle and Ben as she greeted the soft, golden dawn. It filled her with peace and satisfaction. She grasped at it. Satisfaction was so hard for her to hold. Often it slipped through her fingers, but last night's missionary experience had left her with a new peace. The earlier storms of her heart were now as still as this morning. The restlessness that plagued her had not returned. Now, riding in the golden sun, everything felt right with the world. She thought back to her meeting with Toni. She hoped Toni would read the Book of Mormon. Maybe it could help Toni realize her own dream. What was Toni's dream?

Tye turned to Kyle. "What's your dream?" she asked. "If you could have anything you wanted, what would it be?"

Kyle did not hesitate. "I want to ride in the Olympics."

Tye waited for more, noticing a budding intensity.

"I haven't told very many people. I'm afraid they'll just laugh at me. But someday, I hope to have a gold medal." He turned and looked at her, gauging her response.

"I wouldn't laugh at you, Kyle. I believe you're just as capable as any professional rider. I've gone to their seminars, and I've watched you ride for the last eighteen months. I'm convinced you're ready for the professional circuit."

"I don't know, Tye. I've gone to a lot of those clinics too. I always learn so much. I don't think I'm up to their caliber yet."

Tye shrugged. "I'd like to see you go to the Olympics, Kyle. I think it's a dream worthy of your talent."

Kyle looked out over the awakening horizon. "Have you ever thought about riding in the Olympics?"

She shook her head. "No, the Olympics have never been my dream."

"What is your dream?" He asked.

Tye was at a loss. She had never before realized the sacredness of her dreams. Could she tell Kyle about the desire she held for her family? No, he wouldn't understand—yet. Maybe someday he would know the importance of the temple ordinance for which Tye longed. Still, part of her dream was coming true. "I think I'm living part of it," she said.

Kyle laughed. "Riding in the Oregon sunshine?"

"Riding in the Oregon sunshine with you," Tye said. She bit her tongue. The words had just popped out.

Kyle brought Ben to a halt.

Tye met his gaze. Now that the words were out, she wasn't sorry.

"And what's the part of your dream you're not living?" Kyle asked softly.

Tye bit her lip. "It's sacred, Kyle. Something I've longed for all my life."

"And you're not sure you trust me with it."

Tye nodded as she brought Trapper to a halt.

Kyle moved Ben to Trapper's side and faced her. "I would never make light of anything that is important to you, Tye. But I won't push you either. When you feel ready you can share it with me. And I hope someday you'll find me worthy of such trust." He smiled gently and moved Ben into a walk.

Tye caught her breath. She had never shared her most fervent wish with a man. Her dad knew, of course, but he was a part of that dream.

She asked for a walk from Trapper and he complied.

"Do you want to know about the first time I saw you?" Kyle asked.

Tye blinked. Then she smiled. "I don't know. I probably had just taken a spill and was covered with mud, hay, and manure." She laughed.

Kyle joined Tye's laugh, then grew serious. "No. I will never forget that day. It was the most beautiful crisp autumn afternoon and the light was behind you. You had just unloaded Trapper, and you were looking him over for any scrapes, bumps, or bruises. Both you and Trapper glowed—and I could tell it wasn't all from the sun."

Tye blushed. "That seems like so long ago. I didn't know you were watching."

"You were too busy paying attention to your horse, which was how it should be."

Kyle paused. "Can I see you tonight?"

Tye's mouth went dry. She nodded. "I'd like that."

"Can I pick you up around six-thirty?"

"I'll be ready."

For Tye, the rest of the day flew—that is, until now. She was pacing down the hall. She had been ready for thirty minutes, but now that Kyle was to arrive, she felt a tightness in her stomach. Tye heard the knock. Her lipstick! She made a wild dash for the bathroom, and while she carefully put on her lipstick, Meggie answered the door. Tye could hear the introductions being made.

Meggie knocked on the bathroom door and Tye let her in. "You didn't tell me that he's absolutely drop-dead gorgeous," Meggie whispered after she shut the door.

Tye grinned. "I said he was good-looking."

"He's more than good-looking, Tye. My gosh, I can't believe the horses have him all to themselves," she laughed. "If he kisses Trapper, I'd be jealous!"

Tye giggled, appreciative of her friend's easy humor. It eased the tension that fluttered inside.

"You look great," Meggie said as she gave Tye a hug. "Have a good time."

Tye grinned. "I plan on it."

By the time she met Kyle in the living room, the butterflies in her stomach had multiplied. Meggie was right. Kyle was "drop-dead gorgeous." Tye had never seen him away from the barn. He looked fresh, clean, and inviting.

He smiled. "You look great," he said. "I like your hair loose like that."

"Thanks. I never wear it this way at the barn. It would get in the way."

Once in the car, Kyle eased the vehicle into traffic. "I made a vow tonight," he said. "We won't talk about horses. At least not all night."

"That'll be nice," Tye agreed.

"I have reservations at the Fern Grove, then I thought we could go see a movie." He pointed to the movie board they passed on the street. "I've heard that's good," he said pointing to the R-rated movie. "Would you like to see it tonight?"

"I prefer not to see an R-rated movie," Tye replied gently.

Kyle grinned teasingly. "Well, you're over seventeen now. I don't think they'll check for ID."

"No," she started slowly. "You don't understand. I choose not to go."

"Why?" He asked, with a puzzled expression.

"The profanity, the violence, and the sex are all so graphic. I'd rather not see it."

They pulled into the parking lot of the Fern Grove restaurant and were seated at their reserved table by the huge picture window. Even though it was dark, outdoor lighting showed off an abundance of rain soaked ferns. Some hung upside down from mossy tree limbs. They dripped with light, giving the grotto a liquid gold shower.

"It's so pretty here," Tye murmured.

"Yes. It's even pretty in the summer," the waiter said as he handed Tye her menu.

Tye smiled as she took the menu. "It's easy to be pretty in the summer," Tye replied. "But when you find a place that's as lovely as this in the winter, then you know it's special."

The waiter agreed before leaving the table.

After they ordered their meals Kyle continued to question Tye. "I'm curious. What made you decide to never see an R-rated movie?"

"At first I didn't go because my parents said no. After a while I chose not to go. The evening news has enough violence, and I don't appreciate all the sexual content or swearing." Tye leaned back in her chair, surprised at how easy her words flowed. She dated so infrequently that she expected her time away from the horses and with Kyle to be awkward. Instead, she was eager to share. She hoped he felt the same.

The waiter brought a basket of fragrant sourdough bread. Kyle reached in and tore a piece from the loaf.

Kyle was thoughtful. "Yeah, R-rated movies are kind of a mixed bag, I guess. Some have very little swearing or sexual content while others are brimming with it. You never really know until you watch the movie. Still, there are some good movies with an R-rating."

"I'm sure that's true, but I really don't miss it. To be honest I'm not much of a movie buff." Tye continued, "Besides, it's not that unusual, considering how I was raised."

"What do you mean?"

"I'm a Mormon."

"What's a Mormon?"

Tye blinked with her own surprise. "You've never heard of Mormons?"

"No. What's a Mormon?"

"I'm one," she answered. "I mean, it's my religion. I belong to The Church of Jesus Christ of Latter-day Saints. Most people call us Mormons for short."

"Why Mormons?"

"We have a set of scriptures called the Book of Mormon."

"Do you believe in Christ?"

"Yes."

"Then you should be called Christians."

"We are Christians," she said thoughtfully. "Do you believe in Christ?"

He looked at her with a somber expression. "I've never thought much about it. My parents aren't religious. I celebrate Christmas and I know it's in honor of Christ's birth, but that's all I could tell you."

Tye tore her own piece of bread from the loaf. "Have you ever missed anything spiritual?"

He shook his head. "I don't think so. The horses are basically my life. I love my folks and my older brother. I feel complete."

A small corner of Tye's heart drooped with sadness. She wondered if her mother felt complete.

Kyle asked, "Is that why you don't ride on Sundays?"

"Yes."

"How else does it affect your life?"

"Well, the biggest thing is what we call the Word of Wisdom. I don't drink or smoke." She thought about her mother and fought the urge to sniff her sleeve for the familiar stench of cigarettes. She continued, "I try to make Sunday a day of rest. And I believe that Christ is my personal Savior."

"What does that mean?"

"It means that I believe He died for me and that He is my mediator with my Father in Heaven," she answered with gentle conviction.

"Is that why we celebrate Easter?"

"Yes." Tye said with enthusiasm. She could tell that Kyle was at least thinking about their conversation.

"So, what makes you different from other Christian religions?"

"For one, we have another set of scriptures called the Book of Mormon. We believe the Bible and the Book of Mormon to be the word of God."

"What is this Book of Mormon? Is it like the Bible?"

"It's another testament of Jesus, if that's what you mean. We believe that even though Jesus was born of the Jews, after His death and resurrection He visited many people—including people on this continent. The Book of Mormon is a record of that visit to these people." Tye resisted the urge to ask Kyle if he wanted a copy.

Kyle stopped chewing. "I don't know," he said with hesitation.

"You'd have to read it before making a judgment," Tye said.

Kyle nodded slowly. "Yes. I can see how you might be right about that."

The waiter interrupted their conversation by placing their salads in front of them.

Kyle changed the subject. "I know we weren't going to talk about horses tonight, but I was wondering when I could ride with you again?"

The warmth Tye was beginning to recognize in Kyle's company was becoming familiar. Tye nodded. "I would like that," she said.

Kyle nodded. "Are you free tomorrow morning?"

"Yes," Tye said slowly. "But it would have to be early. I could meet you at the barn at six-forty-five."

"I'll be there," Kyle said.

As they ate, the quiet conversation took many different turns. Kyle talked about his family, and the love and admiration he felt for his older brother, who was in medical school. "I always wished I could be more like him," Kyle said quietly. "My folks are so proud of his decisions."

"And you don't think they feel the same way about you?" Tye asked.

Kyle shook his head. "No. They mostly worry about me. They're afraid I'm going to get trampled by some horse. My mom can't even watch me ride anymore. The cross-country course makes her too nervous. They divorced when I about ten, so I don't see either one of them very often." Kyle paused. "Are your folks still together?"

"Yes," Tye said cautiously. "My mom isn't a member of the church though."

Tye recalled Meggie's observation. "But they have a lot in common, and they truly love each other."

"Does your mother's decision to stay out of the church come between your mom and dad?"

Tye thought for a moment. She thought about a day when her family had gone to the beach. Her folks were laughing and playing like a couple of teenagers. She shook her head. "No," she said slowly. "It doesn't seem to. They've been married twenty-four years now. I believe they're happy."

"You'd know if they weren't happy," Kyle said. "I think kids have an uncanny ability to know the currents in the home, even if the parents try to hide it. Even though I was young, I knew something wasn't right. The funny thing is, there wasn't a whole lot of yelling and fighting. The house was quiet. Almost like a tomb. I was almost glad when they finally split. It was like this huge relief. I think that's why they encouraged me to ride. It gave me something else to think about."

"What about your older brother? How did he handle the split?"

"He became quiet. Before the divorce he had been a real outgoing kid. Then after the split, he just got quiet. I think it was because he felt all of this responsibility that was new to him. He was the oldest and a boy, so he felt like he was supposed to look after Mom. No one told him that she could look after herself. So, he grew up thinking he needed to take care of her emotionally. I think it was hard on him, but it's also made him pretty mature. I think that's why he's choosing to be a doctor. He's used to the responsibility."

"Have you ever considered medical school?"

Kyle laughed. "Me, a doctor? No way. I want to ride. I've got several applications out to barns in three states. I'm really hoping for Willoughby stables in Pennsylvania or Seven Gables in Virginia. I know my folks would be pleased if I chose a more traditional job. But it's in my blood now and I know I'd be miserable doing anything else."

Tye and Kyle talked until the waiter interrupted them with the dessert tray. Tye couldn't believe their meal was almost over. She and Kyle had shared fun childhood memories, and even though they had vowed to keep horses out of their conversation they had found themselves discussing the many competitions in which they had participated. After dessert, Kyle checked his watch. He gasped in amazement. "Do you realize it's after nine-thirty?" he asked. "We couldn't go to a movie now, even if we wanted to."

Tye grinned. "Isn't this better than an R-rated film?"

Kyle reached for her hand and looked into her eyes. "Yes," he said honestly. "I've had a wonderful evening."

Tye squeezed Kyle's fingers. "I'm glad," she answered quietly. "It's been nice for me as well."

"I'm going to take you home though," Kyle said. "Otherwise we won't be able to meet for our early morning ride. I've always hated getting up early in the morning."

"You're in the wrong business then. Horses require early risers."

Kyle laughed. "I know. I sure miss sleeping in."

Several minutes later, Kyle walked Tye to her door. "Thank you for coming with me tonight," he said. "It's the nicest evening I've had in a long time."

Tye nodded. "Me too," she said.

He took her hand once again. Tye pressed his warm palm. She wanted to reach out and touch his hair and pull him close. Then she heard someone clomping up the stairs and the spell was broken. Kyle dropped her hand.

Michael and Steve stopped. "Hey, Tye. Who's this?" Michael asked.

"You sure are nosy," Tye replied.

Steve grinned. "We do our best."

Tye made introductions.

"We'll leave the two of you alone. But first we need to ask about Meggie." Steve asked.

"She's fine, but I wouldn't count on any muffins for a while. She's teaching Neil to cook."

Michael shook his head. "I knew that chocolate cake would be the end of the good stuff. I'm sorry we introduced the two of them. Now we're left to our own cooking devices—and that's scary. If anything ever catches on fire, we'll come knock on your door so you can evacuate."

Tye giggled. "Thanks, but maybe the two of you should stick to cold cereal."

Michael and Steve waved as they let themselves into their own apartment.

"They sure seem pretty friendly for just being neighbors." Kyle said.

"They go to my church, but don't tell anybody," Tye grinned. Then she laughed. "They're really a lot of fun, when they're not being annoying. We kind of look out for each other. They're always checking on us and making sure we're okay. If the day has gone by without any correspondence, they'll call and just check or we'll call and check on them. It's a nice way for all of us to keep tabs on each other."

Kyle nodded but Tye could tell that his thoughts were already far away from her neighbors. She waited.

Kyle backed away. "Well, I guess I'll see you in the morning."

Tye watched as Kyle hurried down the stairs and into the windy night. Tomorrow couldn't come fast enough.

Chapter Twelve

Tye arrived early at the barn. She had been so excited about her date with Kyle and their upcoming morning ride that she had barely slept. Finally at 6:00 A.M., she threw off the bedsheets and hurriedly dressed in her breeches, boots, and a sweater before driving to the barn. It wouldn't hurt to warm up Trapper before they actually went out into the wet and fitful morning. As Tye parked her car, she noticed how the cold northern wind pushed the clouds across a sodden sky. The dawn was almost blue from the wind and gray clouds. It was a very different Oregon morning than the one she had shared with Kyle just the previous day. Most folks hated this weather, but Tye found it challenging.

Hurrying to Trapper, Tye let herself into his stall. He looked wonderful, and she was caught in admiration. Often, she would take a quiet minute and gaze in amazement at Trapper. His beauty awed her. His friendship humbled her. Quietly, Trapper nuzzled Tye's shoulder. Tye leaned into his warmth. Then she gave him a quick pat and left his stall for the tack room. She was so involved in collecting her gear that she didn't hear the footsteps come in behind her and close the door.

"Congratulations on your new position as the alternate. I heard

Katie's announcement on Monday."

Tye whirled around, almost dropping her saddle. She smiled. "Thanks, CarrieAnne. I'm looking forward to it. I guess we'll be working together now." She placed her bridle on her shoulder and hefted her saddle into a more comfortable position before moving towards the door.

CarrieAnne blocked her exit. "Not if I have anything to say about it. I should be the one and only alternate," she hissed. "I can't believe that Katie would make me share that position with a sophomore. You think you're so clever. Everyone knows you're seeing Kyle and that the two of you helped Jade with Gypsy. That's the only reason you're riding with the competition team. Katie just wanted to reward you for saving Jade and Gypsy's life. That's all this is. Everyone knows the truth."

Tye's mouth went dry. CarrieAnne's words left her reeling. Is that really why Katie had offered her the alternate position? Because she felt Tye deserved some reward for saving Jade and Gypsy? How could members of the squad know she was seeing Kyle? They had tried to be discreet.

CarrieAnne continued. "I used to date Kyle. He's nothing special. You'll see."

The new revelation felt like a punch in the stomach.

CarrieAnne opened the door and sauntered out of the tack room, leaving Tye with her mouth open as she gripped her saddle. Kyle and CarrieAnne? Was her position as the new alternate really just a reward for saving Jade's life instead of a reward for good riding? Tye tried to recall the interview she had with Katie. It was dim and far away. Katie had thanked her for acting in time to save Jade and Gypsy. She really loved that mare and now her new filly. Maybe CarrieAnne was right.

And what about Kyle? How long had it been since he had dated CarrieAnne? Did he still have feelings for the junior rider?

CarrieAnne was beautiful. Even at the barn when most women looked their worst, CarrieAnne had a natural kind of beauty that thrived in the outdoor surroundings. Tye closed her eyes and tried to remember any rumors about the two. Nothing came to mind. Apparently they were more discreet than Tye and Kyle. Wasn't CarrieAnne married?

Questions swirled around her like a straw caught in a whirlwind. A shiver ran through Tye, bringing her back to the present. It was too cold to be anchored in one place. Her body needed movement. Readjusting the position of the saddle one more time, she hurried to Trapper's stall. He looked at her with the same placid eyes that were so familiar to her, and yet things weren't the same. Methodically, Tye began to saddle her horse. Katie had told Tye that if anyone approached her about the alternate position, she wanted to know. Tye had been expecting some kind of grumbling from the juniors, but when Monday came and nothing was said, she had forgotten about the whole thing. Katie wouldn't tolerate any dissension among her ranks. Should Tye say something?

She cinched the saddle tight and Trapper let out an involuntary grunt. She loosened the buckle a notch. "Sorry, boy," she said absently as she patted his neck. "We'll wait a few minutes for that." She moved towards his head and began placing the bit in his mouth. Trapper accepted it.

Maybe it would be better if Tye didn't say anything. It would look like she was whining. If she ever hoped for real camaraderie with the team maybe it would be good for CarrieAnne to see that she could take a little heat from a fellow member. After all, she could understand how CarrieAnne would feel. She was supposed to move into the alternate position. It was her rightful place as the captain of the junior team. Now that position had been yanked out from under her, and she was made to share with a sophomore. Tye couldn't deny that she would feel a bit unsettled—maybe even angry and jealous. Was that at the root of CarrieAnne's feelings? Was she afraid that

Tye would eventually take the captain position as a junior, leaving CarrieAnne with a blank spot on her resume? Or was CarrieAnne jealous over her relationship with Kyle? Maybe they were still seeing each other. No, that wasn't possible. CarrieAnne was married. What about Kyle? Her thoughts went blank. Dark doubts crowded inside her heart.

"Hey, you ready to go?"

Tye jumped. Kyle was standing in the aisle with Ben.

"Um, yeah. I guess so."

She opened Trapper's stall door and followed Kyle into the blue gray dawn. She mounted Trapper while Kyle mounted Ben. There was no sign of CarrieAnne. Her car was not in the parking lot. "Have you seen CarrieAnne this morning?" she asked.

"No." Kyle gave her a strange look. "Have you?"

Tye wondered what that look meant. She tried to appear casual. "I just ran into her in the tack room." So many questions, but what to ask? Nothing. She needed to think.

Tye pushed Trapper into a walk as she glanced at Kyle.

"She likes to check on Van, her horse, on school mornings before class. She doesn't ride though. Was she cranky? CarrieAnne likes to have the mornings in the barn to herself."

Tye wondered how Kyle could know so much about CarrieAnne's morning habits. She studied him. He was completely at ease, and it was obvious by his expression that the conversation was over. Tye bit her lip and looked ahead.

"How long has it been since you and Trapper have had a good gallop?" Kyle asked.

Tye shrugged, grateful for the change in conversation. "We practiced our cross-country just last week."

"Yes, but you have to worry about obstacles then. What do you say we take our boys to the races?"

As if understanding the challenge, Trapper gave a jaunty trot. Tye had to rein him in. "I guess he's ready." Quietly, she dismounted and shortened her stirrups. Kyle also leapt to the ground and within a couple of minutes, both horses and riders were ready. Tye shortened her reins as she lifted her body out of the saddle slightly, asking for a canter. Dropping her weight into her heels, she grazed Trapper's side with her boot. He shifted into high gear as smooth as a race car and within seconds the landscape was whirring. She knew Ben and Kyle were beside her, matching her and Trapper's pace stride for stride, but she didn't see them.

Tye turned her attention to the cold wind that tugged and numbed her skin. It stung her eyes, forcing tears. She let the tears go. It felt good to cry, even if it was simply an invitation from the biting cold. Trapper immediately found his rhythm. He enjoyed running. Tye enjoyed it too. She could outrun all her cares and worries when she was with Trapper. She asked for more speed and with a burst of muscle and energy, Trapper gave it to her, leaving Ben and Kyle behind. Tye maintained her balance and did not interfere with Trapper's motion. Instead, she kept as quiet as possible and let him run. Her concerns over CarrieAnne, Kyle, and the alternate position dropped away as she felt the freedom that can only come from racing with the wind and sky. It didn't matter that menacing clouds covered her horizon or that her worries would return in a whirlwind of questions. All that mattered now was the cold wind challenging her body and the warm horse that helped her beat that foe.

Chapter Thirteen

Tye walked into the show-jumping arena with her sophomore teammates and looked at the course with a critical eye.

Janna Levin sidled up to her along with her horse, Spud. "Sometimes I wish you hadn't been named as the alternate for the competition team," Janna whispered to Tye. "Ever since Katie made the announcement two weeks ago, she's been as tough as an old spinster school marm."

Tye laughed. "Don't you dare blame that on me, Janna. Katie has always been tough."

Janna gave her a wry look as both women led their horses to the middle of the arena with the rest of the team. "I'll hold Trapper while you walk the course," Janna said. "After all, we'll all want your expert opinion when you're finished," she teased.

Jim Thomas and Nina Simpson, the other two members of the sophomore squad laughed quietly.

Jim continued with the teasing, "Janna, I'll let you hold Trapper this time, but I want my turn. We all want to touch the fabled reins of our esteemed team member who's been named alternate to the competition team."

"All right, that's enough," Tye laughed. But she enjoyed the banter. It helped take the edge off the conversation earlier in the week with CarrieAnne.

If the sophomore team was congratulatory and teasing, the junior team was ominously silent. So far CarrieAnne's hostility was the only open declaration, but no one from the junior team offered Tye a pat on the back or a friendly word. She tried to understand how the junior team would feel. After all, if the situation had been reversed Tye would feel cheated.

Tye hoped Katie's faith in her wouldn't be misplaced. The knowledge that CarrieAnne was waiting for her to make a mistake made the pressure maddening.

Katie walked into the arena. She was a petite woman with short dark hair that hung straight to her jaw line. She was constantly tucking the strands behind her ears. She was dressed in black riding boots, tan breeches, and a dark brown sweater. In spite of her diminutive size, Katie was a powerhouse on horseback. Sometimes if a rider was having trouble with her mount, Katie would ask her to get down and she would sit in the saddle, quietly but firmly working the horse through any misunderstanding.

Tye remembered the first time Katie had ridden Trapper. She and Trapper had been in school for two weeks when Tye had tried to introduce him to a new water jump. For years Tye had ridden Trapper through ponds and creeks—both for fun and for competition. But when he was faced with a false water jump in the show-jumping arena with its bright turquoise tarp simulating water that rattled and waved in the wind, he would have none of it. Tye had become tense and irritated with Trapper. This was only their fourth practice session at OSU, and she and Trapper weren't exactly making a good impression. To make matters worse, the whole freshman squad was watching. Tye could feel her face color with shame. Every time they approached the obstacle, Trapper would come to an abrupt halt and practically sit down on his haunches before traveling sideways. Tye would use her leg against Trapper's side runs, pushing him closer to the obstacle, but he would throw his head and prance in mincing steps that took him in every direction but forward. After several minutes, Tye's frustration made her useless.

Katie moved from the side of the course, and Tye brought Trapper to a halt, several paces away from the obstacle.

"You're not helping him," Katie said. "You're fighting him, and that's not going to encourage him to do it your way."

Tye was humiliated in front of her teammates. "I don't understand it," she said. "He's always so good about doing whatever I ask. What's the matter with him?"

"First let me ask what's the matter with the rider? Look at yourself, Tye. You're so tense that you're gripping the reins with white knuckles. You're holding all that tension in the neck and shoulders, which is throwing your body forward. You're forcing him off balance. So not only are you asking him to jump something he's never seen before—which is okay, he should be able to trust you enough to do that, but you're asking him to jump with you throwing him off balance. That's what his main objection is."

Exasperated, Tye forced out a sigh.

"Dismount," Katie said.

For one brief moment, Tye thought about arguing. She could do this.

"Dismount," Katie repeated.

Tye obediently climbed down from Trapper.

Katie checked the stirrup lengths and then climbed into the saddle. She rode Trapper in a trot for a moment. Tye watched as her horse visibly relaxed under the tutelage of her trainer. His head came down and he began to travel in the correct body posture, which would allow him to use his haunches for take-off over the obstacles. Katie rode him over several obstacles and Trapper sailed over them effortlessly. Then came the water jump with its blue tarp rattling in the wind. Tye's hands began to sweat and she had an overwhelming desire to shut her eyes tight. She forced herself to pay attention. Katie remained calm and kept Trapper well packaged between hand and leg. Then with a few gentle half-halts, she prepared Trapper for the jump. In a blink of an eye he was over the obstacle. It hadn't been graceful, but that would come later. Katie moved him onto the next few obstacles so that Trapper would understand that the work didn't end with the blue tarp. Then she brought him down to a trot and asked for some suppling exercises before bringing him to Tye. She dismounted.

"Your turn," Katie said without any fanfare. "Now, I want you to remember to stay calm. Don't push him out of his line. If he squirms, keep him focused by squeezing him with your leg and giving him a quick half-halt. He knows what it means. So do you. That will set him up properly for the obstacle."

Tye mounted. "Yes, ma'am."

She saw Katie smile briefly before moving Trapper back onto the field. She started the course at the beginning. On the approach to the water jump, Tye could feel Trapper begin to stiffen and begin to push his weight to his front end and to the left. He wanted to run. Tye dropped her weight into her hips and heels and squeezed him into the half-halt Katie recommended. Trapper responded and shifted his weight to his haunches. Then they were airborne. He was over.

"Do it again!" Katie yelled. "Then finish the course."

Tye obeyed. This time Trapper was relaxed and focused.

"Good job!" Katie yelled. "Now bring him in."

Tye did as she was told and after cooling Trapper down, she dismounted. She couldn't deny her humiliation, but she also couldn't deny that Katie would be good for them.

She was leading Trapper into the barn when a fellow freshman teammate walked beside her. "Don't worry," Jim said. "She's already been on Popper's back three times."

Jim, who was leading Popper, moved on ahead, but his words helped put Tye's humiliation in perspective. After all, she and Trapper were both here to learn and Katie was here to teach.

Katie's voice brought Tye back to the present. "Okay, kids," Katie said. "Who's going first?"

The remaining team members voted for Tye, who gave them a grimace before handing her reins to Janna. Once she was on the course though, all other thoughts left her. She didn't see Kyle take a seat in the stand. She didn't notice a look pass between him and Katie. She simply concentrated on her task. Then each of the riders took turns walking the course, deciding how many strides their horse would need between obstacles. After everyone had walked the course, Tye mounted Trapper and circled the course to allow him to look over the jumps.

Using every available inch in the corner of the arena, Tye turned Trapper towards the first obstacle. Maneuvering the course Tye thought this was one of the tougher courses she had seen during her tenure at Oregon State. She pushed her leg into Trapper's side for a tight turn. Trapper responded. He seemed to sense that there was no room for mistakes. To misjudge a fence meant to have a rail down and the penalty of four faults added to the final score. Trapper brought one rail down when his hind leg rubbed against an obstacle. But considering the difficulty of the course, Tye was pleased with their performance.

It wasn't until after Tye was finished and had brought Trapper to a halt that her eyes flickered in Kyle's direction. She didn't acknowledge him. Instead, she concentrated on the other riders. Even though the course didn't change, because each horse and rider team was different, each rider approached the obstacle differently. Some horses were smaller than Trapper and would require more strides in between the fences. Riders needed to know their horse very well, and horses needed to trust their riders. Tye could learn from each horse and rider team that would go through the course.

Jim went next. His ride was a little rough and by fence six, it was obvious that Popper was having a hard time negotiating his big body through the tighter turns. The fence came crashing down. The work crew ran out and put the fence back together while Katie spoke with Jim, who remained on horseback. They started again and this time only rattled the rails on fence six. It remained standing. But he brought two other rails down on fence eight and nine.

Nina Simpson had a clean ride on Tango. Janna knocked down two rails with Spud.

After the lesson was over, Tye and Janna walked side by side, leading their horses.

"You know, I've always wondered why you call your horse Spud," Tye said. "He certainly doesn't look like a potato."

Janna giggled. "He did when he was born," she said. "I was convinced he would be the ugliest horse in the barn. We gave him the name when he was just a baby and it kind of stuck." A dreamy look came into her eyes. "He's beautiful now, though. Isn't he?" She nuzzled Spud with true affection.

Tye stopped at Trapper's stall and waved Janna off. She was untacking Trapper when Kyle came and stood outside the stall.

"You did well today," he said.

"Thanks. Everyone on the sophomore squad is saying that Katie has started making the lessons more difficult because I've been named as the alternate on the competition squad."

"Are they whining?"

"More like teasing." Tye removed Trapper's saddle and handed it to Kyle, who placed it across the bar on the outside door the stall. She began to brush him.

"I'll tell you something Tye. When your team becomes the competition squad, you're going to be the best around. I've watched your team train and they're way beyond where we were. I know that today's course was difficult. In fact it's so difficult we never saw anything like it when I was a sophomore. Katie says that every now and then a group will come along that exceeds all expectations. She thinks the sophomore team is the team that's going to do that."

Tye blinked. The praise warmed her. It felt good to have the confidence of the trainer—especially a trainer who knew her business better than most. Maybe her placement as the alternate wasn't a mistake after all. "Thanks, Kyle. That's nice to hear."

Kyle grinned. "Well, just don't get too cocky. Katie doesn't care much for big egos."

Tye laughed. "It's hard to have a big ego when she's the trainer. I don't care how long I ride, she'll always be better than me."

Kyle laughed. "Why don't you finish up here and we can go grab a hamburger. I'm starved."

Tye quickened her pace. "I'd like that," she said as she began feeding Trapper his apple. "But we'd better go to the drive-up window. I smell like horse."

Chapter Fourteen

Meggie sat in sacrament meeting with Tye and Neil. When she glanced at Neil, he winked. Meggie smiled. For three weeks she and Neil had dated. She could feel her affection for him growing. Their last evening together had consisted of Meggie teaching Neil two muffin recipes. He even whipped up a batch himself, and the success had given him courage to try them at home. Yet in spite of the joy they found in each other's company, Meggie knew that Sammi Rae still resided somewhere in Neil's heart. Often during their evenings, Meggie wanted to pull Neil close for a quiet embrace—yet she never did. If he was thinking about Sammi Rae, Meggie didn't want to compete. How could she compete with a ghost? She wished she didn't want more than Neil was willing to give and yet that was how it was beginning to feel. When Meggie talked with Tye, her friend had nodded her understanding. "Your feelings are completely normal, Meg. The two of you seem to have really bonded."

Meggie had only sighed as Tye hugged her. "Be patient," Tye said. "He has some things to work through, but he may well be worth the wait."

Meggie found it ironic that she had vowed to never wait for a missionary and yet here she was, waiting for a man. A missionary would be easier. At least his heart would belong to the Lord and not some BYU co-ed.

After the Sunday church meetings, Neil asked Meggie if he could take her home. Tye grinned and said, "I won't wait up."

"Well, I hope you will. It's only noon," Meggie replied.

"We won't be late," Neil said. "But it's a beautiful day and some of the daffodils are beginning to bloom. I thought it might be nice if we took a little detour."

"I'd love to," Meggie responded. "If you'd like you're welcome to stay for dinner. I'm baking a chicken tonight."

"Do you want me to put the bird in the oven?" Tye asked.

"That would be great," Meggie replied. "It's been marinating all day. Pre-heat the oven to three-hundred and fifty degrees and put the timer on for an hour."

Tye waved as she moved toward her car, leaving Meggie and Neil in the bright, warm, spring sunshine.

"It is a beautiful day," Meggie said as she climbed into Neil's car.

Neil turned the ignition and the car sprang to life. He pulled out of the parking lot and drove slowly down the residential street. Everywhere spring was beginning to unfold. Front yards, which had lain dormant for months, were beginning to awaken and come to life. Trees were beginning to unwrap their new summer wardrobe, and tender new grass was beginning to clothe the earth.

Meggie rolled down her window and took in a great gulp of air. "It's so fresh," she exclaimed.

"How would you like to go to the beach for a day trip next Saturday?" Neil asked. "I know it's not the ski slopes, but the spring skiing isn't very good this year. I don't make it to the ocean very often and I'd sure like your company. It'll probably be the last time I go before summer vacation."

"Oh, yes. I'd love to."

Soon, they were out of the residential area and into the farmlands.

"I've never gone home this way," Meggie said.

"It's the long route. There's something I want to show you."

Meggie peered through the windshield. "What's growing in that field?" she asked as she pointed ahead.

"That's what I want to show you." Neil drove slowly as they came upon the field of yellow.

"Daffodils!" Meggie exclaimed. "By the thousands."

"Yep. They grow them here and ship them all over. Aren't they beautiful? In a couple of weeks the tulips will bloom."

"I can't believe I've missed this. They're gorgeous."

Neil pulled onto the shoulder and turned off the engine, and together they climbed out of the little truck. Neil helped Meggie step on the bumper so she could sit next to him on the hood. Silently, they gazed at the beautiful display arranged by nature and man. The bright yellow petals were just beginning to trust the warm invitation issued by the spring sunshine and unwrap themselves.

"Next week they'll be in full bloom, " Neil said. He paused. "These last few weeks with you, Meggie, have been some of the most peaceful I've ever experienced. I didn't realize how I missed that peace. When I'm with you like this, nothing else matters."

Meggie pushed away tears. "Nothing?" she asked.

"Nothing," Neil said.

Meggie looked out over the daffodils. She knew what he was saying. But could he be believed? Could he really put Sam behind him? She turned towards him, "Neil—"

Neil placed his fingers over her lips. "Shhhh. We don't need to talk about her, Meggie. I don't want to talk about her."

"But you think about her."

"Not nearly as often as I used to. And soon I won't be thinking of her at all. I can feel it." He caressed her cheek.

Meggie looked down. "What do you think about then?"

Neil smiled and raised Meggie's chin with his finger. "I'm thinking about you." His eyes turned cheerful. "And the wonderful fun we've created together, and the wonderful food you create for me."

Meggie shook her head. "I'm admired for my lasagna. What a horrible fate." She grinned.

"If you cooked in your own restaurant, you'd probably have thousands of admirers."

"I'll never have my own restaurant," Meggie replied. "It's too risky."

"Let's talk about those risks. Sometimes when they're out in the open, they don't seem so bad."

"Well, I haven't told my family yet and I know they'll be disappointed. I don't want to do that to them. Then there's the actual business risk. There are few jobs at the top of the pay scale, but tons of jobs for waitresses and short-order cooks. I don't want to be flipping hamburgers."

"Let's look at the worst case scenario: say you can't get the kind of job you want. Couldn't you always go back to accounting? Or maybe in the process of following this dream, another one would show itself. Dreams are like that."

"What do you mean?"

"Well, I've always dreamed about learning to cook. Not like you though. I just want to be able to succeed in my own kitchen. That dream is being fulfilled. But in the process of meeting that dream, I've discovered another one. I've discovered you, Meg. I needed to learn how to cook and you can teach me. But that was only what brought us together. Now you're a part of my dream."

"What are you saying, Neil?"

Neil became thoughtful. "I'm not sure, Meggie. But in the process of fulfilling one of my dreams I've discovered another one. All I know is that I'm glad we're together. I know neither one of us can tell what the future holds, but we have this moment," he said quietly. "We have these daffodils and we have this sun and right now we have each other," Neil said.

The now familiar concern raced inside of Meggie. Could she trust Neil? She wanted to push him away until she was sure he was over Sam. But she yearned to invite him into her life, just as the daffodils longed for the sun. Gently she placed her hands on his chest and he drew her near in a kiss. A fresh breeze surrounded them and it carried the scent of thousands of daffodils and the promise of spring.

When they drew apart, Meggie felt the thrill of their kiss. It pulsed through her with every heartbeat. Oh, yes, the dream had its share of risks. Just as the daffodils risked being beaten by a hard spring rain, she risked being crushed by Neil's feelings for Sammie Rae. But right now, the risk was worth it and the pain was a distant impossibility.

Neil looked out over the field of yellow. "I'll always remember this moment," he said. "I don't care if I grow to be ninety years old." He smiled. "You and me and the daffodils."

Neil hopped from the hood of his truck and helped Meggie down. "I'd better get you home so you can tend dinner. I like Tye, but I don't trust her with the chicken. It needs your special touch."

Later that evening as Tye finished the dishes, Meggie sat in her room and stared at the pile of completed homework. Dinner had been lively with conversation and laughter. This was the first time Tye had spent any real time with Neil, and they hit it off immediately. After dinner, Meggie had walked Neil to his car. This time he kissed her goodnight. Even though it was only their second kiss, it felt strangely familiar. When she walked into the apartment, Tye had known immediately. "You kissed him. Or he kissed you," she said.

Meggie smiled tenderly. "Yes. It was wonderful."

"I guess so," Tye said.

"We're going to the coast this Saturday and I can't wait."

"Was anything said about his former girlfriend?"

"He doesn't want to talk about her anymore, and neither do I."

"Do you worry about her?"

"I know I should be thinking about that," Meggie said soberly. "But I'm not. I guess it's a risk I'm willing to take."

Tye shook her head. "My best friend accountant, willing to take a risk? Why Meg, that doesn't sound like you."

"Maybe it should sound like me," Meggie said.

She went to her desk and thought about the other risk she was yearning to take. She couldn't deny the satisfaction that filled her when she placed Neil's steaming plate in front of him. She had marinated the chicken in a mixture of soy, ginger, garlic, sesame and olive oil. The seasonings blended together to create a savory and enticing aroma. It was Meggie's favorite recipe; her own special creation.

Right before dinner, Michael and Steve appeared. "We can smell the chicken in the breezeway," Steve said.

Meggie turned to Neil. "Do you mind if they join us?" she whispered.

Neil kissed Meggie's hair. "No." He pulled away and laughed. "I would hate for them to die of malnutrition."

"Pull up a chair," Meggie had replied. The two boys hadn't needed any prompting and the chicken was split five ways, along with the rice pilaf and fresh green beans with butter and lemon-pepper. It was a skimpy meal for five people, but no one seemed to notice.

Meggie closed her eyes. Opening a restaurant was financial suicide. It was out of the question. Sighing, Meggie pulled the Sunday paper from her bed and scanned the help wanted ads. Her folks had offered her a summer job in their office, but they had also encouraged her to work in different accounting firms so that she could get a more general feel for the business. Meggie looked under 'A'. A couple of firms were hiring receptionists. Meggie yawned. How boring. She had done her share of reception work whenever her folks needed help. She didn't want to spend her whole summer stuck behind a desk and phone.

With little interest Meggie read through the rest of the A's. Nothing. Slowly, she scanned the B's. An ad caught her attention and she sat up and focused on the paper. A bed and breakfast was looking for a morning cook during the summer months. The inn was actually an active farm where the maximum of ten guests were invited to participate in the work. Ranch breakfasts were served at six-thirty and nine. Some recipes were provided. Meggie's heart raced. Could she do it? Could she cook for ten people? Scanning the rest of the ad, Meggie read the details. Experience preferred but not required. Three applicants would be chosen to spend the night at the ranch and cook breakfast for the owners.

Hurriedly, Meggie went to her computer and drafted a letter of application. She was about to seal it when she thought about the blueberry muffin recipe she had improved. Quickly, she added it to the envelope and sealed it. Wouldn't it be exciting to cook for a bed and breakfast? She had never considered inn-keeping. There would be so much to learn. Hugging the letter to her chest, Meggie hurried outside and placed it in the outgoing mailbox.

Chapter Fifteen

The following Wednesday, Tye sat on the same sofa in Toni's spotless living room. She noticed that the Book of Mormon and other reading materials they had left were gone.

Toni sat in the chair by the window. "I want to go to church this Sunday," she announced when Tye and Sister Sutton had settled on the couch.

Tye felt warm with relief and happiness.

"That's great, Toni. Can I ask what you've been thinking about this week that made you come to this conclusion?" Sister Sutton asked.

"I read 1 Nephi," Toni said.

"And what was it that impressed you?"

"I'd rather not go into it," Toni said. "But I read 1 Nephi this week, and now I want to go to church."

"I can come pick you up at about ten-forty-five," Tye suggested. "Church is at eleven."

"I'd appreciate that," Toni said. She knew where the church building was located, but she didn't want to go alone. It would be too easy to change her mind. Knowing that Tye was coming to pick her up would keep her from staying home.

"My roommate, Meggie, will be with me, so you'll be able to meet her," Tye said. "You'll like Meg."

Toni smiled. That was even better.

"Would you like to hear about the plan of salvation?" Sister Sutton asked. "It's often called the plan of happiness."

Toni nodded. "I think I'm ready."

Sister Sutton pulled out her chart and began teaching.

Tye listened with real intent, and even though the information wasn't new it was compelling. She wished Kyle could be here—listening to the good news. She wondered how he would react. And how would he react to her dream of being sealed to her parents? She didn't want to think about that.

Sister Sutton asked Tye to read a scripture, so she turned to the chapter and verse and read aloud.

"Did you read about Lehi's dream in the Book of Mormon?" Sister Sutton asked.

Toni nodded. "Yes, I did, but I'm not so sure I understood it."

"Well, it's kind of like the plan of happiness," Sister Sutton said. "We must endure to the end and work hard to obtain that perfect fruit. But that's not the end of the story. Even after we partake of the fruit, we need to continue to strive for perfection. In Lehi's dream some would wander away even after they had eaten. Some were even ashamed. Those who were laughing at them from the tall, spacious building influenced them. When we partake of the fruit, we need to be committed to our Heavenly Father and His plan so that we don't wander in the mist and lose our way."

Toni nodded slowly. "So, the story is really a parable." She became quiet and looked down at her hands. "I'm going to be perfectly honest with you sisters," Toni said. "I'm not worthy to partake of that fruit."

"What would make you say that?" Sister Sutton asked gently.

"Well, I've got a beer in the refrigerator right now. Several beers to be perfectly honest, and a bottle of wine too. I'm not an alcoholic, but I drink a couple times a week. And when I was in high school, me and my boyfriend ..." her voice trailed off. "Let's just say we drank."

"What about your current boyfriend?" Sister Sutton asked.

Toni's shoulders slumped. "I lied about that," she murmured. "I'm not seeing anyone." She sighed and then looked at Tye and Sister Sutton. Her eyes were filled with tears. "I'm one of those people in the spacious building," she said. "When I was in high school, I used to laugh at the Mormon kids. Because I knew what Mormons believed, I knew just where they were vulnerable." She cried. "I used to say horrible things."

Tye felt her own tears. Toni was truly anguished over her past deeds. She was facing them. What about Tye's past deeds? There were sins of omission as well as commission. The thought cut off Tye's breath. Had she neglected some important part of her relationship with her mother?

Toni's countenance changed and she became angry. "It's all my father's fault," she snapped. "He never bothered to take me to church when I was a kid. He didn't even stay at home on the weekends. I basically could do whatever I wanted. What do you think any sixteen- or seventeen-year-old kid is going to do under those conditions? Of course I drank—not a lot, but enough. Of course I fooled around. Why not? He never took the time to teach me about the facts of life so I figured it out on my own."

"Did you take drugs?" Sister Sutton asked.

Toni's anger dissipated for a moment. "No," she said. "I never bothered with them. I went to a party once where a bunch of kids were stoned, and it didn't look like that much fun. I saw a kid vomit right where he was sitting and then he rolled over in it."

"How would you feel if we went into the kitchen and dumped out the alcoholic beverages?" Sister Sutton asked.

Toni thought for a moment. Then she shook her head. "No. I might want a beer after you sisters leave." She didn't smile.

"The choice is yours, of course," Sister Sutton said quietly.

Toni was surprised at Sister Sutton's response. It left her feeling strangely empty. The anger and bitterness that had always been her fuel was now spent. She had no argument. Silence filled the room. The soft, peaceful spirit that the sisters brought with them was gone and Toni felt trapped by her isolation. If anything the distance between her and the sister missionaries was made even more prominent by their presence. She would never be able to be like them. This whole thing had been a bad idea. Now she had made a complete fool of herself in front of two strangers.

She stood. "Listen, I appreciate you taking time out of your busy schedules to come and talk to me, but maybe we just shouldn't meet anymore. I shouldn't go to church this Sunday, either. I don't belong there."

"That's not true!" Tye leaned forward in her intensity. "Don't you see? That's exactly what Satan would have you feel. Okay, maybe you've done some things, but they can be overcome. Church isn't for the perfect, you know. It's for those who are simply trying to do the best they can. You're trying to do your best. You belong."

Tye was shocked at her own outburst. What was she doing? She was supposed to follow Sister Sutton's lead. She calmed down. She should know that church wasn't for the perfect. Didn't she go every week? Tye pushed that away. During the evening, she had sat silent—watchful and listening—determined to allow Sister Sutton to handle the situation. But the very idea of Toni giving up caused her panic. Now both Sister Sutton and Toni were staring at her. There was nothing to do but forge ahead.

Tye continued, "When we walked in here tonight, you were

interested in attending church. You must've spent the last week coming to that decision. Don't let a few minutes of anger dismantle everything you've been studying and working towards. I would almost guarantee that if we leave tonight and you've decided not to go to church, you'll regret it. Oh, you might say you're not sorry and you might convince yourself for a little while that you did the right thing. But deep down, where it counts, you'll regret it." Tye was silent for a moment, then asked, "May I ask you a personal question?"

Toni was caught completely off-guard. She nodded with hesitation.

"Why did you make fun of the Mormon kids in high school?"

Toni's eyes filled with tears. How could she tell this woman that her desire to bring them down came from the walls she had built to protect herself? That her taunting and jibes came from her only allies—bitterness and jealousy. She turned away.

"Everyone did it," she mumbled.

She looked at Tye. It was obvious that the stake missionary didn't believe her.

Tye nodded. "You're not in high school anymore, Toni. Say you'll come with me on Sunday."

Toni studied Tye for a long minute. She liked the way Tye met her eyes when they spoke. It reminded her of one of the Mormon girls in high school when Toni used to tease. Some of them would duck or take a side path if they saw Toni coming, but not Allison Thayer. She would face Toni and her insults with firmness. Toni came to grudgingly respect Allison, and by their senior year, they had an unspoken truce.

"Does Allison Thayer go to your ward?" Toni asked.

Tye whispered the name and thought for a moment. "No," she said slowly. "I don't believe so."

Toni breathed a sigh of relief. She didn't want to see anyone from high school. Not yet. She couldn't face them—especially in church. "Okay," she said quietly. "I'll go with you on Sunday."

A wave of relief washed over Toni. It surprised her. Relief was what she had expected to feel if she decided not to go to church. It would have allowed her to quit thinking about the painful reality of her family. No longer would she have to wrestle with the Book of Mormon and Nephi's story, which tried to show her a different path. It would certainly be easier to pull away from this challenge of a better way. But now that she had committed to attending church she relaxed inside. It was just as Tye had said—deep down, where it counted.

Chapter Sixteen

When Kyle arrived the following Friday, Meggie had conveniently gone to the library to study. Tye was making a spaghetti dinner. It smelled good. Italian seasonings and fresh, sourdough bread filled the room with its inviting spicy fragrance. Still, for the first time, Tye wished she could cook like Meggie.

From her position behind the stove, Tye glanced at the table. Two candles were offering a dim, romantic light. She had put out their best dishes. Nothing matched, but under the soft glow of the candles, they still shimmered. On Kyle's plate was a wrapped gift. All week Tye tried to think through the urge to give Kyle a Book of Mormon. After all, this was only their second real date. But still, as the days brought Friday closer, Tye was compelled to find a copy and wrap paper that matched the budding spring. The green ribbon gave off a rich shine under the candles.

Tye wiped her perspiring palms on her pants. She wasn't sure why she was so nervous. Was it because she was cooking for Kyle? Or was it the Book of Mormon that was lying on his plate, waiting to be discovered?

The knock on the door startled her. Wiping her hands once

again, she answered the door.

Kyle stepped in. "This is so nice," he said in his usual quiet voice. "Where's Meggie?"

"She's at the library," Tye replied. "She'll be back around nine. Can I take your coat?" she asked.

"Oh, sure," he said as he handed it to her.

Tye hung it in the closet and then went back to the stove.

"Let me guess," Kyle said as he followed her in the kitchen. "Spaghetti."

Tye smiled as she nodded. "I hope you like it. I made it myself. Meggie's the real cook in this house, but tonight I tried my hand at scratch cooking. Meggie would've thrown me out if I had even considered bottled sauce."

"Spaghetti is my favorite. It smells great."

"Thanks. I hope it turned out. Can you please get the plates? I'll dish it up in here."

Kyle walked to the table. He looked at the package. "Is this my seat?" he asked.

Tye nodded.

Kyle picked up the gift.

"It's for you," Tye said.

Kyle was completely taken by surprise. "Tye, I don't know what to say."

Tye walked to where Kyle stood. "You can open it now, if you'd like."

Kyle glanced at her and then gently unwrapped the gift. The sturdy little book looked right in his hands. He traced the gold-embossed letters.

"We talked about this last week, didn't we?"

"Yes, we did," Tye said, her eyes meeting his. "I wrote something on the title page. Take a look."

He opened the cover and read aloud. "This book holds many truths. It will teach you of your brother, Jesus Christ. Of this I testify. Love, Tye." Kyle's eyes softened as he looked at Tye. "It's really beautiful. Thank you, Tye."

She studied him carefully for some spark. "You're welcome," she said.

Tye moved to the kitchen. Kyle followed her with the plates where she dished up the spaghetti before bringing it to the table. They both sat down.

"This book means a lot to you, doesn't it?"

"Yes, it does."

He tightened his grip on it. "I really do appreciate the thought."

Tye could tell that he didn't know how to respond. For a moment, she hesitated, then she reached across the table and placed her hand on his. "I'm truly committed to my way of life, Kyle, and this book is a big part of the foundation. Do you understand?"

Kyle became pensive. "I don't know, Tye, but I've always known that you're different from other girls, and if this is part of the reason then I guess I owe it to myself to look into it."

It was all she could hope for. Was she really different from other girls, as Kyle had said? Was she different from CarrieAnne? She pushed that thought away as she squeezed his hand.

Kyle placed the book on the table and the conversation lightened as they ate spaghetti by candlelight.

After dinner, Kyle helped Tye with the dishes, then went to the window. "There's a full moon out tonight," he said. "It has a ring around it."

Tye joined Kyle at the window. "That means the weather is

going to change."

Kyle faced Tye. "I know it's cool outside, but let's go to the barn and check on the horses. I think the car ride would be nice. What do you say?"

"I'll get our jackets." Tye returned a few minutes later dressed in her coat, scarf, and gloves.

In the truck, Kyle popped in a cassette and classical music softly filled the cab.

"This music is pretty," she said.

"The composer is Strauss," Kyle said. "I used excerpts from it for a competition."

"Did you do dressage to music?" Tye asked excitedly.

Kyle grinned. It was obvious he was proud. "Yeah. There aren't many competitions here for that sort of thing, but I thought it would be a good experience for Ben and me. We worked up a routine to this music. You'd think I'd be tired of listening to it, but I just love it."

Tye was intrigued. "How did the competition go?"

"We didn't place, but I wasn't disappointed. We'd never done it before. It's a very subjective division, and we mostly did it for the experience."

"What kind of routine did you work out?"

Kyle became animated. "I kept it very simple. I believe that horses have a natural sense of rhythm. I mean, it only makes sense when you think of the way they travel. Everything has a beat. So, the challenge is finding the music that can match your horse's natural sense of rhythm and then using that natural ability to create something beautiful. Kind of like a horse's dance." He grew pensive. "In many ways our relationship with our horses is like a dance. I've never considered Ben a subject or just an animal. I know that several trainers just look at horses as commodities to be trained, bought, and sold. And I also know that when the time comes for me to start training, I'll have to look at other people's horses that way. But Ben and I—we're partners. Participating in that exercise to music was a celebration of that partnership." He smiled. "The best part was the extended trot. I believe he was really listening because he moved with the music. It felt great!"

"I've watched a couple of those competitions and I've wondered how Trapper would do." Tye became thoughtful. "I understand what you're saying about you and Ben being partners. It's the same for Trapper and me. I guess that's part of the reason why I'm not all that interested in moving east and competing nationally. I'd be happy just settling down someplace where I could teach others to enjoy horseback riding. Don't get me wrong. I want to be good at what I do, and I enjoy competition, but I'm more interested in folks who feel the same way about their horses as I do. I don't look at Trapper as a business. I look at him as a friend."

Kyle pulled into the barn parking lot. It was dark. He kept the headlights on so that he could find the light switch, just inside the large sliding door of the barn. Once the lights were on, Tye turned off the headlights and joined Kyle. The smell of sweet hay, sawdust, and warm animals greeted them. Even though Tye was familiar with the smell of stabled horses, she always enjoyed their sweet earthy aroma. It had been such a part of her life for so long that it reminded her of home. No matter where she traveled, horses and barns would always smell the same.

"What are you thinking?" Kyle asked.

Tye laughed. "Nothing much. Just about the familiar smell of the barn. When I was a kid, my folks were sure the smell would discourage me from riding. When they discovered that I actually liked it, they would tease me about being switched at birth. They were sure that I had been born in a barn. Neither one of them can tolerate the smell."

Kyle laughed. "I've always believed that we come to this earth with a great deal of our personalities already intact."

Tye looked at Kyle. "Do you believe that you lived before you came to earth?" she asked.

Kyle shook his head. "No. Nothing like that. I just think that we take the traits of our families from long ago and mingle them with the present. You're probably a throwback to some great-great grandfather who used horses on a farm."

Tye liked that thought. Then she smiled. "I bet you're right," she paused. "You did live before coming to earth, you know."

Kyle looked at Tye. She was taken aback by the deep color of his eyes.

"Is that what Mormons believe?" he asked.

"Yes," Tye replied.

Kyle nodded.

Tye could tell that he was uncomfortable with the conversation. Part of her was saddened by his lack of desire to explore the concept. But she tried to understand. She shouldn't be pushing him. Placing her arm through his, she grinned. "We should go check on those horses."

Slowly, they walked down the aisle. Horses whinnied and nickered in greeting. They reached Ben's stall and the horse looked up from his watering bucket. Kyle handed him a sugar cube and laughed when the horse's ears perked up as he reached for the sweet treat. Kyle gave him a pat through the bars of his stall.

They found Trapper, looking out of his stall with sleepy interest.

"I think we interrupted his nap," Kyle said.

"We've always been early birds," Tye said.

They came to Jade and Gypsy's stall. The foal came to the bars and sniffed with purpose. Kyle rubbed the filly's nose. "It's amazing how quickly these little ones grow. Look at Gypsy, would you? She's all legs now."

Tye laughed. "They're just like kids. They go through that gangly stage. I remember being all arms and legs."

Once Gypsy recognized Kyle and Tye she moved back to her mother's side and watched the pair with interest. Jade's nose was buried in sweet alfalfa.

Continuing down the aisle, they came to the end. Kyle threw back the door to the outside arena and stepped into the cool moonlight. Tye followed. The moon threw their shadows against the dark earth.

Carefully, they picked their way across the cold ground and leaned against the fence. The deep cold seemed to settle the evening into a quiet trance.

"When the weather is nice, this is where I like to sit and watch," Kyle said.

"Now that I think about it, I can remember seeing you sitting on the fence and watching our team go through their paces."

"I am always trying to learn."

"Even from a bunch of freshmen and sophomores?"

"Sure. We're all horse people."

"That's a great attitude, Kyle," Tye replied as she shivered in her coat. "And you're right, we can all learn from others."

Kyle placed his arm around her. "Maybe coming out here was a bad idea. The cold has never bothered me, but I forget that it's not for everyone."

"I like warm summer days."

"Every season has its trade-off, I guess. In the summer, it's warm and riding is easier, but we're stuck with flies. In the winter, it's cold and harder to get going, but the flies are gone."

Tye grinned. "That's a good way to look at it."

Kyle pushed himself away from the fence and gently placed his warm fingers on Tye's cheek. "Will you be riding in the morning?"

Tye nodded, then looked down.

Kyle tilted her face towards his. "May I join you?" he asked.

"You don't have to ask anymore," she said. "You're always welcome to come with me, Kyle."

Tye felt Kyle's arms encircle her waist, and she drew near to him in a tender embrace and lingering kiss.

"I've wanted to do that for a long time," he whispered in her ear.

Tye didn't answer. She allowed the moment to swallow her in its joy.

Kyle drew away from Tye and placed his hands on her shoulders. "I know I probably don't have any right to ask this, Tye, but…" he hesitated. "Are you seeing anyone else? I guess I need to know because… " he fumbled for the right word.

"Why?" Tye asked gently.

"Because I think I can feel myself wanting to have something exclusive with you. I have no interest in other women. I've watched you for a long time now, and I guess I always hoped it would come to this. The other day you said it was no secret that you admired me. Well, I've kept a big secret. I've wished to get close to you since the first day I watched you unload Trapper."

Tye blinked. She had no idea that Kyle had harbored such feelings. The worries of CarrieAnne dissipated in the moonlight. Then a new worry crept into her heart. "Kyle, I know we've talked a little about my religion, and I hope you understand how important it is to me. But there's something else." She hesitated. "I can't give you the physical love that you might expect. Do you understand?"

He nodded. "Yeah, I understand. You mean no sex."

"That's right."

Kyle kissed her gently. "I know, Tye. Somehow I've always

known."

Tye pulled Kyle close. "I'm not seeing anyone else," she whispered in his ear.

Kyle pulled away and searched Tye's face in the bright moonlight. Then he smiled as he placed his arm around her shoulder as her teeth began to chatter. He grinned. "You definitely don't like the cold. We should've had this conversation in a nice warm restaurant. That would've been more romantic."

"I'm not sorry we're here. I can't think of anything more appropriate than sharing this moment in a place we both love." Tye said. "I'm just not used to spending my winter evenings out in freezing weather. I spend too many days out in the cold. My nights are reserved for hot chocolate."

"I bet we could scrounge up some hot chocolate. Do you want to go to Missy's Diner and grab a mug?"

"How about if you take me home and I'll make some."

They began walking through the barn towards the truck. "I like that idea even better."

Meggie was home when Tye and Kyle arrived.

Meggie made an excuse and was about to go into her bedroom when Tye stopped her with an invitation to join them for hot chocolate. Meggie took little convincing—she dropped her books on the table, went into the kitchen cabinet, and pulled out three mugs while Tye warmed the milk on the stove.

"Don't you girls believe in the microwave?" Kyle asked.

Tye giggled. "Meggie's a purist. She only uses the microwave when absolutely necessary. She thinks hot chocolate will stay warmer longer if it's been heated on the stove. She also mixes the cocoa with the sugar. It's got to be just right."

Kyle raised his eyebrows. "I'm impressed!"

Tye could feel Meggie's unsolicited glances. Was it so obvious that she and Kyle had become a couple? Is that what had just happened? It almost seemed unreal, but the feeling in the cab of the truck had been different on their way home. The few words that had passed between them had somehow bound them together. It exhilarated Tye. And it frightened her. There were so many unanswered questions. What about CarrieAnne? Would she try to come between them? What would happen after graduation? How would Kyle respond to the church? Suddenly that question loomed in front of Tye as large and seemingly insurmountable as some of the obstacles she faced with Trapper. But through her bond with Trapper, they were able to overcome. Could she and Kyle form a partnership that would be as successful?

Kyle didn't stay long. He complained about Tye's early morning habits after he drained his hot chocolate and rose. Tye walked him out to his car and, with the hot chocolate warming her, she was able to kiss him goodnight without shivering.

When she walked back into the apartment, Meggie was standing over the sink washing out the mugs.

"Hey!" protested Tye. "I thought cleaning up was my job."

"Just what happened between the two of you tonight?" Meggie returned, ignoring her roommate's empty rebuke.

"You noticed?"

"Noticed! The air was so full of electricity; I thought my hair would stand on end."

Tye grinned. "He asked to see me exclusively, and I said yes."

Meggie's mouth dropped open. "Oh, Tye. I don't know if I should be happy or sad. I mean, what are you going to do about the fact that he's a non-member?"

Tye shook her head vigorously. "I don't want to think about that," she said.

"But you're going to have to think about it," Meggie persisted.

Tye was silent.

"I'm sorry," Meggie said. "I shouldn't be so difficult. I'm just scared for you, Tye. That's all."

"I know," Tye said. "I'm scared for me, too. It's all happened so fast, but I can't deny that my feelings for him have grown stronger every single day. I've never felt like this before. It's so new and wonderful."

A few minutes later, Tye bid her friend goodnight, but she wasn't tired. She knew she should consider putting in some time on her homework, but she couldn't concentrate on studies. All she wanted to think about was Kyle. Had she done the right thing by making her promise? She wasn't seeing anyone before him, so it wasn't like she would be missing out on chances to date other men—non-members or members. Or was she? Tye wished it mattered. But if she were to be perfectly honest, she would have to admit that it didn't matter. She wanted to be with Kyle. He surrounded her with his deep, thoughtful voice and their mutual respect for horses. She had always known that he was gentle and kind, but to feel the warmth of that gentleness inside was powerful. It made all other concerns shrink. But for how long?

Tye stood and wandered around the apartment. Did she want to be like Toni? Inactive and lonely? Did she want to live like her father? In a marriage that could only promise earthly bonds? Is that what would happen if she chose to be with Kyle? Tye shuddered. Being involved in a part-member family was difficult at best. Would she do that to her unborn children? Risk everything she loved for a different love? The reality came back with new force. Could she ever consider a serious relationship with a non-member? Isn't that what she was doing? No, she was getting ahead of herself. After all, she and Kyle were hardly talking about marriage. But this was how non-member marriages began, wasn't it?

Tye went to the window and watched the clouds play with the moon. She could not deny the tenderness she felt towards Kyle—the desire to be with him, the pull that lingered in her whenever she looked into his black eyes. It almost made Tye willing to forget the importance of the gospel and rush headlong into whatever awaited her with Kyle. Almost.

Tye left the window and began to pace. The haunting feeling of dissatisfaction came creeping back like tendrils on a vine. No, she wasn't supposed to feel this way—so unfulfilled. Where was this yearning coming from? Tears of frustration welled up in her eyes. Just when she thought she had beaten it down with the promotion on the team, a new calling, and her new love for Kyle, she found it lurking like the morning fog.

Sitting down on the couch, Tye felt something push into her back. She leaned away from the couch and turned. The Book of Mormon she had given to Kyle was standing against the cushion. He had forgotten her gift. The tears Tye was trying to deny came rushing back. How could he forget these precious words she had given him? Didn't he understand that this wasn't just a book? It was a part of her soul and her dream.

The gentle knock on the door startled Tye. It was late. Who would be coming to the apartment? She wiped her eyes, softly walked to the door, and looked through the peep hole. It was Kyle. She opened the door and allowed him to enter. He looked sheepish.

"Um, I think I forgot something," he said.

"Oh?" Tye tried to sound casual.

"Yes. The book you gave me. Have you seen it?"

"I think it's on the couch," Tye said.

Kyle grabbed the book, then faced her. "In a way I'm glad I forgot it," he said. "It gives me the excuse to come see you again."

As Kyle kissed her goodnight, Tye's heart warmed, but some stubborn part of her would not let go of the yearning she didn't understand.

Chapter Seventeen

Meggie closed her eyes and listened to the rolling surf. Its rhythmic pulse lulled her into tranquility as she leaned against Neil. If she sat very still she could hear the steady beating of his heart. It kept time with the waves and added to her sense of peace.

The spring morning was cold, but there was no bite to the ocean air. Sunshine began breaking through the thick fog, sending prisms and beams through the heavy mist. The long stretch of sandy beach was deserted and surrounded by the fog. Meggie felt as if she and Neil were the only two people alive. The bonfire crackled and hissed as it gave out its cheery warmth, chasing away the wet cold. It seemed to beckon the sun down from its heaven.

They had come early and had built the bonfire in the gray dawn. The day had begun to break clear and gold, but then the sea brought the misty fog, shrouding every surface it encountered with a fine liquid lace. Now with the help of the bonfire, the sun was chasing the mist back to the sea. Meggie's skin began to warm under the brightening rays of the morning sun, and the fire.

Neil stirred and tightened his arm around Meggie. She huddled against his warmth. "I applied for a summer job," she said quietly.

"Oh? I thought you were going to work with your parents."

Meggie hesitated. "I'm not sure," she said. "This job doesn't have anything to do with accounting."

Neil broke away from Meggie and looked at her intently.

"It's for a morning chef position in a bed and breakfast."

Neil slowly smiled as he hugged Meggie. "I think you'd make a great breakfast chef. If they're anything like the dinners your produce, you'll get the job for sure."

Meggie was warmed by his confidence.

"Have you told your folks?"

Apprehension filled Meg. "No. Not yet. I didn't see any point in discussing it with them until I get an interview. Nothing may become of it."

"But something already has become of it."

"How so?"

"You're considering other options. You're allowing yourself to think beyond accounting. If this job won't pan out, then another one will."

Meggie hugged her knees. Her teeth chattered, but it wasn't from the cold. How could she tell her parents that their hopes weren't her hopes? "I just don't know if I can say anything to them just yet. My brother Justin didn't follow in their footsteps and neither did my sister Mattie, although she tried. How can I tell them that I don't want what they have to offer? It would feel like I was rejecting them."

"You're not rejecting them. You just want to find your own way. Meggie, don't you think it's a bit unfair that your parents have mapped out your future without consulting you?"

"I don't think that's how they look at it. They simply want what's best, and grooming me to take over the business would certainly give me a worry-free future."

"Have you told your parents that you don't like accounting?"

Meggie became defensive. "I wouldn't go that far," she said. "Accounting has given me a good life."

"But does that mean you owe it the rest of your life? You've told me that numbers give you a headache. You don't have any enthusiasm for your classes. Something is speaking to you and you need to listen."

Meggie stood and pulled her jacket close. "Well, maybe I'm not ready to talk back." She held out her hand to Neil, who allowed her to help him stand.

Quietly, they walked along the golden shore. Neil was the first to break the silence. "I received a letter from Sammi Rae."

Meggie caught her breath, but bit her tongue.

"She didn't say much. It was just a newsy letter, really."

"How did that make you feel?" Meggie asked.

"I'm not sure. My first reaction was to grab a piece of paper and write her back, but I didn't."

"And how are you feeling right now?"

Neil sighed. "I'm glad I didn't write her." He turned and faced Meggie. "Whenever I'm with you, Sam seems so far away and separate from me. It's as if she can't touch me, and the hole she has left inside of me has started to fill."

"But you don't feel like that all the time, do you?"

Neil shook his head. "No. I'm working on it, Meg."

"Maybe it shouldn't be so hard."

Neil shook his head. "Everything since Sammi Rae has been hard."

Meggie said nothing. Some small part of her hoped he would share Sammi Rae's letter, but the rest of her didn't want to hear it. She didn't want to know about the claim this woman had. "I'm sorry,

Neil. It must be hard to have her come back into your life."

"In some ways it's like she never left." Suddenly, he realized what he had said. "I didn't mean it like that, Meggie. I-I…"

Meggie shook her head. "Don't Neil. Don't start covering up your feelings. If we can't be honest with each other, then what's the point?"

"No wonder I feel so comfortable around you. You seem to understand me."

"I'm your friend, Neil. Above all else I'm your friend."

Neil smiled and took her hand.

Could she do it? Could she be his friend when she wanted to give him so much more? Could she make a place for herself in his life by helping him push away Sam? Could she risk her heart in such a venture? She smiled to herself. That was the accountant in her head talking, and she didn't want to listen to that familiar voice. She sprinted away. "C'mon, I'll race you to the waves."

"Meggie, that water is freezing."

She shed her jacket, quickly removed her shoes and socks and pushed her pants up to her knees. "We'll warm up by the fire," she yelled above the surf as she moved towards the water.

Neil stayed rooted so Meggie ran to him and caught his hand, pulling him towards the surf.

"Wait! I didn't bring extra shoes."

"Then you'd better take those off."

Neil quickly removed his shoes and socks. Then before he could protest, Meggie was pulling him towards the water. The surf lapped over their ankles.

Neil sucked in his breath. "It's so cold."

"Be patient and after a minute, you'll get numb and won't notice."

"Oh, that'll be a pleasant alternative," Neil said, but he was smiling.

Meggie dashed away from him. He grabbed for her but missed.

As they chased each other through the splashing surf, Meggie forgot about her accounting class and the expectations of her parents. She forgot about Sammi Rae and the letter. Laughter mixed with the rhythm of the crashing surf, filling Meggie's heart with the intensity of the moment. She pulled the carefree feeling close and allowed her delight to overshadow the future.

Chapter Eighteen

Tye drove into the barn parking lot and was surprised to see several cars. Saturday mornings were usually hers alone, until she started sharing them with Kyle. Now it looked like the whole junior team had arrived.

Hesitantly, she walked into the barn. If Katie was holding an informal meeting, she didn't want to interrupt. Instead, Tye was greeted with the usual noise of people laughing and the jangle of bits and spurs.

Tye smiled, "Hey, Denise. What's the junior team doing here this morning?" She asked. Her voice echoed in the sudden silence. No one replied.

CarrieAnne came out of the tack room, holding her saddle and bridle. She gave Tye an appraising look. "Katie called an extra dressage practice for the junior team," she replied as she stood before Tye.

"Oh, I didn't know," Tye stammered.

"Guess you don't know everything," CarrieAnne replied.

The rest of the junior riders watched the confrontation. There was no question about their support.

Tye opened her mouth to speak, but was interrupted.

"You're not the only one who doesn't know everything. I'm beginning to wonder about Katie. I can't imagine her choosing you over a junior for the alternate position. But I suppose she'll learn." Denise said. She was CarrieAnne's best friend.

A flash of anger exploded in Tye. "And what exactly is she supposed to learn?"

"Oh, I don't mean any offense, Tye. We all know you're a good rider. But you're just not prepared for competition. She'll figure it out during your first show— if you get to show. Kyle won't even be able to save you then."

CarrieAnne smirked with an air of superiority.

"I don't even see a need to respond to that," Tye said with more conviction than she felt. Willing her legs to work she turned and went into the tack room to gather her belongings. She was supposed to be going on another Saturday morning ride with Kyle. She prayed he would be late. Gathering her saddle and bridle, she moved into the barn. She didn't notice CarrieAnne until it was too late. The girl grabbed Tye's arm, sending her gear sprawling.

CarrieAnne bent down at the same time Tye did. "Oh, I'm *so* sorry," she whispered with mock sincerity. "It just gets so crowded in here. Don't you agree?"

Tye shot her a look, and CarrieAnne rose to her full height and laughed.

Tye bit her tongue. She gathered her belongings and stood. She couldn't stand it another minute. Looking CarrieAnne straight in the eye, she said, "I can't imagine why the junior team needs an extra dressage practice. What a disappointment." Her voice dripped with honey. She moved into Trapper's stall and closed the door behind her. She felt ill. Red shame enveloped her and made her both angry and weak. She had lowered herself to CarrieAnne's level. CarrieAnne had baited her, and Tye had hooked herself. She willed the tears away and went to Trapper. He was fidgety as he picked up on Tye's obvious anxiety. Taking several deep breaths, Tye forced herself into calmness. Trapper began to settle down.

Tye heard Katie arrive and she breathed a sigh of relief. As soon as the trainer was in the barn, the junior team got down to business and finished tacking up their horses. They passed Trapper's stall on their way to the arena. Tye kept her eyes on her work, but from her peripheral vision she could tell that no one looked her way.

Several minutes later they were warming up their horses when Kyle arrived breathlessly. "I'm sorry I'm late," he said hurriedly. "I forgot to set my alarm clock. It's Saturday after all. I'll have Ben tacked up in a minute. I'll meet you outside. It's a beautiful day." Before Tye could say one word, he was gone. She took another deep breath and lead Trapper outside. It was a beautiful day. A March gift of sun and blue sky. Even the air had softened and lost its bite. Tye thought of Meggie and hoped she and Neil were having good weather at the coast.

Quietly, Tye mounted Trapper and asked him for a walk. He complied and she moved toward the open field. Part of her wished she could be alone for a while. She needed to sort out CarrieAnne's attack and the junior team's response. She wasn't shaking anymore, but the confrontation, although brief, had been intense and had left Tye tired and drained.

She was so involved in her thoughts that she didn't hear Kyle on Ben trot next to her and Trapper. "Hey, do you plan on going without me?" Kyle asked.

Tye looked at him. He was serious.

"No. Not at all. I'm sorry."

"Are you okay?"

At that moment Tye decided to keep the incident to herself. Involving Kyle would only complicate matters.

"Did the junior team say anything?" Kyle asked.

Tye looked at him. "What would make you ask that?"

"I noticed they were here in force this morning, and I thought maybe they had something to say about your appointment to the squad."

Tye desperately wished to share the confrontation with Kyle, but stuck to her original decision to keep it to herself. What would Kyle's involvement solve? "Well, I don't think they're too happy about it. They're not exactly my new best friends."

"Will you let me know if anything is said? I know how difficult, I mean, I think I know how hard this can be on everyone."

Tye looked at Kyle. "How would you know that?" she asked.

"CarrieAnne can be a real fireball, and she's the definite leader of the junior squad."

Tye raised a noncommittal eyebrow and waited.

Kyle continued, "CarrieAnne and I used to be real close for a while." He grew silent. "It's a long story."

"What do you mean by 'real close'?" Tye asked.

Kyle stopped Ben. "We used to go out," he answered hurriedly. "Tye, can I ask you something? Do you regret what we talked about last night?" he asked, his voice barely above a whisper.

Tye brought Trapper to a halt and looked at him. "No," Tye said emphatically. "What would make you think that?"

"You're kind of distant and aloof this morning."

Tye immediately felt a pushing desire to ask Kyle about his relationship with CarrieAnne, but thought better of it. "I wasn't expecting the junior team to show up en masse," she replied. "It just surprised me, that's all."

She reached over and placed a gloved hand on his arm. "I'm sorry," she replied. "I guess I'm still used to coming out here alone in my own little world. I'm not used to being with a man, you know. I have a very short dating history."

Kyle smiled and gently took her fingers into his own. "You're not the only one," he said as he squeezed her hand.

Tye removed her fingers. Pictures of Kyle with CarrieAnne surfaced in Tye. "I think you may know more about dating than I do," she replied. "It sounds like you and CarrieAnne were quite an item."

He looked thoughtful. "What would make you say that?"

"CarrieAnne told me," she confessed.

Kyle pulled at his upper lip and sighed. "CarrieAnne," he whispered before facing Tye. "Don't worry about my past with CarrieAnne," he replied. "We only lasted three months before she went back to Jonathan and married him. I wasn't exactly a priority in her life. I think she just used me to get Jonathan's attention. He wanted her to give up her horse and her spot on the team. She wouldn't do it so she found someone who would make allowances for her relationship with Van. Who better than a man from the team?"

"That's how you see it from CarrieAnne's perspective. What about you, Kyle? How did you feel about CarrieAnne? How do you feel about her today?"

Kyle was silent for a moment as he looked over the glorious March morning. "I won't deny that it hurt me," he said quietly. "Relationships aren't easy for me and once I pledge myself, I believe in that relationship and I am committed." He looked at Tye. "Do you understand what I'm saying?"

Tye swallowed. The weight of Kyle's words and the promise they had made to each other the previous night settled in her heart. She nodded.

Kyle reached out his hand and Tye grasped it. "Really, Tye. There is no room for CarrieAnne. My only concern is that she doesn't make your tenure as the alternate a difficult one."

Tye brought Trapper to a halt. "She has made it difficult, but I don't want any involvement," Tye said. "Not from you or from Katie. I want to handle this."

Kyle dismounted Ben and held Trapper's reins so Tye could also dismount. "What happened?" he asked.

"I'd rather not go into it, Kyle. She…it…it's just stupid. Please, just trust me to take care of it. Remember how you trusted me with Jade and Gypsy? Trust me with this."

Kyle shook his head. "This is different, Tye. This kind of strife can lead to all kinds of problems, and we need to be a smooth operation when we compete. I'm the captain of the team, which makes the team my responsibility. Beyond that, my professional future depends in part on how well we do this season. I can't leave that to chance."

"I'm not asking you to leave it to chance. I'm asking you to leave it to me. Don't tell Katie or anyone. I want CarrieAnne to come to respect me because of the way I ride, not because you or Katie push her. Respect can't be forced."

Kyle drew in a breath. "You're not the only one this affects. What about the other team members? Didn't Katie tell you to keep her informed about any difficulties?"

"Please, Kyle."

Kyle nodded slowly. "Okay," he said. "But for the record, I disagree. I think Katie needs to be informed. It's only fair."

"Noted. Now can we please get back on horseback? I'm about ankle deep in mud. Trapper is much better equipped to handle this kind of footing."

Kyle's face lost some of its tension as he gave Tye a quick kiss. They moved to a grassy knoll and began scraping the mud from their boots before mounting their horses once again.

Tye smiled as the sun's warmth began radiating from her chest. It was going to be okay. The earlier concern of CarrieAnne and the junior team began to shrink. The morning's incident felt galaxies away from this moment. Right now all that mattered to Tye was the warm sun, this warm horse that patiently stood in its rays, and the man who shared them with her.

Chapter Nineteen

Toni sat next to Tye in the middle of the chapel. She had met Meggie when the two girls had come to the house to pick her up for church and had immediately liked her. She had warm brown eyes and soft curly brown hair that went to her shoulders. She was prettier than Tye who had long honey-blonde hair and snappy green eyes.

Neither girl wore very much make-up, which made Toni feel like a neon sign with her heavy foundation and bleached blonde hair. She had chided herself when the girls came to the door, looking scrubbed and clean. After all, she wasn't attending a night club act. This was church. She had glanced at her watch in hopes of having time to wash her face and reapply her make-up, but the girls had arrived right on time. Toni set her jaw. She would just have to suffer through. Besides, this was how she always looked. She was happy with the new dress she had bought. A soft blue sweater dress which clung to the lines of her figure modestly and fell below her knees. Both girls had complimented her on the dress.

That had helped for a moment, but her stomach still fluttered. It had been ten years since Toni had stepped inside a latter-day saint chapel. She pushed that thought away and the anxiety that came along with it. She was not an eleven-year-old child anymore, having to worry about her mother dragging her out of church. Still, when Tye pulled into the parking lot, Toni found herself looking for the old black Mustang her father used to drive. The strange old longing seeped inside as she remembered wishing for his presence and hoping against it. She missed him now. Since she had been reading the Book of Mormon, the longing for her family often came to her unbidden, but she always denied it entry into her heart. It followed on the heels of the many memories that seemed to flood every conscious moment. She tried to slay them too—even the happy recollections. It was too painful to remember any of it. But some little piece of her wished to explore them. To remember in the fullness of the light of day, instead of pushing them under the dark lid in her mind.

As Tye parked the car, Meggie chatted about school, asking Toni about her major. Toni was grateful for the conversation. It helped unloosen the knot in her stomach.

All three girls climbed out of Tye's car and hurried to the chapel, where Toni was introduced to Neil, Steve, and Michael. The three boys moved over to make room for the girls. Toni noticed that Meggie sat next to Neil and the young man took her hand.

The opening hymn startled Toni's thoughts and she took her half of the hymnal. As she looked up at the chorister, she noticed Sister Sutton and her companion, Sister Kohler, sitting on the stand. She had only met Sister Kohler once, but their inviting demeanor helped put her at ease. They seemed genuinely happy to see her. The music was familiar and she remembered her mother's sweet soprano voice mingling with her father's tenor. Tears came again. Oh, this was hard! Everywhere she turned there were memories. Even the building looked the same with its plain lighting fixtures and wooden pews. Toni pushed at the memories that were like walls in her mind. If she were to let them in, the weight of them would press the life out of her. Their power was frightening.

Tentatively, Toni mingled her soprano voice with Tye's soprano and Meggie's alto. It felt good to sing. A tendril of hope overcame Toni's immediate worries as her voice sang in harmony with new voices.

When the sacrament came around, Toni felt a new stab of anxiety. She wasn't worthy to partake of the bread and water, yet she wished for it. Long forgotten Sunday School lessons and Primary talks came back to her. She recalled the day she was baptized. Wasn't that what the sacrament was about? Remembering the promises that were made at baptism? Toni passed the bread and water to Tye. What were those promises? Words dimmed by time and pain started filtering through Toni's heart. Baptism was about taking on the name of Jesus. That was it! Yes, she remembered now. When she was eight, her Primary teacher had spent the whole year teaching about baptism. Sister Roarke had also been the lady who had braided Toni's long brown hair. Oh, that had been wonderful.

"My girls won't let me do this," Sister Roarke had murmured as she ran her fingers through Toni's thick, long, healthy tresses.

Toni's mother had worked in the Primary then, and she would come to Toni's classroom after church to find her sitting on a chair with Sister Roarke braiding her hair.

She would smile and both women would comment on the beauty of Toni's long, glossy hair.

When Toni moved to Corvallis, she cut her hip-length hair short. Her dad certainly didn't know how to braid and Toni couldn't do it by herself. There was no point to having long hair. She wanted to rid herself of everything that reminded her of Idaho. Besides, her father had encouraged the change. As the strands fell to the floor under the barber's scissors, Toni looked resolutely in the mirror. She was convinced that this act would change everything. No longer was she the naive youngster who believed all those silly words about a loving Heavenly Father. If there really was a God, then why would He let her family fall apart? Why did He allow her, an innocent victim, to feel such pain? Where was He when she needed Him? Toni had turned away from God that day. As she watched the barber sweep up the remnants of her past life, she was determined to bury it forever and leave it behind. With her hair neatly bobbed to her ears, Toni felt ready for her new identity.

But the old identity held on with stubborn tenacity. At night, Toni would dream about her mother. And in those dreams, Toni would have long hair. It was as if her dreams were stuck in time—reliving those happy days before the divorce. Then the dreams began to be a mixed bag of present and past. She would see faces of her schoolmates from Corvallis but they would all be on the farm in Idaho. The morning Toni woke and recalled a dream with her year-old bob, she counted it as a triumph.

Her mother had cried when she had seen Toni's shorn locks the following summer. Toni didn't care. Her mother was part of what she was trying to leave behind.

Toni shifted uneasily in her seat. She was getting warm, but the memories kept coming. When Toni turned eighteen she let her hair grow to her shoulders and bleached it blonde. It looked brassy and the ends were damaged because of old perms and bad bleaching jobs but Toni didn't think about her hair much anymore. She was sorry she had bleached it. It was more trouble than it was worth. But blondes were supposed to have more fun, and Toni was determined to have fun.

She glanced at Tye. Her hair was naturally blonde—dark honey blonde. It was long and today Tye was wearing it in a French braid that reached the small of her back. A few strands had pulled loose around her face and delicately framed her green eyes. Toni felt like a tinny imitation next to this young woman. Everything about Tye reminded Toni of what she would never be—loved, fulfilled, strong. Toni knew very little about Tye, but she was sure that she came from a loving family, who had raised her in the bosom of the gospel. Tye was everything Toni had come to despise in high school. And yet, here she was, sitting next to her in church. Why? Why couldn't Toni muster any of that old sarcasm and hate that had served her so well in the past?

It was a question Toni didn't want to answer. But the truth was, she was tired. Tired of always being defensive. Tired of being alone.

Toni squirmed in her seat and tried to focus on the talk being given from the pulpit. She didn't come here to daydream. But why had she come to this place? What was beckoning her? It wasn't Sister Sutton or even Tye. It was something from inside; something that was becoming more incessant in its cry to be heard. It had started when she had graduated from high school and her father had told her that he was going to start his new job in Texas. The one remaining piece of her family's puzzle had now slipped through her fingers.

Toni thought back to Nephi and his own personal family crisis. Did he feel that way when he had been forced to leave his brothers? Did he feel like a fragmented piece of a greater whole that would never be able to fit together again? She didn't know for sure, but she imagined he did. At least he never had to go to high school. But that comparison wasn't fair. At least her family never tried to kill her as Nephi's brothers had tried to kill him. Still, the separation of his family had to hurt. He must have grieved—just as she grieved. Was her grieving over? Toni shook her head. She didn't want to think about that.

Tye gently touched her hand. "Are you okay?" she asked.

Toni glanced at Tye and nodded, but the truth was, she wasn't okay. She was hot and felt penned in—like a bird that needed to fly. This place had brought up too many old ghost-like memories. Their empty shells marched forward to their own cadence, void of their former vibrancy and vitality. They came rushing in from under that lid she kept closed in her mind. They begged to display themselves and return the pieces of her life that she buried the day she had cut her hair. They wanted Toni to paint them to their fullest color and bring them life.

Suddenly, Toni felt claustrophobic. Tye, Meggie, and the boys seemed to have trapped her in the middle. Had they done this on purpose? Was this a trick to keep her glued to her seat for the duration of the meeting? Suddenly, Toni had the overwhelming desire to flee—to stand up and run out of the meeting. It was hot in the chapel and it became hard to breathe. She fanned herself with the program but to no avail.

She saw Tye shoot worried glances in her direction.

She tried to calm down, but it was as if her nerves were no longer under her command. She jiggled her foot.

Finally it overwhelmed her. She stood. Suddenly, she wasn't sure what to do. Then she plowed her way down the row and with as much dignity as she could rally, walked into the foyer where she took great gulps of air.

She didn't know how Tye came to be beside her, but she felt the young woman's arms go around her shoulders as she led her to the couch.

Tye's cool hand reach up and touch her forehead.

"My goodness," Tye said. "You're positively burning up."

Toni closed her eyes and fell against the back of the couch. "I'm okay," she gasped. Embarrassment flooded through her. She did the very thing her mother had always done. She ran. "I'm sorry," she mumbled.

"There's nothing to be sorry for," Tye replied. "Just sit here and rest for a minute."

Toni closed her eyes. She was weary and wrung out. She wanted to take a nap—to lose herself in the oblivion of sleep.

"Maybe I should go home," Toni said.

"Are you sure?" Tye asked.

Toni nodded. "I'm sorry. It means you'll have to miss part of your meetings. Maybe if I could just go out to the car, I could wait for you there."

"Nonsense," Tye said. "If you're not well, I'll take you home. I don't mind."

"I should've driven, I guess."

"Don't worry," Tye said. "This is no big deal. I don't have to teach or anything."

Still, Toni made no move to get up. She wasn't sure her legs would hold her. She sat against the back of the couch and willfully slowed her breathing.

Tye was in no hurry. She sat beside Toni quietly.

Finally Toni stood and the two women walked to the car.

Tye turned into the traffic and kept silent for several minutes. Then she asked, "How are you feeling?"

"Better."

"You're not sick, are you?"

"Not physically, no."

"I know it's none of my business, but if you want to talk about it, I'd be more than willing to listen."

Toni turned to Tye. "What would you know about divorce? What would you know about losing a family?" she asked bitterly.

Tye said nothing.

Toni sighed, "I'm sorry. I shouldn't be attacking you like that."

"No. You shouldn't," Tye said. "The truth is, I've never experienced that kind of pain. So, I don't know what it feels like to lose a family." She paused, "I bet it's horrible."

"It is horrible," Toni said vehemently. "I have no family, Tye. I haven't seen my mom in years and it's been six months since I've talked with her on the phone. I see my dad maybe six days out of the year—if I'm lucky. I'm alone in the world and I have been since I was twelve."

Tye pulled into the driveway and shut off the engine. "I'm so sorry, Toni. I didn't realize."

Silence hung in the air, but Toni found comfort in it. The car smelled like a barn and then Toni remembered Tye had said she was on the equestrian team. The silence continued and she appreciated the girl who was next to her, who didn't seem to feel any anxiety about the lack of conversation.

Toni looked out the windshield. "What's your family like?" she asked quietly.

"My folks have been married for about twenty-five years. I don't have any brothers or sisters. My dad is a member of the church, but my mom isn't. She smokes." Tye sighed. "That was hard as a kid. I was always so aware that my mom was different than all the other moms at church."

"Do your folks get along?"

Tye nodded. "Yeah. They've always been close."

"You don't know how lucky you are," Toni's voice took a hard edge.

Tye stared at Toni for a moment. Lucky? She had never considered herself lucky. Her dad and mom weren't sealed in the temple. Her mother had a terrible smoking habit. But when she compared her family life to the little she knew about Toni's life, maybe she was lucky.

"How do you think I came to be such a good rider?" Tye asked.

Toni blinked. "I don't know."

"Because I spent every free minute at the barn. I never wanted to go home. My mom's smoking habit drove me crazy. I'd rather smell horse manure all day than cigarette smoke. I worked to buy my horse so that I wouldn't have to be at home. I used Trapper as my escape. That's why I got so good at riding. I rode all the time." She turned and looked at Toni. "What are you good at Toni? What was your escape?"

The question hit Toni like frigid water. She searched her mind, but she didn't have to search very hard. She knew her allies—sarcasm, bitterness, and jealousy.

Toni looked down at her hands. Tears welled up in her eyes and flowed down her cheeks. "I can be so hateful," she whispered quietly.

"Yes, I imagine that's true."

Toni looked up and noticed Tye's steady gaze.

"The other night when I was here with Sister Sutton, I could tell you were fighting the urge to throw us both out on our backsides."

Toni laughed, then grew somber. "My isolation has been my escape," Toni replied softly.

"But it doesn't work anymore does it?"

"No," Toni sighed. "It hasn't worked for a long time. I just haven't noticed."

"Until now."

Toni hated the fact that this young woman was right. But she was right. Ten years of keeping herself apart from the very things that mattered had left her empty and isolated. And it wasn't even something for which she could blame her father. She alone was responsible for it.

The tears continued—coming faster. Soon, Toni was sobbing. She couldn't remember the last time she had cried—honestly wept. Maybe never. Maybe she had been so busy pushing away the pain that she never really faced it. Now it was facing her and there was no way to dodge it. It loomed in front of her like a huge tidal wave—sucking her under in a torrent of grief. She wished she had strength to open the car door and flee into the house, but the tears took everything.

She felt Tye pull her into an embrace, and Toni grasped at her fiercely. The embrace was comforting and familiar. Her mother used to hug her often before the divorce. But that was ages ago. Her father rarely touched her.

Now, Tye was offering her a shoulder to cry on. Toni held on to Tye for a long time. After the sobs subsided, she pulled away and hastily wiped her eyes. She knew she looked a mess with mascara running down her cheeks and her make-up smeared. When she looked up at Tye, she noticed the same thing. Her mascara was also smudged. She was wiping her eyes. Had Tye cried with her?

Gently, Tye placed her hands over Toni's. "I'm so sorry," she murmured. "So sorry about your family, Toni."

Fresh tears came to Toni's tired eyes as she squeezed Tye's hand. "Thank you," she whispered. "Thank you so much. You're the first person who has ever bothered to say they're sorry and yet in many ways, something has died. Something precious and important."

"Yes, I can understand."

"I don't think I've ever grieved," Toni said quietly. "I was too busy being angry."

"Maybe you were too busy just trying to survive."

Toni nodded. "There were days when that took everything I had." She sniffed and wiped her eyes again. "I need to let you go pick up Meggie. She'll wonder what happened to you."

Tye glanced at her watch. "I've got about fifteen minutes." She paused. "I hope you'll come again next week, Toni."

Toni hesitated. She couldn't go through this every week.

"It won't be like this all the time," Tye said quietly. "It'll be hard, I know. But let the gospel teach you a new way. Don't rely on your old allies any longer. Hate has its own agenda. It isolates you and holds you back from finding anything remotely precious. The church can never replace your family. Nothing can. But it can aid in your healing."

"Yes, I know," Toni replied slowly.

"How do you know?" Tye asked.

"Nephi told me," Toni said.

Tye nodded. "Yes, I believe he has."

Toni reached out and hugged Tye quickly. "I'll come next week," she said. "But I'll drive myself," she smiled.

"I'm glad I drove today," Tye said. "I hate to think of what we would've missed if we'd been in separate cars."

Toni smiled. "Tell Sister Sutton that I'll be planning on seeing the two of you next Wednesday."

Tye grinned as she started the engine. "She'll be pleased to hear it."

Toni stepped out of the car and waved as Tye pulled out of the driveway.

After picking up Meggie, and driving home, Tye went straight to her bedroom. She picked up the phone receiver three times and then returned it to its cradle. Finally on the fourth try, she dialed her home number. Her mother answered the phone.

"Hi, Mom."

"Well, Tye. I'm surprised to hear from you. Your dad's at church."

"I know," Tye said quietly. "I called to talk to you."

"Are you okay?" Trudy asked. "What's happened?"

"No, I'm fine. Nothing's wrong." She hesitated. "I just needed to call." The earlier warm feelings were dissipating and being replaced by the same old questions. Why didn't her mother join the church? Why did she have to smoke after all these years?

"How is Trapper?" Trudy asked.

Tye was grateful to be on familiar ground. "Trapper's fine," she said before launching into the details of horse care. She spoke about the upcoming season and her belief that Trapper was ready.

"Oh, I forgot to tell you that I'll be coming home next weekend."

"That is good news. What's the occasion?"

"Meggie has a job interview down there and I'm coming along. Kyle said he would take care of Trapper."

"Good! We'll look forward to a visit. Your dad will be thrilled."

"Well, I'd better go, Mom. I can't have a big phone bill."

"I know, honey. It's good to hear your voice. We'll be expecting you Friday evening, then."

Tye hung up after a quick goodbye.

It had been good to hear her mother's voice. But it was awkward to call and talk to her without talking to her dad. Tye sat on her bed. Why did some people turn to the gospel while others continued to turn away? What was reaching Toni that hadn't yet touched her mother? Trudy had read the Book of Mormon. She knew all about Nephi. Tye sat in silence. What converted people? Toni had been a member all of her life but was just now starting the conversion process. Trudy had been exposed to the church for years and still wasn't interested in what it could offer. Then there was Kyle. Would he allow the spirit to touch him the way Toni was allowing it into her life? That was it! The Holy Ghost. Reaching for her scriptures, Tye turned to Moroni 10:5 *"And by the power of the Holy Ghost ye may know the truth of all things."*

Tye sniffled and tears pricked her eyes. Even though things were clearer, they still didn't make sense. Tye thought about all the missionaries who had visited the Jorgenson home and how angry she had been with them when her mother continued her refusal to join the church. Somehow Tye had considered them to blame for her mother's lack of enthusiasm. But it wasn't the missionaries at all. Tye would never dare take credit for Toni's experiences that were leading her to the gospel, neither could the missionaries who had taught her mother be responsible for her decisions. A missionary was simply a messenger. But oh, how she loved the message! It brought her the greatest satisfaction. Tye sighed deeply. Whenever she thought about Toni and the missionary work she was doing, the restlessness would leave her. Only then was Tye completely at peace.

Chapter Twenty

Meggie stood in the unfamiliar kitchen and tried to take everything in.

Pots and pans hung above the stove. A double oven was built into one wall. A huge industrialized dishwasher and a double stainless steel sink completed the picture. It made her pulse race. So did her reason for being here. Soon after she had sent her letter of application, the owner of the inn, Eilene Anderson, had called and invited Meg to come cook.

Meggie had danced around the room and hugged Tye until she couldn't breathe. Then the nerves set in. What if she burned the omelette? How would she ever remember where everything was located?

Tye had sat with Meggie and helped her combat her doubts. "Meggie, you know how to cook. You'll just be doing it in someone else's kitchen that's all. If you're afraid you'll forget something, then just line up everything before you start."

Meggie had hung onto that idea. Now, as she looked over the kitchen of the Farmer's Bed and Breakfast, she mentally tried to place all the necessary equipment.

"Our cook has gone home for the day," Eilene explained. "She comes in about five in the morning and leaves around noon. After you get settled in your room, we'll have you come down and we'll ask you some questions. Then you can do the cooking."

"What's on your menu?" Meggie asked.

"Depends on the season," Eilene said. "Berries aren't ripe yet, but they will be this summer, so we'll make a lot of Belgian waffles with berries and cream. Your muffin recipe was a big hit, by the way."

Meggie smiled with pride. "Thank you."

Eilene continued, "We have blueberry, strawberry, raspberry, and more than our share of blackberry bushes. You'll be responsible for picking what you need for the guests. We suggest you do it the day before."

"Since the berries aren't producing yet, we bought some blueberries at the store and tried your muffin recipe. They were the most tender and tastiest muffins I'd ever eaten. It's part of the reason we asked you to come down."

"How many applications did you receive?"

"About a dozen. Now I'll show you upstairs and you can settle in. Then we'll start our interview about three."

Meggie picked up her overnight bag and followed Eilene up the stairs to a small room with flowered, Victorian wallpaper and a private bath. The window looked out over the fields where sheep grazed. The hills were alive with fresh green grass and the sheep looked like cotton balls against the velvet pastures. A spring breeze freshened the room as Meggie sat by the open window.

It felt good to in her home county, even if she wasn't here to visit her parents. She loved the green pastures dotted with sheep and cows. The only thing that had tempered Meggie's enthusiasm for her job interview, and her visit, was the discussion she was going to have with her folks. When she had told them about her application and subsequent interview, there had been a stunned silence on the phone. "Don't you think it would be best if you worked in an accounting office?" her father, Jacob, had asked. "In fact, I was thinking we'd have an opening for you at our office. One of our assistants just gave us a two-week notice. She's moving to Seattle. We were planning on using a temp agency until you came home for the summer. Then you could have the job until school started in September."

"Dad, I'm not sure I want to work in the office this summer. I've been working in your office since I was fourteen. I want to try something different."

"Really, Meg, you should be thinking about your future," her mother, Melissa, said.

"I am thinking about my future," Meg said. The words popped out and hung on the line. Meggie could picture her folks standing with separate receivers, looking shocked.

"The office is your future," Jacob said. "You know that, Meg."

Meg felt her mouth go dry. This wasn't where this conversation was supposed to be going. She wasn't prepared to tell them of her doubts. Not yet. What if she didn't get this job? What if she hated cooking for strangers and on a schedule? "Dad, I'm not so sure I want to work in the office. I'm not sure about anything. I need some new experiences—something different."

"Well, of course, if you would like to try something different, I suppose we can get along without you this summer," Melissa's words trailed off.

"How are your classes going?" Jacob asked. "Is that why you're so worried about working at the office? Are you having trouble in your classes?"

"No, my classes are fine," Meggie hedged. "But I have to admit, I don't enjoy them."

"School is never fun," Jacob said. "Not if you do it right."

"I'm not so sure about that," Meg said. "Tye works hard, but she loves what she's doing."

"Yes and that horse of hers will eat all her profits. She's a wonderful gal, Meg. We couldn't ask for a better friend for you, but she's always been a little short-sighted when it comes to Trapper."

"Tell us about Neil," Melissa said. "Your letters say he transferred from BYU because of some girl."

Meggie wondered if her folks were really interested in Neil or just trying to figure out why she wasn't willing to work in the office. She tried not to sound too gushy. "He's really nice, Mom. We went to the coast last weekend and had a wonderful time. He was engaged once before but it didn't work out. That's why he left BYU." Meggie was grateful she hadn't gone into the details of Neil's relationship with Sammi Rae.

"Is he a cook?" Jacob asked.

"No. He's majoring in pre-med."

The approval was tangible. Meggie could feel it coming through the line. It irritated her. She should be glad that her folks approved of Neil's schooling decisions, but she didn't want their opinion of him based on his desire to be a doctor. Did that mean they would disapprove of her if she decided to become a chef? Well, they certainly would disapprove of the decision. But would they disapprove of her? Meggie closed her eyes. She didn't want to disappoint her folks, but she didn't want to be chained to a career for which she felt a growing desperation.

"You know, Meggie, I wanted to be an airline pilot when I was your age," Jacob said.

Meggie was shocked. "I didn't know that, Dad."

"Yes. Back then most airline pilots were recruited from the Air Force, so I knew I'd have to join the military after my mission."

"Why didn't you?"

"Your grandpa wouldn't hear of it. He made me realize that it would be difficult to have a family under those circumstances—always leaving home to fly. I'd have to live in a big metropolitan area in order to be available for my job. Then there are the dangers of the military to consider. He made me see the sensible side of life," Jacob said.

Meggie sighed. "I'm sorry you didn't get to be a pilot."

"It turned out for the best, really," Jacob said. "The office has afforded us a good life. You'd do well to remember that."

"Is that what Grandpa said to you?"

"Yes, and he was right."

Things became clear to Meggie. Her folks were only doing what they thought was best. Her father had been coerced into accounting—the safe and predictable lifestyle. They wanted the same for her—safety—and a predictable income. But Meggie wasn't ready for those things. Not now. Maybe not ever. "I need a challenge, Dad," she said softly. "I'm going to come home next weekend and see if I can get this job. Don't hold the job at the office for me. If I don't get this position, I'll try someplace else. I need to make my own way."

"You're as stubborn as Justin," Melissa said. "Running off to become an auto mechanic of all things."

"He didn't run off, Mom. He lives right there. Besides, he always loved working on cars. He's good at it too. He'd probably make a poor accountant."

"He didn't even try," Melissa said. "Your father and I have worked our whole lives in hopes of turning this business over to you kids, and you don't even appreciate it. Most children would be overjoyed for such an opportunity."

"Then sell it to someone who feels that way, Mom. I want to be a chef." The words stopped everyone, including Meggie. She bit her lip. She hadn't meant to be harsh. But now that the words were out, she didn't take them back. Her long hope was finally out in the open. The burden she didn't even know she was carrying was suddenly lifted and Meggie felt as light as feathers.

"Well, Meggie," Jacob began. "We'll look forward to having you come home. Tell us about this bed and breakfast."

Meggie could hear the disappointment in her father's voice, but her folks acted interested when she told them about the letter she had written and Eilene Anderson's response. They knew the inn and had driven by it often.

Now she was sitting in a lovely country room looking over a spring afternoon. She wasn't nervous about the interview. After the grilling she received from her folks, talking to Eilene would be a snap. She was worried about her cooking. She didn't have any credentials. Just instinct as to how things should go. Would it be enough? It was enough to get her this interview.

She glanced at her watch. Two-forty-five. Meggie stood. She should change her clothes and freshen up before going back downstairs.

∼

Tye looked out the window and saw her mother sitting in the late afternoon sun that filtered weakly through the clouds. She held a cigarette between her fingers. An ashtray was on the table.

Familiar disappointment crowded Tye's heart. She opened the sliding glass door and found a chair. She sat down beside her Mom on the opposite side of the smoke.

"It's a lovely afternoon," Trudy murmured. "A real treat for early April." She reached over and patted her daughter's knee. "Having you home for a short weekend is a real treat as well. How is Trapper?"

Tye grinned. "He's fine. Kyle's looking after him while I'm

here."

"Tell me about Kyle," Trudy said.

Tye's guard went up. What could she say? "Well," she began slowly. "He's kind and gentle. He loves his horse and we ride together often."

"Is that how you spend most of your time?"

Tye nodded. "Yeah. We go out to dinner sometimes, but we're both so busy that if we want to spend time together, it has to be on horseback."

Tye could feel questions still lurking in her mother, but Trudy remained silent for a moment. When Tye didn't volunteer anything more she changed the subject. "What's this job interview Meggie is all excited about?"

"It's for a cook at the Farmer's Bed and Breakfast."

"I know that place," Trudy said. "They used to serve dinner, and your father and I ate there a couple of times. It's very expensive. What made Meggie want to cook?"

Tye looked out over the budding yard. "I think she's always wanted to cook but she just didn't know what to do about it until now." She became thoughtful. "Mom, what would you and Dad like to see me do with my life?"

Trudy blinked. "That's a weighty question. I guess we've just always wanted you to be happy."

"Do you ever regret allowing me to ride?"

"I wouldn't say we regret it," Trudy said slowly. "We worry for you. Riding is such a dangerous sport, but it brings you such happiness and I'd never want to be responsible for holding you back." She paused. "Are you wanting to compete for a living?"

"No," Tye said thoughtfully. "I still want to teach."

"You don't sound too convinced. What brought this up? Does

Kyle want you to compete?"

Tye shook her head. "No. It really doesn't have anything to do with Kyle. It's Meggie. She's sweating bullets over this decision to apply for a position as a chef."

Trudy gave her an inquiring look.

Tye continued, "Her folks want her to take over the accounting business."

"Yes. I know that's always been the plan."

Tye shook her head. "Not Meggie's plan. Jacob and Melissa's plan."

"I see," Trudy said slowly. "I know Meggie has always liked to cook and bake. Do you remember when she spent the night here, and we woke up to bran muffins right out of the oven?"

Tye grinned. "You hired her on the spot."

"Well, I tried. For all of my years in the kitchen, I could never match Meg. She's good."

"Do you think she'll get the job?"

"I think the owners would be foolish not to hire her. Anyone who can make bran muffins as light and delicious as she, deserves to cook for a crowd, if it's what she wants."

"What if I decided to become a cook?"

"Then I'd help you choose your classes and sample all your dishes."

"What if I chose plumbing?"

"I'd ship you off to school in a pair of coveralls and then show you the leaky pipes under the bathroom sink when you came home."

Tye laughed. Then she sobered. "And what if I decided to compete in three-day-eventing instead of teach?"

Trudy grasped Tye's hand. "Then, I'll hope for the best teachers and pray that the Lord will look after you and keep you safe."

Tears came to Tye's eyes as her spirit warmed to her mother.

"I guess that's why I'm so concerned about your relationship with Kyle," Trudy said cautiously. "All we want is your happiness, Tye, and we all know how important the gospel is to you."

She nodded thoughtfully. Yes, the gospel was important.

"I know how distressed you've been over my smoking habit and the fact that I'm not a member. I don't see why that would be any different for Kyle."

Tye sighed. She had no argument. "It's not different," she said. "And you're right."

"I hope you're not thinking you can change him," Trudy said.

Tye laughed at her mother's revelation. "Doesn't everyone think that way?" she asked lightly.

"People change only when it's what they want," Trudy said. "Not because it's what someone else wants. I'm the perfect example."

"Mom, why do you continue to smoke when you know it's shaving years off your life? Don't you love me and Dad enough to quit?"

"That's not fair, Tye, and you know it."

"It seems fair to me. I don't want to lose you like this."

"Like what? Unsealed?"

"Don't you know how much that means to me? If you would join the church we could be sealed as a family. Don't you believe in the truthfulness of the gospel?"

Trudy crushed her cigarette in the ashtray and took both of Tye's hands into hers. "I hope it's true, Tye. I hope."

"Oh, Mom, it is true. I don't just hope. I know."

"That's why you have the testimony and I don't," Trudy said

quietly.

Tye squeezed her mother's hand. The familiar sorrow came ebbing in, but a new feeling rose with it. Ever since Tye was a teenager, she believed that Meggie's family was perfect. There were many things that were right with Meggie's family. They were active in church. They were sealed in the temple. But there were things that were right with her family as well. Her folks put aside their own fear and allowed Tye the right to choose her own path. They supported her in the decisions she made and were truly interested in her personal happiness. "Mom, I just want us to be together. I wouldn't trade you," Tye said quietly.

Tears came to Trudy's eyes. "You haven't always felt that way."

Tye bit her lip. "I know," she said.

"Well, I'm glad you feel that way now. That's all that matters."

Rex came through the door, carrying a tray of lemonade. "I thought we could all use some refreshment," he said. He sat the tray down on the table and Tye picked up a beaded glass of lemonade.

Her father sat down and all was quiet in the spring evening; for the first time, Tye felt as if she were truly home.

⁓

When Meggie came the following morning to pick Tye up, she got out of the car and stood in the brilliant sunshine. Tye stood on the porch with her overnight bag in hand.

"You are looking at the new morning chef for Farmer's Bed and Breakfast," Meggie said as she threw her hands in the air.

Tye gave a delighted laugh and ran down the porch to hug her best friend.

"I start June fifth."

"Did you tell them you could only stay on through the summer?" Tye asked.

Meggie nodded. "They only need someone for the summer. Their cook is going on maternity leave. It's perfect!"

Tye looked up to the porch and saw her parents standing beside each other. Her father had his arm around her mother.

"Congratulations, Meg!" Trudy said. "I told Tye just yesterday that they would be foolish not to hire you. I'm glad to see they recognize talent when they see it."

Meggie grinned. She couldn't stop grinning.

Tye ran back to her folks and gave them each a hug. "I'll be home before you know it," she said quietly.

"Goodbye, dear girl. Be careful. We love you," Trudy whispered in her ear.

Her father held her close for a long minute, then turned her loose. Tye waved to them as Meggie backed out of the driveway.

Once they were on the freeway, Tye asked, "How did your parents take the news?"

Meggie's gleeful mood dampened. "Well, I think they were hoping I wouldn't get the position so that I would have to go back to work at the office. I know they think the office is my future and that it's best for me, but I'm not sure I see it that way."

"Did you talk about it at all?"

"Yeah. They think it's just a phase and I'll get over it once I get 'this cooking business' out of my system."

"Is that what they call it? This cooking business?"

Meggie nodded. "And who knows? Maybe they're right. But I need to find that out for myself." She paused. "I really love my folks. This must be a terrible disappointment for them. They've spent years building up this business so that the three of us could inherit an easier life. Now nobody wants it."

Tye touched Meggie's arm. "It'll work out."

"I hope so."

Both girls became silent as Tye watched the passing landscape. Spring was unfolding like a treasured gift newly unwrapped, and she gloried in the bright morning sun and rebirth of land. She looked for new lambs and calves in the pastures and even noticed a few foals. She thought about Trapper. How was he? Tye settled into her seat. He was fine. Kyle was looking after him and in the last few weeks she had known Kyle, she had come to understand that when it came to horses, he was very single-minded. He had promised Tye to make sure that Trapper was able to have some pasture time. A rare treat. Tye smiled. She knew what Trapper would do. He would go down for a good roll in the grass. Hopefully it would be grass and not mud.

Her thoughts turned to Kyle. What was he doing this weekend? The show season was scheduled to begin the following Saturday, so there was plenty of work that needed to be done. Ben would have to be clipped and groomed. Boots, bridles, and saddles would need to be cleaned and polished. All equipment would have to be looked over for weak buckles, stretched leather, and anything else that could possibly snap or break during a show. He would have his hands full. Tye felt a bite of apprehension. CarrieAnne would probably spend a great deal of her time at the barn too. Tye shook her head and turned her thoughts to her own gear. She also had equipment that needed some cleaning and care. Even though she was just the alternate, her horse and equipment needed to be in top shape.

"Do you think we'll get back in time for church?" Meggie asked.

"I hope so," Tye replied. "Toni is going to be there."

"So is Neil," Meggie murmured.

Tye wondered what it would be like to go to church with a man. What would it be like to go to church with Kyle? Would she ever know? Her mother's words echoed in her thoughts. The gospel was important to her. Kyle was becoming increasingly important. How could she deny those feelings? In many ways, Kyle was her soulmate.

He understood her deep and abiding love for Trapper. He appreciated her work ethic and worked just as hard. He understood her moral views and respected them. He didn't begrudge the time she spent in church activities. Weren't those qualities of value? Was it enough?

The deep longing she felt for a sealed family rose in her like the tide. How could she deny her own children the very thing she wished for so fervently? She clamped down on that thought. She wasn't thinking of marrying Kyle. That was completely out of the question. Then what was the point of their relationship? It had gone beyond just going out to have fun. Their promise to be exclusive with one another extracted any thoughts of casual dating. Did she love him? The question dangled. She respected him. She reveled in his company. She longed to be with him when they were apart. Was that love? It was a close relationship maybe. Did he love her? She honestly couldn't say. Did she want him to love her? It was a delicious thought, but it was also scary. He certainly didn't see her religion as something that could come between them. He respected her choices, but he didn't understand them. Could he change? Tye thought about her mother. She hadn't joined the church. For the longest time, Tye believed it was because her mother didn't love her enough to want to be sealed. She loved her cigarettes more. Would Kyle love her enough to join the church? Is that what she wanted? The questions became like jackhammers.

She turned towards Meggie. "How are you feeling about Neil's letter from Sammi Rae?"

Meggie swallowed. "Scared. Apprehensive. Jealous!"

Tye arched her eyebrows. Then she thought about CarrieAnne. Kyle had said there was nothing for her to worry about. But the shared history still nagged at her sometimes.

Meggie continued quietly, "I wonder if she'll write him again."

"Do you think she will?"

Meggie nodded as she stared out onto the freeway, "Yes, I do."

"What are you going to do?"

Meggie shrugged. "I can't do anything. It's up to Neil." She continued, "I hate the thought of losing him. We've become so close and he's been so supportive of my desire to cook. I don't think I would've even applied for this job if it weren't for Neil." She flashed a grin. "You too."

"Me! What have I done?"

"Every day I see you doing something you love and it's given me courage to try something I love. And you've let me talk about my worries."

Tye smiled. A feeling of warmth replaced her earlier shadows. "You're a good friend, Meggie. I have a feeling we're going to need each other in the next few weeks."

Chapter Twenty-One

Walking up the stairs to their apartment, Meggie and Tye discussed sacrament meeting.

"Where did Toni go?" Meggie asked.

"I guess she hung out in the bathroom for a few minutes, but at least she came back. Last week she went home. I think she's really trying."

"I saw her talking to Steve after sacrament meeting," Meggie said. "Do you think he asked her out?"

"I don't know. He walked her to her car though."

"Do you think she'll start staying for the full three hours soon?"

Tye shrugged. "It would be nice if she could come to Relief Society. Maybe next week. She always looks so worn out after sacrament meeting. I don't blame her for going home." Tye paused as she unlocked the door and she and Meggie moved into the apartment. "How's Neil?" she asked.

Meggie smiled. "Fine. It was good to see him. I know we were only apart a couple of days, but I missed him more than I realized."

"What did he say about your new position as the breakfast chef?"

Meggie grinned. "He was so excited! He says he wants to have a celebration, but I don't know when we'll be able to do that."

A knock on the door interrupted their conversation.

"I bet that's Steve and Michael, hoping they can come over for dinner," Tye whispered.

Meggie answered the door.

"Surprise!"

Meggie counted. Michael, Steven, Toni, and Neil stood at her front door. Steve was holding a chocolate cake in need of repair. "Do you think you can fix it?" he asked.

"I don't think it needs to be fixed. It's perfect!" Meg replied.

Neil moved to the front and pulled Meggie close. "We wanted to congratulate you on your new job."

Michael looked sheepish. "We baked this cake yesterday," he said. "We were hoping for a celebration when you got home, but we thought it might be consolation if you didn't get the job."

Meggie's heart warmed as she threw the door wide. "Come in!" She looked at her roommate. "Tye. Did you know about this?"

Tye shook her head. "No one said a word."

Toni smiled. "They made me keep it a secret on the pain of death. Are you surprised, Meggie?"

Meggie nodded.

"I'm sorry about the cake," Steve said as he handed it to Meggie. "We did our best."

Meggie looked down. Canned frosting couldn't cover the crack the size of an earthquake fault that ran down the middle. "It'll taste the same," she said.

"I told them to buy two cans of frosting," Neil said. "But they didn't believe me."

"One can would've been enough if we didn't have to fill that crack in the middle," Michael said.

"I just appreciate you thinking of me," Meggie said. "That's what counts."

"I bet that's not all that counts in your job. The food you serve will probably have to be pretty when it comes out of the kitchen," Michael said.

"Tell us about your job," Toni said as she sat down on the couch.

Meggie grinned. Her heart began to soar. She sat in a chair and leaned forward. "Well, I have to be there by five in the morning."

Collective groans came from the crowd.

"The menu will rotate depending on what seasonal fruit is available. They have berry bushes and a couple of peach and pear trees, and I'm responsible for making sure all the fruit is picked for the day before I cook with it."

"What kind of things will you be creating?" Steve asked.

Meggie thought for a moment. "Let's see. Their summer menu revolves around fresh fruit. I'll be making banana sourdough pancakes and coconut French toast, along with Belgian waffles with berries and cream. Ham with a hot apples and cinnamon, and eggs. Lots of eggs. I'll be responsible for a variety of muffins and breads. The only bread they buy is croissants. They take forever to make and require special equipment."

"Will you be making all of these things every day?" Toni asked.

"Oh, no. One day it'll be Belgian waffles, then the following day it'll be eggs with hollandaise sauce and bacon. It varies."

"Well, you can practice on us anytime," Steve said.

"Oh, no," Neil stepped in. "If she practices on anyone, it'll be me."

"Wait a minute," Tye said. "I live here. She's going to practice on me."

Everyone laughed.

"Well, if you don't mind having breakfast for dinner, I'll probably practice on all of you."

"We don't mind. Do we, Michael?" Steve piped up.

"You'll all have to pitch in for the cost," Meggie said.

"Done!" Neil said.

Tye sat back and smiled. Everyone was having such a good time. She glanced at Toni. Her face was relaxed and open. She had lost her earlier pinched look that she had at church. But Toni wasn't the only one changing. Sharing the gospel with her had brought more joy than Tye imagined. She looked forward to her Wednesday night visits, even if she wasn't sure what to expect—but that was part of what she came to enjoy. Ever since her missionary contact with Toni, Tye felt a new openness about the gospel. True, she had only been out with the sisters three times, but she found herself intrigued by the Spirit that seemed to linger whenever they were around. She could feel a remnant of it now. Could Toni feel it? Would Kyle feel it?

Tye stood. Maybe she should call Kyle and see if he would be willing to come over. A small thrill pulsed through her. She never saw him on Sunday and this would be the perfect introduction to the gospel—just good friends sitting around—enjoying each other's company and celebrating. She had called him earlier to check on Trapper, but because she was getting ready for church their conversation was brief.

She hurried to her bedroom and placed the phone on her lap before dialing.

"Hello?"

"Kyle?"

"Tye?"

"Yeah, listen, I was wondering if you'd want to come over. A bunch of us have gotten together to celebrate Meggie's new job. We'd love to have your company."

Silence came between them.

"Kyle?"

"Yeah. Um, Tye. I was just on my way to the barn. You barely caught me. It's such a beautiful afternoon I thought I'd take Ben out for a long ride. Listen, why don't you come with me? It's such a beautiful spring day. Trapper would be happy to see you."

A mixture of feelings tumbled inside of Tye. The weather was inviting. So was Kyle's gentle voice. But she had a house full of guests and Toni was among them. This was where she belonged and this was where she wanted to be.

She thought of Trapper and a trace of guilt threaded through her. She should go check on him. But she didn't have to do that now. Kyle had told her he was fit and had enjoyed the weekend off. "I don't ride on Sundays. Remember?"

"Oh, of course. I'm sorry. I honestly forgot. It's just such a beautiful afternoon." Kyle became pensive. "Don't you miss Trapper?"

"Sure, I miss him, but you told me he was doing fine and I believe you. Besides, I really can't leave, Kyle. It wouldn't be nice to just speed out on Meg and we have a small houseful of people. This is where I belong right now."

"Of course. I understand. It was just a thought. Listen, I'd better go. These days are short and I want to catch as much sunlight as possible. I'll see you tomorrow?"

"Sure."

"We've got a busy week ahead. The show season starts next weekend. Have you checked your gear?"

"No. I'm going to do that this week."

"Well, if you need any help, let me know."

"Okay."

After a quick goodbye, Tye hung up. She could hear the laughter coming in from the front room, but her conversation with Kyle had dampened her enthusiasm. Tye walked back out into the living room to see everyone was gathering around as Michael cut pieces. Everyone wanted a piece with frosting so they decided to draw straws. Toni and Tye drew short straws and were given pieces without frosting.

After everyone sat down with their cake, Toni asked, "So, how do your folks feel about your new job? It must be nice to go home and have a job waiting. I'm sure they appreciate that."

Meggie exchanged looks with Tye. "It's not that simple," she said quietly. "My folks want me to be an accountant so I can take over the business when I graduate. They were hoping I'd work in their office or possibly find a job in another accounting firm. They never intended for me to go to work in a Bed and Breakfast."

Toni felt as if she had stumbled into personal business. "I'm sorry," she murmured.

Meggie nodded. "So am I. But it will work itself out somehow." She smiled and bit into her cake. "This is good," she said. "I appreciate you boys thinking of me."

"It was fun. We ought to think of you more often," Michael teased.

"And it was easy. We just bought a mix and added two eggs." Steve added. "Mike is right. We should think of you more often."

"Not too often," Neil said as he put his hand over Meggie's.

⁓

An hour later, Toni drove home in the quiet hush of a Sunday spring evening. The earlier warmth was dissipating and being replaced by a heavy chill. But the air still held the aroma of the day—with its budding wildflowers and new spring grass.

When she stepped out of the car, she lingered in the driveway and then walked to the back deck. The smell of earth and renewal surrounded her. It wasn't the same as the arid and light spring she remembered in Idaho. Springtime in Idaho had a mixture of odors—manure that was being used as fertilizer would mingle with fresh mountain air. Toni never minded the fertilizer but she was always glad when that part of the season was finished and she could concentrate on the blossoming warmth and the promise that accompanied it. Then cherry blossoms would fill the valley and their delicate fragrance and pink petals would be the highlight of the season. It wasn't time for cherry blossoms yet.

Toni thought back to the day when she and her dad moved into this house. Her eyes were drawn to the corner of the yard that needed a cherry tree, but she never asked for one. It would just be a silly reminder of her life in Idaho. The life she was trying to forget.

Toni surveyed the corner by the wooden fence. That's where the tree would go. It was a bright, sunny location that was sheltered from the wind.

Toni shook her head. No. No cherry trees. No pink blossoms and no reminders.

With quick motions, she turned her back on the deepening spring evening and the vacant corner in her yard and in her heart.

Chapter Twenty-Two

Kyle glanced at Tye. She sat in the passenger side of his truck, looking tense and drawn. He had called her at six in the morning. Kyle's teammate, Jenny, had been loading her horse in preparation for the first show of the season when the gray gelding shocked everyone by rearing. He hit his head on the ceiling of the trailer as he tried to lunge away. In his obvious fear, the horse accidentally stepped off the ramp, threw a shoe, and went down to his knees before the episode was over. Jenny was shocked. Her horse had never acted this way before. He was trembling and skittish for several minutes. Jenny tried to calm him while Kyle searched the trailer. It didn't take him long to find the reason behind the horse's fright. A medium sized snake was coiled up in the hay that was sitting in the trailer. It was a harmless garden snake, but it had slithered into a coil just when the horse was being led into the trailer. It had been enough to send him into a panic. After the incident was over, Jenny tended the sharp cut in her horse's knee. It was deep and blood was running down his leg.

"I'm glad Jenny is going to have Dr. Robinson look at her horse's knee. That gash looked pretty serious to me. I think he's going to need some stitches."

Kyle nodded. "It looked like it could go either way. Sometimes those injuries can look worse than they really are. Jenny wasn't too happy. Sitting out the first show of the season made her irritable." He placed his hand on her knee. "I'm sorry I had to call you so early."

Tye smiled for the first time all morning as she placed her hand over Kyle's. "It's okay. I'm the alternate, remember? It means I'm on call for this kind of thing. Actually, I'm kind of glad to go. It means we can spend the day together."

"Then why do you look so anxious?"

"You noticed, huh?" She sighed. "Being dragged out of bed and told to be at the barn in twenty minutes so I can ride with the competition team is enough to make anyone tense." She tried to smile but couldn't pull it off. "Truth is, I'm nervous," she said. "I know Trapper and I are prepared and our gear is in fine shape." She breathed a sigh of relief. "I'm so glad I took Tuesday evening to go over my gear." She paused. "But there's a lot at stake here. If I foul up, I'm not the only one who will look stupid. Katie will look stupid too. CarrieAnne is waiting for me to show badly."

Kyle squeezed Tye's hand. "It's not like you to worry about someone else. You didn't get to this level of competition by worrying about other people, Tye. Who cares what CarrieAnne thinks? Katie can take care of herself and CarrieAnne too, if necessary. You just worry about you doing the best job you can. You'll pull through."

"I don't want to look like a fraud, Kyle," Tye blurted out.

Kyle stared at her for a moment. "A fraud? Tye, you may be many things, but you're not a fraud." He turned his eyes back to the road. "You've worked hard for this. If you didn't know what you were doing, don't you think it would have been obvious by now?"

Tye breathed the tension out of her neck and shoulders. "Yes. You're right about that."

"Since you've never competed with a team before, let me tell you about the routine once we get to the grounds," Kyle said.

Carefully, Kyle began to explain the process. The team was already registered but Katie would have to go to the show organizers and make sure Tye and Trapper's names were placed on the roster. Meanwhile, Tye would be leading Trapper to his rented stall. Katie would return with the day's schedule. Then they would all walk the cross-country course together, as a team. This would be their opportunity to ask Katie her opinion and test their theories about the course on other riders. Then each rider was responsible for walking the course alone. It would be the same in the show-jumping arena.

Tye nodded as she listened to Kyle. It all sounded pretty straightforward. She knew the routine of the three-day-event—usually crammed into one long day for the sake of convenience. That was what would be happening here.

Kyle slowed the truck and checked the trailer in his rearview mirror. Ben and Trapper were together in the back.

"We're almost there," Kyle said. "We'll get these boys settled and then get started."

Tye breathed easier. Just listening to Kyle's gentle voice explain the process helped calm her nerves.

Kyle parked his truck next to Katie's vehicle and Tye hopped out. She couldn't look nervous now. Other team members would be watching to see how she handled the stress of being called out at the last minute. She could feel CarrieAnne's eyes on her as she dropped the ramp of the trailer and helped Kyle unload the horses. She had gone through this so many times that her body was on automatic. She ran through the checklist in her mind: settle Trapper in his stall, make sure he has enough hay and fresh water, check in with the organizers, and then prepare for the competition. Just putting her body into the routine tasks gave her confidence. Kyle was right. She knew what she was doing.

Leading Trapper down the aisle, she found Jenny's name and number on the rented stall. She led Trapper inside with a flake of alfalfa. He sniffed his water bucket and then buried his nose in the sweet-smelling feed. Tye gave his shoulder a pat. He knew the routine also. To him this was just one more competition. She should feel the same.

Moving away, she found Katie standing in the aisle with the rest of the riders. Katie handed Tye a copy of the schedule. Jenny's name had been crossed out and hers written in the space above. She glanced through the schedule looking for her name and breathed a sigh of relief. She had pulled her favorite order. Show-jumping would be her first element. That would allow Trapper to work off some of his show energy. Dressage would be next. Then the cross-country course. Perfect.

Every rider had a preference as to how they approached the competition. Some liked to get the cross-country out of the way while their horses were fresh and full of excitement. Others like to work through the more disciplined rhythm and balance of dressage so that they could focus on the more adventurous elements—the show-jumping and cross-country.

Tye preferred to work out some of Trapper's verve on the show-jumping course, which required his concentration, but also allowed him to expend his energy. Then he would focus better on the dressage. Trapper loved the cross-country course the best. He was free to gallop between fences, and he found the courses challenging and exciting. She could tell by the way he pranced before the gun went off and the way his ears would prick forward whenever the new fence was sighted. This schedule was in Trapper's favor.

Quietly she moved towards Kyle. "My schedule is good. What about you?" she asked.

"I run cross-country first. I'd rather do dressage, but that's the way it goes. Ben's up to it though."

They read through the schedule together. Kyle would be able to watch Tye's dressage test and show-jumping but he would miss her cross-country run.

Moving with the rest of the team, Tye began walking the cross-country course. When they reached the first fence, she squatted near the take-off point and checked the ground. It was saturated from a rainy winter; after a dozen horses passed this way, the clay-like mud would be slick. Tye dug into the soil and rolled it around her palm. She would need to screw cleats into Trapper's shoes. She sized up the fence. It wasn't difficult. Usually the first fence of the course was one of the easier fences. It would be the invitation to the horse to begin the course. It was a plain log jump with a brushy evergreen hedge in front.

For an hour, Tye walked the course with the team, looking at each fence with the same scrutiny. She checked the soil and measured the width of some fences—determining her take-off point by the numbers. She checked the slope of the ground around each fence and looked for trouble spots. Were there bare spots where puddles of water would form as the horses beat down the sod? Would the grass hold up? Tye was convinced that by the time she and Trapper rode the cross-country course, the ground would be thoroughly chewed up. She would have to pay special attention to the turf.

She walked the show-jumping course with the same concentration. It didn't look difficult compared to the courses Katie had been putting together at home. Suddenly, Tye was grateful for Katie's tough-minded exactness. She required her students to work harder at home, which gave them confidence for the show. Not that it would be easy. Tye would have to pay attention, but her conviction that she could get through this course returned.

After the team was finished with the show-jumping course, Katie gathered them together near Trapper's stall. She gave special instructions for them to walk the course in pairs or alone. She cautioned against the slippery field and suggested that each rider screw cleats into their horse's shoes. She reminded them that they were coming into this first competition as last year's champions and that they needed to be professional both on and off the field. She told the riders where she could be found for questions or problems and then left them to individual preparations.

"So, what do you think?" Kyle asked.

"I feel better," Tye said.

"You'll be fine," Kyle said with a smile. He checked his watch. "We don't have much time before the show starts. We ought to look at the cross-country course once again. Do you prefer to go with me or alone?"

"You know Trapper well. I'd appreciate your input."

As Tye and Kyle walked the course again, it began to feel more familiar. Each fence has its individual characteristics but there wasn't anything new for Tye to worry over. It was a difficult course made dicey by the weather but none of this was new to Tye, Trapper, Kyle or Ben.

After they were finished, they hurried to the paddock to prepare their horses for the day of competition.

Methodically, Tye began to saddle Trapper. She checked the cinch, placed the bit in his mouth, and made sure the buckles were all tight.

Trapper was eager to begin his day. Tye grinned. Trapper had a competitive spirit. He fed on the energy that came from the show. Tye talked in whispers to Trapper as she checked her stirrup length and gave the buckles one last look. She talked about the upcoming competition. She spoke about the slippery sod on the cross-country course and the tight turn between fences four and five in the show-jumping ring. She knew Trapper couldn't understand her words, but he did seem to pay attention—catching her voice with a flick of his ears.

Giving Trapper a pat on the neck, Tye led him out of the stall to the outdoor warm-up arena. There were several riders putting their horses through their warm-up exercises that would help them prepare for the day ahead. Tye began her routine with Trapper. She paid special attention when she asked him to move to the right. He had stiffened during the ride in the trailer. It wasn't unusual, but Tye thought about the tight turn between fences four and five in the show-jumping arena. It was a right turn. With patience, Tye asked for twenty-meter circles and serpentines. After several minutes Trapper improved. Soon, he was bending around Tye's leg and she could feel that he was supple and moving without stiffness.

Moving out of the warm-up area, Tye dismounted and led Trapper to the show-jumping area. She always liked to arrive a few minutes early so she could watch a couple of her competitors. She didn't know the young woman who was negotiating the course on a dappled gray, but she watched carefully as she negotiated her horse through the course. Fence four came down. It was the fence that worried Tye; a vertical that stood four-and-a-half feet with planks hinged on flat cups. It looked like the merest of breezes would knock it over. Coming off a tight right-hand turn, Trapper would be facing the exit, which would give him the impression that he was finished with the course. If he wasn't paying attention, he would focus on the exit. With his concentration lost, they could easily plow into fence four. That's what had just happened to the rider who had finished. She couldn't get her horse's attention until it was too late and he crow-hopped over the fence, bringing it down with a crash.

Tye watched the next rider negotiate the course. He managed to keep his horse's attention riveted onto the task and he rode a clean round.

Tye was next. Checking the girth once again, Tye mounted and rode into the arena. She looked over the small crowd of horses and riders and was able to pick out Kyle, Katie, and CarrieAnne. CarrieAnne had lost some of her smug look and was watching intently. Katie looked calm but alert.

Suddenly, the noise dropped away. It happened every time Tye competed, allowing her to completely focus on her job. Nothing else mattered except the course. Quietly, she pushed Trapper into a canter and rode around the arena, allowing him his first look at the course. The faces around the edges of the course faded from view as Tye turned Trapper to the first obstacle. For one brilliant moment they were airborne and Tye caught her breath. That first glorious moment in the air was heaven. It only lasted a second. She had to focus on the second fence before she even landed—giving Trapper subtle signals with her hands and body that would allow him to understand the direction of the course.

Tye handled each fence that way—always looking ahead and telling Trapper through her aids what he was to do next. They were a horse and rider partnership who listened to each other and met the challenge.

In mid-air over fence three, Tye asked Trapper for a hard right turn by pushing her right leg into his side. She kept contact with his mouth through the reins, and as soon as Trapper landed she gave him a half-halt to keep his attention focused on the fence. She could feel him getting strong in the mouth. He wanted to run for the exit. Tye gave another tug on the reins coupled with a push from the leg. Trapper moved into the bit, made the turn and took off over fence four. Tye's world was completely silent. All she heard was the sound she and Trapper made as they greeted the wind that met them at every fence. After she landed she pushed Trapper towards the rest of the course, which was away from the exit, and gave him some rein. After the last fence, Tye encouraged him to pick up speed and canter by the automatic timer.

Tye didn't have to look back to know that she had run a clear round. Tears came to her eyes as she patted Trapper on the neck. Her time flashed up on the board. She had come in second. Relief and happiness flooded through her. There were several horse and rider teams still left to compete on the course, but Tye had shown well. One-third of her competition was over and she hadn't embarrassed herself—or Katie.

Giving Trapper a long rein, she allowed him to stretch his neck as he walked towards the exit. Katie greeted her. Kyle had left to prepare Ben and CarrieAnne had gone with him. Tye dismounted.

"Good job," Katie said. "You handled fence four like a real pro. I'm proud of you, Tye."

Tye beamed and leaned against Trapper. "Wasn't he wonderful?" she asked.

Katie nodded. "Yes. He was remarkable."

Katie checked her watch. "You've got twenty minutes to kill before the dressage test. Keep him warm and interested in his surroundings."

Tye nodded as Katie hurried away. She looked for Kyle, but then remembered he had to prepare for his show-jumping test.

The rest of the day was spent moving from one arena to the next. Tye was one of the last riders on the cross-country course; as expected the ground was muddy and chewed. But by using control and good judgment she and Trapper were able to get around the course without any mishaps. Their time was slow though. Tye had opted for caution instead of speed, and she came away with time faults. She didn't care. Any sensible rider had to take the footing into consideration. Tye was pleased with her and Trapper's overall work. Their show-jumping score had been excellent and her second-place rating had remained. She had come in first in the dressage test where Trapper's ego really came through, and even though she didn't show as well as she knew she could in the cross-country, she had used common sense. Her score there had come out somewhere in the middle. By the time the team was leading the horses up the ramp for their long ride home, they knew they had come in first place.

Tye breathed a long sigh of relief. She hadn't embarrassed herself or Katie. The team had been able to hold on to their number one ranking. Tye and Trapper had been tested and they had met the challenge. Tye could feel the bond between her and Trapper grow stronger as she fed him his apple. He was an incredible equine with a heart to match his ego. He would do whatever Tye asked and because she was so keenly aware of this, she never asked for anything he couldn't do. It was this attitude that allowed them to trust each other.

After the horses were secured in the trailer, Tye climbed into the cab of Kyle's truck and laid her head against the headrest. It was over. Suddenly the fatigue dripped through her as the adrenaline dissipated.

Looking at Kyle, she placed her hand on his arm. "I'm so glad you're driving," she said with a smile. "I might just fall asleep before we even get to the highway."

Kyle squeezed her hand. "Well, you've earned a good nap."

"Maybe, but I'll wait until I get home. How do you feel about the show?"

"I think as a team we were great. It was a solid performance. I want to improve my dressage though. Maybe you could give me a few pointers."

Tye laughed. "Yeah, right! I'm going to teach you about dressage."

Kyle looked at her. "Why not? You did come in first, and Trapper was absolutely spectacular."

Tye laughed. "Trapper has an ego. He knows he's worth watching. Whenever he's at a competition and he steps inside the arena, he knows it's show time. It's one of the things I love about him."

Kyle was thoughtful. "You know, I think that's it. Somehow he reads the energy and attention from the crowd. You should've seen the way the people reacted to him. There was this reverenced awe. He sure has a unique trait, but remember, Tye, it doesn't all come from him," Kyle said. "Trapper wouldn't be so free to act that way if he didn't completely trust you. He acts like he doesn't have a care in the world because he knows you'll look after him. The two of you have a real special bond. No wonder Katie thinks you'll be going places. I bet she spotted Trapper's ego from the very beginning."

Tye nodded. "Yep."

"I just can't get over how he puffed out his chest and acted like he was the best thing on hooves. Katie grinned the whole time and CarrieAnne was completely quiet."

Tye fiddled with her blue ribbon from the dressage test. "I guess that's part of the reason I don't want to train horses full-time. I'll never meet another horse quite like Trapper."

Kyle agreed. "That's true. But you could meet other personalities with different strengths. Ben isn't like Trapper. He doesn't have that ego, but he is the most obedient horse I've ever worked with. He has never refused an obstacle or a request."

Tye thought about the day Katie had worked with Trapper over the blue tarp. "I see what you mean."

"I really look forward to the day when I can train other horses and bring out their best qualities."

"I can't think of a better job for you, Kyle. You'll be a very good trainer. It's nice to be able to see your dream unfold, isn't it?"

Kyle nodded. "And what about your dream, Tye? You said that riding in the Oregon sunshine was a part of that dream. Today it was cloudy but you rode well. That must bring you some satisfaction."

"Yes, that's true. But it's not my most important dream and it's not what brings me the most satisfaction."

"Do you feel ready to share that with me?"

Tye nodded. "My most important dream is to someday be sealed to my parents," she said quietly.

Kyle was genuinely interested. "What does that mean?"

"We believe that couples can be married and sealed to their children for time and all eternity. It doesn't make sense that the most precious relationships we have on this earth would end with death. We think they can continue if couples are married in the temple through the proper authority. That's what I want. I love my family and I want to be sealed to them. My mom isn't a member of the church so that dream hasn't come true yet."

Kyle was thoughtful. "Why isn't your mother a member?"

Tye shrugged. "She doesn't have a testimony," she said. The words hurt Tye, but she accepted them as truth. "She also has a smoking habit. That goes against a principle called the Word of Wisdom."

"I remember you telling me the first time we met that you didn't drink or smoke because of your religion."

Tye nodded.

"So, when you marry, will you want to be sealed in a temple?"

Tye's mouth went dry. "Yes."

"I like that idea," Kyle said slowly. "I like the idea of being with someone forever. It makes sense that the relationships we cultivate would be able to continue."

"It's very important and sacred to me."

"Yes, I can tell." He paused. "So, what brings you the most satisfaction? I can't imagine anything more satisfying than a day like this one."

Tye thought about her missionary experiences and the message she felt privileged to share. "In a way it's like training," she said. "But it doesn't have anything to do with horses. Once a week I go out with the missionaries from my church and I teach people about the gospel. It's been the most satisfying experience I've ever had."

Kyle looked shocked. "You mean it's better than this?"

"It is to me."

"Then why do you ride?"

"I love riding. It's another piece of my life. A very important piece of my life, but it isn't my whole life."

"I guess I was under the impression that it was your whole life. You're a much better rider than I was at your age. I just figured you would have to dedicate your whole life to it."

"No. I do love it and I have a passion for it. But I have a passion for the gospel too."

"So how did you get to be so good at riding?"

"I'm ashamed of this now, but it was a way of punishing my mother. I hated her smoking habit and I stayed away from home because of it. I felt she was choosing cigarettes over me and I wanted to make her pay."

"That's pretty harsh."

"And very uncharitable. I understand that now." She glanced at Kyle. She had shared some of her most important thoughts with him. She had told him about her worries over CarrieAnne and he had kept it to himself. Now she had shared her dreams and hopes and it seemed right.

Kyle geared the truck down as he pulled off the freeway.

"I'm glad I told you," she said quietly.

Kyle placed his hands over hers, covering up the deep blue ribbon. She studied his fingers and rubbed the back of his hand with her palm. She could feel the delicate veins through his warm and dry skin. An overwhelming fatigue began to rise in Tye. She continued to stroke Kyle's hand. "This has been an important day."

"I agree," Kyle said as he placed his arm around her shoulder.

Chapter Twenty-Three

Walking inside the church building, Toni noticed Tye, Meggie, and the two sister missionaries standing in the foyer waiting for her. Their familiar faces made it easier to breathe.

Tye grinned and the new familiarity of her smile calmed Toni's racing heart.

"Hi everybody," she said quietly.

"Hi, yourself," Tye said. "You look great!"

Toni was pleased that Tye noticed. Toni was wearing the same blue dress she had worn before, but she had put on her make-up with a more sparing hand. Her skin gleamed fresh and clear. She felt younger and prettier than she had in years.

Toni followed Tye into the chapel and waved as Sister Sutton and Sister Kohler moved toward the pulpit.

Toni had wanted to sit on the end of the pew, but she made the decision to sit in the middle. She would not run out on the meeting again. It was disruptive and rude. It was also cowardly.

Sitting straight against the pew, Toni pressed her back against the hard wood of the bench as she allowed a new determination to steal into her soul. It would work. Church would no longer be a battleground. In a growing recognition, she was glad to be attending. It would allow her to put away the memories forever. If she could beat them here, they would be permanently defeated.

As the meeting progressed Toni sat still with her hands folded in her lap. She didn't listen to the speakers. She couldn't as memories of her youth and her family bubbled incessantly to the surface of her mind. Without being asked, the images presented themselves. Oh, this was hard and so bittersweet! Yet something deep inside recalled happy moments. Toni allowed herself to remember the yearly cherry festival when her family had picked cherries for the church budget program. She had loved climbing onto the tall ladders and plucking the sweet sun-ripened fruit. It was her favorite event of the year, when members of the ward would gather in the orchards under the benevolent summer sun of late June. Her father would send her up the ladder first, and then he would stand behind her and hold her legs while she reached for the ripest cherries that were at the top of the tree.

The smell of trampled grass, ripe cherries, and sun-warmed dust would fill her. Her father's strong, warm, and sturdy hands would hold her ankles, keeping her steady as she reached higher into the tree without fear. Sometimes Toni would have to fight the obnoxious crows for the fruit, so she would wave her arms around and shoo the birds away until they swept their wings in flight, complaining with vexatious cawing and black feathers.

"Don't you get too rambunctious up there," her father would call.

Toni would smile and throw her head back to look at the blue, Idahoan sky through the dancing green leaves and ripening fruit of the cherry trees. How she wished she could fly. Sometimes she almost felt like she might. When the breeze would rustle the leaves in the tree, lifting Toni's hair and brushing against her cheek, she often wished for feathers that would carry her in flight.

Toni shook her head to dispel the memories. Silly childhood dreams. If one thing had been made perfectly clear to Toni in the last few years it was that she was definitely earthbound.

Toni tried pushing the memory away but it continued to demand her attention. She remembered the contest at the end of the day, when every family would bring their boxes and buckets to be weighed. One year Toni's family had picked the most cherries—Toni was so proud! Their family of three had beaten other families with more children! It was a day of intense exhilaration for Toni, and she had strutted through the cherry orchard with her blue paper ribbon.

The sacrament was passed, but Toni still didn't feel worthy to partake of the bread and water. She passed them on to Tye while other memories called. They whispered to her with the echoes of merry laughter and the delight of a well-worn path under her bare feet. Toni smiled. It had felt good to be barefoot in the fields with the sun throwing its rays across her eight-year-old arms and legs. Sometimes she would sit in the field and dangle her feet in the irrigation ditch that crossed her family farm, watching dappled water move in its predestined path to enrich the earth and give life to corn, alfalfa, and cherries. Its cool movement against her warm sun-drenched skin would refresh her. As noon approached, she would go home for lunch, and her mother would run her fingers through her long, tousled, brown hair that smelled like sun and hay. She could still hear her mother smile and say, "You're going to be as brown as a little berry. We might want to put some sun block on you."

But Toni would scamper away before her mother made good on the threat. She didn't like the feel of sun block on her skin. She wanted the sun to embrace her and bathe her in its warm light.

Toni closed her eyes, surprised at feeling wet lashes. No! She wasn't going to do this anymore. She wasn't going to torture herself with painful reminders of what would never be again. Reaching for her purse, Toni dug out a tissue, wiped her eyes, and blew her nose.

She glanced at Tye, who was sitting next to her.

Their eyes met and Toni could see Tye was concerned. She patted Tye's arm. "It's okay," she whispered.

Tye looked doubtful, but Toni smiled. *I should be thinking about the speaker*, she thought. She put her purse down and turned her attention to the young woman who was speaking. It was hard to follow the words. Toni hadn't been paying attention and she found it difficult to listen, but she kept trying. She sat still and concentrated on each individual word the young woman was saying. It didn't matter that she didn't understand. It kept her mind occupied.

After the meeting was over, Toni breathed a huge sigh of relief. She had sat through the whole meeting. That was a triumph even if it was a tired victory. She didn't want to stay for Sunday School. "I think I'm going to head home," she said to Tye as they walked out of the chapel. "I really am tired."

Tye nodded. "Three hours of church can be difficult at first." She changed the subject. "You will be up to coming for dinner though, right? It wouldn't be the same without you. Meggie is making eggs benedict."

Toni grinned. "I wouldn't miss it."

Driving home, Toni snapped the radio on to give her something to dwell on besides her thoughts. The distraction didn't work.

As she pulled into the driveway, she realized she had forgotten to turn on the car heater. No wonder she was shivering. Rain dumped on her when she opened the car door and the wind whipped around her in a frenzy. She was soaked before she could push open the door. Hurrying into the house, she glanced at the answering machine. It was blinking. Pushing the rewind button, Toni sat down with a dish towel and began wiping her hair. She stopped when she heard her father's voice.

"Hi, Toni girl. Just thought I'd call and let you know I'm going to be coming into town next week. I'll only be staying for a few days, but I thought I'd give you some warning this time so that you can stock the fridge." He laughed.

Toni froze as the message continued, "My flight lands in Portland at two o'clock in the afternoon, this coming Thursday. I should be home in time for dinner. I thought we could spend a long weekend together." The fake cheerfulness became subdued and Anthony's voice changed. The message continued, "Um, Toni, there's something else I need to tell you. Gloria and I got married last week. I'm bringing her with me." The feigned cheery voice came back on the tape. "See you Thursday. I'm anxious for you to meet my new bride."

Toni's mouth went dry. Her father was coming home and he was bringing his "new bride"! Toni closed her eyes and tried to draw in a breath. It stuck in her throat. Absently, she wiped the water that dripped onto her face. She looked at the floor and noticed the puddle that was forming on the hardwood floor. Automatically, she bent down to wipe it up, but stopped. She should leave it. It would ruin the finish if it was left standing long enough. Her father would be livid when he saw the ruined floor the size of a hand towel. He would demand to know how this happened, and Toni could say that she was shocked beyond thinking when she got his message. Quietly, Toni turned her back on the puddle and walked out of the kitchen and up the stairs.

Chapter Twenty-Four

Meggie opened the oven door. The aroma of melting cheese in a cream sauce over potatoes greeted her warmly. She breathed deep. She couldn't see the bubbling scalloped potatoes because of the lid that was tightly placed over the casserole dish, but the smell told her they were ready. She checked the clock. Almost five-thirty. Perfect. She turned off the oven and pulled out the potatoes. They could cool while she finished poaching the eggs. The hollandaise sauce had been made earlier and was keeping warm on the small back burner. Meggie could smell its lemony aroma mingle with the rich scent of potatoes, cheese, and cream.

Tye was setting the table and pouring water into glasses.

"I hope everyone remembers their money and their own plates. We don't have enough," she said. "Also, I would hate for us to have to come up short financially because you're feeding so many people."

"It'll be okay. I doubt anyone will forget. You told Kyle, didn't you?"

Tye nodded. "Yep. Four bucks." She grinned. "Pretty good deal when you consider what he would probably be eating."

"What would that be?" Meg asked.

"Canned stroganoff."

Meggie made a face.

The rap at the door caught their attention. Tye answered it. Steve and Michael stood in the doorway with plates and crumpled dollar bills in hand.

"You're early," Tye said wryly.

"We know that," Michael said. "We wanted to make sure we got the fresh stuff. It doesn't do any good to be late for breakfast."

Tye grinned. "This is dinner."

"Don't confuse us," Steve said as he walked past Tye and plopped his money and plate on the kitchen counter. "Fill 'er up."

"Didn't your mother ever teach you any manners?" Meggie asked. "Stack your plate right here. I'll prepare it before bringing it to the table."

Michael moved next to Steve. "Now make sure we're not at the bottom of the plate pile," he said. "After all, we're first."

"No. You're early," Meggie said with a hint of irritation. "There's a difference."

Soon, everyone else arrived. Neil and Kyle showed up about the same time. Introductions were made as everyone waited for Toni. She came several minutes later, apologizing profusely and complaining about the difficult traffic for a Sunday evening.

Meggie started serving the plates.

Everyone complimented her on the presentation of the meal. Fruit and mint sprigs rounded out the meal of eggs benedict with hollandaise sauce and scalloped potatoes.

"I'm going to have to go on a diet after this," Toni said. "My jeans are already getting tight. I don't know if I can continue doing this favor for you, Meggie."

Steve laughed. "I'll eat your share."

"Not tonight," Toni warned as she pointed her fork in Steve's direction. "I've been trained to use this as a weapon," she giggled.

Everyone laughed and Steve grinned.

∼

Toni was glad she had decided to come for dinner. When the shock of her father's message had worn off, she had just wanted to crawl into a warm bed and go to sleep. Instead, she combed out her wet hair and changed into dry clothes. Tonight it would be best to be among hopeful new friends.

Now she sat at the table in Tye and Meggie's apartment and willfully chased her darker thoughts away. It was easier in the company of such gaiety.

Tye's boyfriend, Kyle, didn't seem all that willing to give in to the happy mood though. Toni thought he looked reserved and unsure. Maybe he wasn't used to seeing Tye in this kind of environment where she was so relaxed. Toni imagined that things could be pretty stressful in the barn with everyone so geared towards competing. She watched as Kyle whispered something into Tye's ear.

After the meal, everyone pitched in and helped with cleaning the table and dishes. Meggie's cooking efforts received rave reviews.

It was Kyle who broke up the evening early. "I really need to get back to the barn and take one last look at my horse," he stated. "We got back from our show pretty late last night." He stood.

Tye followed his example. "I'm going to see Trapper," she explained. "I've missed him over the weekend. I won't be too late." She grabbed an apple from the refrigerator.

Everyone said a quick goodbye to the couple as they headed out the door.

∼

Later that evening, after Kyle and Tye had checked their gear and horses, they both sat on a bale of hay and listened to the quiet in the early spring evening. Frogs were beginning to call outside and Tye smiled at their familiar pond song. She looked into Kyle's eyes and saw his warm emotion. She sighed, happy to be in this man's company.

She smiled, "What are you thinking?"

"It's more about what I'm feeling," he stated. "I know we haven't been together very long, Tye, but I can tell that you're unique. Your relationship with Trapper is a fine thing." He paused. "And I believe that our relationship is a fine thing also. Sometimes…" He became quiet, searching for the right words.

"What is it?"

"Sometimes I'm overwhelmed with the feelings I have for you. It scares me."

Tye didn't know what to say. Her feelings for Kyle scared her too. Part of her wanted to run from Kyle and his offering. Most of her wanted to stay. She looked forward to the moments they shared. She placed her arm through his. "No one understands my relationship with Trapper like you do," she said gently. "People accept it. My family and Meggie know how much it means to me and they support me, but they don't understand it. You do. That is a completely new experience for me, Kyle. But I get scared too." Sometimes I feel so…" She paused, trying to find the right world. "I feel so unfulfilled. Do you ever feel restless?" she asked.

Kyle furrowed his brow. "No. What do you mean?"

The vague feeling began to well up inside, demanding to be explored. "Do you ever wish for something and you don't know what it is?"

Kyle shook his head. "No. I know that I feel anxious sometimes. Right now I'm worried about graduation and whether I'll have a job when I get out of school. I haven't heard from any of the barns where

I've applied and that makes me restless."

"Yes, I can see how it would. Maybe it's the same thing that I feel."

"Does this have something to do with your own personal dreams?"

"Maybe," she said slowly. "Sometimes I feel so restless. It's hard to explain. It's like there's something out there—something I need to be doing and I'm missing it."

"How often do you feel this way?"

Tye shrugged. "Not as often as I used to. Since I started my missionary work—" Tye stopped. Yes, her missionary work. That had squelched the restlessness.

"What is it, Tye?"

She shook her head. "I'm not sure," she replied thoughtfully. "I just realized that my missionary work is what squelches the restlessness."

"I don't think I understand."

"Do you remember last week when we were talking about what brings me the most satisfaction and I told you it was my missionary work?"

"Yes."

"Well, that satisfaction is what brings the restlessness to heel. When I'm with the sister missionaries I feel completely satisfied. Not even riding can do that for me."

"Missionary work must be a pretty powerful experience for you."

She nodded thoughtfully.

"Is that why you're interested in me?"

Tye looked at him. "What do you mean?"

"Do you hope to convert me to your church?"

Tye thought for a moment. Then slowly said, "I can't deny that I wish you were interested."

"I wish I understood exactly what—"

Headlights interrupted their conversation. They waited in silence as a car door slammed and CarrieAnne appeared in the doorway. She laughed. "I can't believe the two of you can't find a better place to hang out. Pretty cheap date, wouldn't you say, Kyle?"

Tye noticed the teasing look in CarrieAnne's eyes as she flashed a relaxed smile toward Kyle. There was no biting sarcasm in her tone, but the words held their own venom for Tye.

Kyle laughed. "This is where we're the most comfortable."

CarrieAnne smirked. "You could always opt for a motel."

Kyle stood. "That's enough from you, CarrieAnne. You have no basis for such a comment."

She smiled as she moved passed them towards the tack room. "Maybe I do."

Kyle moved towards her. "Look, I don't know what's eating you, but don't spread your brand of poison around here. My relationship with Tye has no room for you, CarrieAnne."

"What a pity," she said.

Tye and Kyle exchanged looks.

CarrieAnne stopped and turned to Tye. "Someday you're going to be working directly under me. Next year Kyle will be gone and I'll be the captain of the competition team. I just want you to know that you're not my golden girl. Kyle may think the sun rises and sets with you and Trapper, but as of next year, he won't be here to protect you. So, you'd better kiss up."

Tye looked directly at CarrieAnne. "What do you want from me?" Tye asked.

Kyle interrupted. "You don't have to put up with this, Tye."

"No. I really want to know. What do you want from me?"

"I want you to go away," CarrieAnne answered. "I don't like you. I've never liked you. In fact, I despise you."

"You don't have to like me."

"Well, thanks for your permission." CarrieAnne turned to walk away.

Tye continued, "Oh, and one more thing, CarrieAnne. I'm not going away."

CarrieAnne faced her. "We'll see about that."

"Yes, I suppose we will," Tye replied.

CarrieAnne disappeared into the tack room, leaving Tye and Kyle alone.

"Maybe we'd better go," Kyle whispered.

"Are you finished checking on Ben?"

Kyle nodded. "Is Trapper okay?"

Tye nodded, but a new thought crept into her heart. "You don't think CarrieAnne would try to hurt Trapper, do you?" Fear rose into Tye's throat, cutting off her breath.

Kyle grew pensive. "You want to hang around until she leaves?"

Tye was already walking towards Trapper's stall. Kyle caught up with her and opened the horse's stall door. Trapper looked at both of them with sleepy interest as they closed the door and settled into the corner. Both of them kept silent as they listened for CarrieAnne. After several minutes, they heard her car door slam. The car pulled away from the barn.

Tye breathed deep.

"I think we both need to go to Katie about this," Kyle said. "CarrieAnne has threatened you, Tye, and although I don't think she would hurt Trapper, I think Katie needs to know so she can be aware. There are going to have to be some decisions made about Trapper's well-being and your peace of mind. Katie needs to be part of that."

Tye was trembling. "Maybe you're right, Kyle." she said.

Kyle nodded. "I need to see her as the captain. You need to see her as a member of the team. We'll go separately."

Tye nodded.

Kyle pulled her close and Tye surrendered to his warmth and strength. "I'm scared for Trapper," Tye said.

"Of course you are."

Tye broke from their embrace and went to Trapper, placing her arms around his neck. Silently, she began to weep.

"It's okay," Kyle said as he moved beside her. "We'll take care of this, Tye. Don't worry."

Tye nodded and tried to dry her tears, but she still clung to Trapper.

Kyle pulled a carrot stick out of his coat pocket. "I've been carrying this carrot stick around for the last three days." He fed it to Trapper. "Now, don't you tell Ben, Trapper. This is between you and me."

Tye giggled through her tears as Trapper happily chewed on the unexpected delight.

She embraced Kyle. "Thank you," she murmured.

Kyle stroked her hair. "It'll be fine, Tye. No worries."

Chapter Twenty-Five

Meggie bit her lip the minute she heard her father's voice on the line.

"How are you?" Jacob asked.

"I'm fine, Dad. How about you?"

"Oh, we're all fine here. Anymore news about the job?"

Meggie's defenses began putting on armor. "No," she said slowly. "I really don't expect to hear from Eilene until I'm home."

Silence filled the line.

"Where's Mom?" Meggie asked.

"She's meeting with the stake Relief Society presidency today," Jacob said. "And I was kind of missing my family. Things sure are quiet around here now that you and your brother and sister are out of the house."

"How is Justin?"

"Oh, he's fine. He's met a new girl. He's convinced that she's the one."

"Is it serious?"

"I never know about Justin," Jacob said. "Mattie keeps trying to talk him into moving to Utah to find a wife. She's convinced that he needs to move to the mountains if he wants to find a decent mate. Justin isn't so sure. He thinks he'll find someone here and he gives it a good try. He attends the single adult ward and stays busy with their activities. Tell me about your Neil?"

Meg blushed. "He's not really my Neil," she said.

"Would you like him to be?" Jacob asked.

"Yes," Meggie said quietly. "But I try not to think about that. Neither one of us are really ready for that kind of commitment," Meggie said. But inside, she could feel herself readying for the kind of commitment that would require Neil to be hers.

Jacob changed the subject. "Meggie, I wanted to talk about your job for a minute."

Meggie closed her eyes. So that was the purpose of this call. Would he try to talk her out of it? It wouldn't work. This new job was a lifeline and Meggie could not be talked out of it. She waited patiently.

"I guess I really don't know where to begin." He paused. "Do you remember when I told you that I wanted to become an airline pilot?"

"Yes?"

"Well, I didn't tell you the whole story. I didn't tell you how disappointed I was in your grandfather's approach. He literally refused to even listen to me."

Meggie closed her eyes and pictured her grandfather with his piercing blue eyes and neatly trimmed gray mustache. She could see him sitting behind the big mahogany desk in his office. He wasn't a big man, but he had a presence that was hard to ignore.

Jacob continued, "Whenever I would bring up the topic, he would turn to me with that look he gets and say, 'The subject is closed.' Finally I knuckled under and quit talking about it. It was just easier." Jacob became quiet and his voice was barely a whisper. "But I've always wondered what it would be like to fly those big jets. Whenever I get the opportunity to fly, I buy a first class ticket so I can be close to the cockpit. As I board the plane, I walk slowly so I can take a look inside and see what the pilots are doing." He paused. "Then that old desire comes back. I don't think I'll ever get over that regret."

Meggie ached for her father.

"Well, I started to think about your desire to cook and my desire to fly, and I realized that I was doing the same thing to you that my father had done to me. So, I went and spoke with your grandfather. I told him that you had decided to cook at the bed and breakfast on Sunnyvine Road and you were going to try some new things."

Meggie felt a shock wave move through her. "What did he say?" she asked breathlessly.

"He talked about the importance of the Stewart name and how we've been in the accounting business for over fifty years. He reminded me that he started the firm and that this was more than a job—it was a family tradition. He told me that he wanted to see you when you came home."

A sense of dread filled Meggie. Grandpa could be stern. She loved him dearly and had always known how to make his blue eyes twinkle, but he could also be a strict disciplinarian. He was used to getting his way.

Jacob continued, "I told him that you would be happy to see him but that he was not to pressure you into anything. I told him that our family was starting a new tradition and that I was going to allow you the freedom to choose your own path. I told him that I would not discourage you as he had discouraged me."

"Oh, my."

"Yes, well, then he ranted for a few minutes about how he knew what was best for me and that I wouldn't have amounted to much if

I'd been allowed to chase my own fool dream and how if you didn't straighten up you'd be faced with financial ruin. He said that the restaurant business was too risky for his granddaughter."

"I might not even go into the restaurant business," Meggie said in exasperation. "There are a lot of things I can do if I decide to become a chef."

"What kind of ideas do you have in mind?" Jacob asked.

Meggie hadn't really thought that far ahead. She hadn't even thought beyond the school year, but as she searched her heart, she came up with alternatives she hadn't even considered. "I could cater parties and weddings. Maybe I could own a bed and breakfast or some kind of inn. Maybe I could specialize in truffles or cheesecakes and ship them all over the country." Meggie's heart beat faster. Yes. The possibilities were truly endless. It all depended on what she chose.

"Those are wonderful ideas, Meg," Jacob said. "Catering and specialty items probably wouldn't take as much investing capital as an inn. Maybe the two could be combined. Maybe you could have an inn that specialized in a certain item or maybe a catering business that specialized in desserts."

Meggie blinked. "Do you think that would work?"

"Well, I think you'd have to find just the right item. You'd have to do a lot of market research and study out the shipping issues. You'd have to work out a conservative business plan, but sure I think it could work."

"What are you saying, Dad?"

"Meg, I'm saying that whatever you choose to do, we'll support you. I told your grandfather that this meant a lot to you and that as a family we would support you. Your mother and I will help however we can." Jacob chuckled. "Justin is tickled. He wants to be a taste tester."

Meggie laughed. "So does everyone here. I've been practicing my breakfast cooking on Neil, Tye, and some other friends. So far I've gotten rave reviews."

Jacob was quiet for a moment, then he continued, "Meggie, we know you'll succeed at whatever you choose to do."

"What about Grandpa?"

"We'll go see him together when you get home. He doesn't have to see things your way. Chances are he won't. He's always wanted complete control. He about went into cardiac arrest when Justin decided to be a mechanic. But as you can see, he's recovered and he doesn't love Justin any less. He was against Mattie's marriage too. He thought the business should take precedence over any plans she and her husband might have. But now that she has given him two great-grandchildren, he thinks her husband is the best thing that ever happened to her. I wouldn't worry too much about Grandpa." Jacob was quiet for a moment, then continued, "I'll tell you true, Meggie. Your mom and I truly would love to see you take over the business. We feel like it can offer you a stable future, but if you don't enjoy accounting, it could also be what ruins you."

Hot tears spilled onto Meggie's cheeks. "Thanks, Dad," she murmured. "Thanks for understanding."

Jacob laughed. "I just hope you remember this when you start making those sourdough pancakes you've mentioned. I don't want the guests at Farmer's to get all of your energy. Breakfast is one of my favorite meals."

"I promise to make you the best breakfast ever," Meggie said.

"And remember, Meggie. The business is still an option, but only if it's what you decide."

"I'll remember."

"Well, I'd better go. Give Tye our love, will you?"

"I will," Meggie said.

After a quick goodbye, she hung up the phone. Glancing at her watch, she realized it had been a busy day and evening. The meal had gone well and everyone appeared to have had a good time, except for maybe Kyle. He looked a little uncomfortable and seemed to be in a hurry to leave and take Tye with him.

That wasn't Meggie's biggest concern though. Neil had received another letter from Sammi Rae. This was his third. After everyone had left, he had sat next to Meggie and told her that Sam wanted to hear back from him. Up to this point he had not written her and she had not asked for any correspondence. Now she was asking for his address at college so that her letters wouldn't have to be forwarded from his home. She was hoping he would want to write her back.

Panic and fear had constricted Meggie's throat and she swallowed hard before asking her question. "How do you feel about that Neil?"

"I don't know what to do," he said.

"What do you want to do?" Meggie asked.

"I don't know." He paused. "Maybe I shouldn't even be telling you about this."

Meggie grabbed his hand. "Don't ever hide things from me, Neil. Trust is the biggest part of what we have; if you start hiding this, that trust will be damaged beyond repair."

Neil had nodded. "Do you want to read the letters?" he asked.

Meggie closed her eyes. She was torn. She did want to read them. She wanted to interpret the tone Sam was trying to set and she wanted to understand Neil's reaction. But somehow she already knew that it would hurt. And she desperately wanted to spare herself that pain. "How do you feel about sharing them?" she asked.

"I think I'm ready for that," Neil replied.

Meggie nodded. "Then, yes. I would like to read them," she said.

Neil promised he would bring them over.

The conversation turned toward dinner, but Meggie's heart wasn't in it. All she could think about was the letters that held Sammi's words.

Neil had kissed her gently and they had embraced for a long time. Meggie prayed it wouldn't be the last time.

Chapter Twenty-Six

When Tye stepped into Toni's house the following Wednesday, she immediately sensed something was wrong. Toni looked anxious and drawn. Even though it had only been three days since they had last met, Tye could have sworn that Toni had dropped five pounds.

"You okay?" Tye asked as she made her way to the now familiar living room.

Toni sat for a moment and then stood. She began to pace.

Tye and Sister Sutton followed her with their eyes, patiently waiting.

"My father's coming into town!" Toni gasped. "He'll be here tomorrow."

"Okay," Tye said slowly. "This isn't the first time he's come into town, is it? What makes it different?"

"He's *married*!" Toni practically screamed.

Tye and Sister Sutton exchanged looks.

"I see," Tye said quietly. "This does change things a bit, doesn't it?"

"You bet it does. And I'll tell you something else," Toni pressed. "He's bringing her with him."

Tye bit her lip. "Okay, let's talk this through."

Toni closed her eyes. "There's nothing to say." She steadied herself against the green marble of the fireplace, then sat down on the cold stone of the mantle.

"There's plenty to say," Tye responded. "How do you feel about this new marriage?"

"I don't feel anything. I've never met her," Toni said flatly.

"You're acting awfully anxious for someone who doesn't feel anything," Sister Sutton said quietly.

Toni began playing with a tissue, tearing it into little pieces and dropping them on the floor.

"She might be nice," Tye suggested.

"If she's anything like the women he used to bring home she'll be nothing but a painted tart," Toni said vehemently.

Tye said quietly, "Maybe he's changed."

"Yeah? Well, maybe he hasn't. Then what?"

"I don't have any answers," Tye paused. "But you can stay with me and Meggie if you don't want to be here."

Toni blinked. "You would offer your home to me?" she asked.

Tye nodded. "Yes. Usually I don't speak for Meggie, but I'm sure she would understand. If Meg were here, she'd be in complete agreement."

For one brief and shining moment, Toni felt hope. For days she had been drowning in anxiety, and now someone was offering her a life preserver. Staying at Tye's would give her the distance from her father that she was craving. But she couldn't do it. Slowly, she shook her head as a new and tentative calm struggled to surface. "Thanks, Tye. You don't know how much the offer means to me, but I can't do that. I've been running all my life. I ran away from Idaho and my mother. I can't run away from this."

"What will you do?" Sister Sutton asked.

"Nothing," Toni said. "I can't do anything. This is his home. He pays the mortgage. I'll meet his new wife and I'll take it one day at a time." She stood. "Thanks for coming this evening," she said. "You've really been a big help."

"We haven't done anything," Sister Sutton protested.

"Yes, you have. You've done more than you know. But right now I need to ask you to leave. I need to be alone for a while."

Sister Sutton looked at Toni. "Maybe we'd better stick around," she said.

Toni shook her head. "No. I'll be fine. I just need to make some plans."

"Okay," Sister Sutton said. "Would you mind if we said a prayer before we left?"

Toni was grateful for the offer. She bowed her head and quietly concentrated on Sister Sutton's words in her behalf. The tentative calm Toni had felt minutes earlier grew stronger. Would it really be all right? Somehow, she could sense that she would get through this. She didn't know how or what shape she would be in when it was all over, but with Heavenly Father standing beside her, she would manage to live through this weekend. She could sense it. She wondered if Nephi had ever seen his two older brothers after he had fled from them. Tears came to Toni's eyes. Tears that were for both her and Nephi. The destruction of that family had led to centuries of war. Would her father's visit mean war for Toni? She pushed the tears back and the calm feeling came again—stronger this time. The sureness of it came to her and beckoned like the memories that whispered gently and played within the sunlit halls of her mind. Toni didn't fight the feeling of security. She welcomed it and begged it to stay. She needed it desperately.

After Tye and Sister Sutton left, Toni walked into the kitchen. She opened the refrigerator and looked at the bottles of beer and wine. She pulled out a bottle of beer, opened it, and without a second thought poured the contents down the drain—the carbonation making a fizzy sound as it was swallowed by the sink. One by one, she emptied the contents of all of the alcoholic beverages in the refrigerator and with it she washed away her desire to run. She would stand this time. She would face her father and ask the hard questions.

Chapter Twenty-Seven

Toni walked into the house with a grocery sack. A rented car was in the driveway and she could hear the television blaring.

"Hi! I'm home!" she yelled.

"Hey, Toni girl. Let me help you with that bag," Anthony said. He stepped forward and Toni unloaded the bag into his arms. When their arms briefly touched, her father pulled away.

Closing the door behind her, Toni followed her father into the kitchen. It felt odd to have someone else in the house. Toni wasn't used to the noise or the static energy that pulled her close and pushed her away at the same time.

She looked around the room. Only her father was there. Maybe Gloria had decided not to come. It was a fervent wish.

Anthony placed the grocery sack on the counter and moved away. Toni methodically began putting the groceries away.

"Gloria thought it might be best if we had a few minutes alone before she came down," Anthony volunteered. Then he laughed. "I told her it wasn't necessary. She's part of the family now."

"Family?" Toni asked incredulously. "What family?" She bit her tongue.

"I see you had an accident with the floor," Anthony said as he moved towards the ruined wood floor. "What happened?"

A genuine sorrow washed over Toni. She had completely forgotten about the floor. Now her earlier bravado seemed weak. "I'm sorry, Dad. I shouldn't have been so careless."

"Well, you got that right. You should be more willing to take care of this house. I didn't raise you to be careless. Most college kids would give their right arm to live in a place like this, and you don't even have the sense to mop up the floor."

Toni's temper flared. "Problem is, Dad, you didn't raise me at all," Toni said with a level stare.

"Damn it, Toni. How dare you treat me this way? Haven't I always provided for you?"

Toni felt her face tighten. She purposely relaxed her jaw. "Dad, there's more to raising a child than just providing for them. You were never here. I've been alone for the longest time. Was it so terrible to spend time with me?"

Anthony looked up at the ceiling with an anxious expression. "Don't you dare cause any trouble with Gloria, you understand?"

"This isn't about Gloria!" Toni's voice was on the rise.

"What's that supposed to mean?"

Toni fought the urge to scream. Instead, she kept her voice level, almost gentle. "You never come home, Dad. I haven't seen you in over a year. Now you give me three days' notice and show up with a new wife and expect me to be *pleased*? We're not a family, Dad. We haven't been a family since the divorce."

A knowing look came into Anthony's eyes. "Oh, I see," he said. "You've been talking to your mother."

Toni shook her head. "I haven't talked to Mom in over six

months."

Anthony ran his hand through his graying hair. "Look, maybe I should've told you about Gloria. Maybe I should've invited you to the wedding. You would've been able to meet your step-brother and sisters. They're real nice kids. You'd like them. One of them is a business major at University of Texas. Gloria can tell you all about them."

Toni closed her eyes. He didn't get it. He just didn't get it. She opened her eyes. "Dad, why did you leave Mom?"

Anthony's face became hard. "That's between your mother and me."

"Maybe it was at first, Dad, but not anymore."

"I'm trying to protect you, Toni."

Toni shook her head. "No," she said slowly. "I don't think so. I think you're trying to protect yourself." Toni felt tears come to her eyes. "Please, Dad," She said gently.

Anthony shrugged with open palms. "I don't need any protection. Your mother isn't the easiest woman to live with."

"I know. I'm the one she dragged out of all those meetings, remember? Believe me, I understand what humiliation can be like in her hands. But that still doesn't answer my question. Why did you leave Mom?"

"Well, just multiply your humiliation by ten. Then you'll have a pretty good idea about why I left your Mom."

"She humiliated you?" Toni asked quietly.

"Every chance she got," Anthony said bitterly. "It didn't matter where we were or what we were doing. One time we went to the movies with another couple and she spent the whole time in the car telling everyone about how inept I was as a farmer." He threw his hands in the air. "I was doing the best I could. I was from the city streets of Los Angeles. What did I know about farming? When her dad died and turned the farm over to us, I wanted to sell it and invest the money, but she wouldn't hear of it. She was determined to raise her kids as she had been raised—on the farm. It didn't matter that I had never even had a vegetable garden. I tried to learn. I tried to do it. But I never pleased her. She wasn't even happy when I got a good crop of alfalfa one year. I can remember standing in the middle of that field of green one evening just at sunset. I was filled with satisfaction. Finally I had gotten it right. Then I saw your mother coming through the field and I was so glad she was there. I wanted to share this moment with her. But before she even reached me, she started in again. This time it was the cherries. I had forgotten to spray the trees and the bugs had moved in. She gave me a tongue-lashing I'll never forget. That's when I knew I'd had enough."

Toni closed her eyes and leaned against the counter. Yes, her mother was capable of such things.

"Your mother didn't have a loyal bone in her body, Toni."

"Yes," Toni said slowly. "I can see the truth of that." She thought back to unhappy memories. Her mom's disapproval of a decision her father had made about the farm. It was a vague recollection, washed in shades of white and gray. But other memories rushed forward with their brilliant and shiny colors. "But, Dad, we had some good times too. Those are the things I want to remember. Don't you remember the day when we played in the hose and—"

"I'd really rather not talk about that Toni. Those memories don't have anything to do with Gloria and I don't want her to feel left out."

"Left out? What about me? Why don't you ever worry about me feeling left out?"

"You're my daughter," he said. "You'll never be left out."

Toni shook her head. "I've been left out for many years, Dad. The fact that you didn't tell me about the wedding proves my point."

Anthony opened his mouth to respond, but changed his mind as Gloria walked in the kitchen.

Anthony immediately diverted his attention to his new wife. With a quick step, he walked to Gloria and put his arm protectively around her. Toni felt bereft. Her father never touched her. He hadn't even hugged her this afternoon. It hadn't always been that way. When she was a child her father had often given her hugs and kisses. What had changed? She wished she knew. She wished she could reclaim some pieces of the puzzle that had slipped away, but maybe they wouldn't fit anymore. It was hard to say. She bit her lip.

Swallowing, Toni looked at the woman standing in the crook of her father's arm. She was as tall as he was with bleached blonde hair that went to her shoulders. Toni immediately became aware of her own hair. The shades were practically identical—as if they had come out of the same bottle. It looked metallic on Gloria. Toni didn't fool herself. It looked metallic on her, too.

"Toni, this is Gloria," Anthony said proudly.

Toni shook Gloria's hand. It was warm and dry. Pulling away from the couple, she did a quick study of her father's new wife. A brassy blonde with tight jeans tucked into cowboy boots and a western-style blouse with fringe completed the picture. Gloria was not slender, and she looked uncomfortable in the tight clothing. Toni wondered if she could breathe.

Both her father and Gloria looked at Toni expectantly. She swallowed hard and pasted a smile on her face. "Nice to meet you," she said quietly. She turned toward the groceries. "I bought ingredients for spaghetti. How does that sound?"

"Gloria is a wonderful cook," Anthony said. "Maybe she could make dinner tonight?"

A territorial feeling came over Toni. This was her kitchen. Just because her dad paid the bills didn't mean his wife could step in and make herself at home. "Aren't you tired, Gloria?"

"Well, I am a bit fatigued," she said quietly.

"Besides, Dad, she doesn't know where anything is stashed. I'd have to be in here anyway. I'll just put together some spaghetti."

Anthony laughed. "Well, I sure hope your cooking has improved over the years, Toni. I remember the quiche you made last time I was home. It practically ran all over my plate."

Tears came to Toni's eyes. It was a small, innocuous comment, but it stung. Her mother wasn't the only one who could be disloyal. "And you talk about Mom," she said quietly.

Anthony's face went white. Gloria looked from Toni to Anthony with concern. "Well, we should leave Toni to the cooking," she said. "After all, she knows where everything is in the kitchen. I'd probably just make a big mess. Spaghetti sounds wonderful." Placing her hand on Anthony's arm, she led him into the family room where the news was blaring on the television.

Impatiently Toni continued to brush the tears away as she began preparing dinner. Why was her father here anyway? His sudden appearance was frightening. She grabbed a napkin and dabbed her eyes. She would not cry. It wouldn't do to come to the table with red-rimmed eyes. After they left she would have plenty of time for tears. Clenching her jaw she forced the tears down. As she made the tossed salad, she finally calmed herself so she could use the knife without fear of cutting herself.

When she was finished in the kitchen, she called her father and Gloria to the dining room. The meal was mostly a silent affair. Toni was grateful she had bought bottled sauce so her father couldn't comment on her cooking.

Gloria mentioned her children, and Toni looked at pictures of three step-siblings. It was obvious that Gloria was proud of her children. One had graduated from college with a degree in engineering, and the other two were business majors. Toni feigned interest, but she couldn't help but wonder what her father said about her when he was back in Texas. Did he talk about her horrible cooking? Already she felt inferior to the smiling adults she saw in the pictures. She toyed with the food on her plate.

"Toni, there's something Gloria and I need to tell you," Anthony said.

Toni looked up.

Gloria placed her hand on Anthony's arm. "Maybe this isn't the time," she said.

Anthony shook her off. "No, Toni needs to know so she can start making plans."

Toni's mouth went dry. Plans?

Anthony took a deep breath. "Now that Gloria and I are married, we're going to sell the house."

For a moment, the news didn't sink in. "Which house?" Toni asked. "Do you have a place in Texas? I thought you were living in an apartment."

Anthony rushed ahead before Gloria could stop him. "Yes, we do. I mean we're going to be selling this house. We'd like to put it on the market while we're here."

Toni blinked. She looked at Gloria, who gave her a desperate, sorrowful look.

"I'll pay for your rent when the house sells. So, I don't want you to worry about the finances. I'll make sure you make it through school. But we're hoping to buy a place in Texas. Right now the market favors us. It's a seller's market here and a buyer's market in Texas. If we sell now we'll do well."

Toni's jaw dropped. She looked at Gloria, who was concentrating on her plate.

"That's why you came here, isn't it?" Toni asked. "You came here to put the house on the market. You didn't come to see me or even to introduce Gloria. You came to sell the house," her voice got quiet.

"That certainly wasn't the only reason," Anthony said. "Don't be ridiculous."

Sadness and anger flooded Toni like a cold river hitting red-hot lava. She stood. "I've hardly had the opportunity to be ridiculous," she stated. "Why did you bother coming at all? A simple phone call would've sufficed. Why, you didn't even have to call me. You could've just talked with the realtor, and handled everything through them." She threw her napkin onto the table and pushed her chair back. It fell, clattering against the hardwood floor.

When Toni reached her room, she pulled her duffel bag out of the closet and began packing her clothes. Tye had said she could stay with them if things got too difficult during her father's visit. Well, that's what she would do. Her dad and Gloria could have the house during their stay. Then she stopped. No. She would not run. All her life she had been running. She ran from Idaho and her mother. She ran from the gospel and the church.

Quietly, she got down on her knees. Prayer was still new to Toni. It felt clumsy, but the need outweighed the awkwardness as Toni poured her heart out to her Heavenly Father. Soon the tears began. She didn't push them back. They overwhelmed her. In her desperation, she clung to the only thing that made sense—her Heavenly Father and the prophet Nephi. Through sobs, she prayed for understanding. Why did her family have to be torn apart? Why was she the only remnant of a once-loving relationship between her mother and father?

Slowly the memories began to show themselves once again. Toni fought them. This wasn't the time. She couldn't deal with them right now. The bittersweet longing would crush her. But the memories would not leave. They crowded around her and brought golden sunshine on gilded leaves. Yes, she remembered that special light that bathed the earth only at sunset; that golden hue that threw long shadows and softened the angles of the mountains and made the leaves look like green silk. The cherry orchard was her favorite place during the summer sunsets. After dinner, she would walk alone through the fields until she came to the cherry orchards. There, she would climb one of the sturdier trees and rest in the branches—surrounded by the warm evening and the last rays of the sun. Sometimes, she would tilt her head back and watch clouds turn from golden to pink, then a deep magenta as the sun bade them goodnight. Climbing as high as she dared in the tree, Toni could catch the last glimpse of the light as it slowly disappeared behind the western horizon, leaving her alone in the lengthening evening. Then her mother would call. Her voice would sound far away, but clear, and Toni would clamber down from the tree and race home to whatever dessert her mother had been baking. Then under the cheerful light in the farm house she would sit at the table and eat the sweets with her parents.

As the memories washed over her, Toni realized that she was not the only remnant left from her family's love. There were the memories. They were also orphaned and looking for a home—someplace or someone they could call their own. Fresh tears came to Toni's eyes. For years she had tried to bury this precious part of her life—afraid of the pain, afraid of the sorrow that would remind her of the hopelessness. But this time they didn't bring hopelessness. Hopelessness was down at the dinner table. Tentatively, she turned to her memories for comfort and they rushed in like lonely siblings.

Her father was young and vital. She remembered him toiling in the hot sun. His hair was thick and dark and his smile was perfect. Back then he had never been too tired to play with her. She would anxiously await his arrival from the fields and orchards so that he could drop on all fours and be her horsey. He would gallivant around the living room and whinny and snort. The very picture of it was so vivid and comical that Toni laughed out loud. She could see her mother, leaning in the door frame, smiling as she watched father and daughter.

She remembered cherry cobbler with homemade ice cream. She

thought about her best friend, Connie Walker, in the first grade.

One by one the memories revealed themselves and surprised her with their clarity and freshness. Walking down dirt roads with her dad, carrying buckets of cherries to the house and holding hands. Cousins, aunts and uncles all gathering at her home for her sixth birthday. Her first bicycle with its pink frame and white basket with yellow plastic flowers.

Not all of the recollections were happy. She remembered the day she was standing on the front porch with her Aunt Jenny, Uncle Chad, and cousins Jenna Lee and Jackson. Her father was trying to wind the hose and everyone was watching. The hose became difficult and snake-like as it twisted out of his hands. In exasperation, her mother stomped to Anthony's side and snatched the wily hose away from him. With practiced moves she wound the hose into a neat coil. Dusting her hands off, she laughed at her husband. "Why, he can't even wind a hose much less keep the irrigation canals running. I've got to watch him every minute." Behind the teasing, Jolene's voice was hard.

Everyone laughed, except Anthony. Her father seemed to shrink before Toni's eyes, and she remembered being filled with both compassion and loathing.

She wondered how much of that humiliation her father had suffered before calling it quits. She wondered about his retaliation. Undoubtedly, his and Jolene's memories would be different than Toni's. But that didn't mean her memories never happened. It didn't mean she couldn't find solace in them.

Breathing deep, Toni curled up with her pillow. No. Not every memory was happy. But she could choose to remember the happier times. At last she could look back on her childhood and pull strength from what it offered her. Holding her pillow tight, Toni remembered her prayer. It had been answered with a resolution that had been there all along.

Chapter Twenty-Eight

Toni was awakened by a gentle knocking on her door. Her head was pounding and her eyes felt like someone had rubbed sand in them. Slowly, she propped herself on one elbow and looked at the clock: six o'clock A.M.

The knock sounded again.

Toni pulled herself into a sitting position and ran her hand over her face. It was puffy and swollen from last night's tears. "Come in," she said in a raspy voice.

Her father entered and looked around. He smiled. "I haven't been in here for years. In fact, I can't remember the last time I was in your room."

"Neither can I," Toni said.

Anthony sat on the edge of the bed.

Toni watched her father. He was fully dressed. He looked tense.

She wanted to ask if he had more bad news, but she bit her tongue. Instead, she waited patiently.

"Gloria cleaned the kitchen as best she could," he started. "But she wasn't sure where things belonged."

"I'm sure it'll be fine," Toni said.

"I think it would be best if Gloria and I moved on," Anthony said. "She's never seen the Pacific Ocean and we're not that far from the coast. We'll take care of the business we have with a real estate agent this morning and then head over to Lincoln City for the rest of our stay."

Toni licked her dry lips. "Dad," she began. "Don't go. Please, don't go. I hardly ever see you. I want to talk about Idaho."

Anthony held up his hands. "I don't want an argument, Toni. I can tell you don't care much for Gloria, and I really don't want to ruin her vacation by making her tense."

Toni shook her head. "I wish you were half as concerned with me as you are with Gloria." She sighed, "Besides, it has nothing to do with Gloria." Toni smiled briefly. "Dad, do you remember picking cherries?"

Anthony moved to the window and looked out at the gray dawn. "Cherries," he spat out. "I've seen enough cherries in my life. I can't even stand to look at them in the grocery store," he said bitterly.

Tears stung Toni's eyes. Couldn't he put the pain away for just a little while?

"Don't you remember anything good?" she asked desperately.

Anthony turned towards his daughter and for the first time, Toni noticed the lines on his face. He looked old and worn. But a slight smile touched his lips and softened his features. "Yes," he said quietly. "I remember the first time I held you in the hospital. You were minutes old and the doctor placed you in my arms. It felt like a miracle."

Tears spilled onto Toni's cheeks.

Anthony sat beside her. "Don't think about those memories, Toni. It's over. Nothing will come of remembering them."

"Oh, Dad, you're wrong," Toni said gently. "They have so much to offer us. They're what binds us together."

Anthony shook his head as he stood. "No, they don't." He moved towards the door and turned and gave Toni a sad and lingering look. "I'll call you when we get back to Texas and we can talk about moving your things." He paused. "I guess this is goodbye, Toni girl. Maybe you can come to Texas for a visit after we get a new house. By then you will have had some time to get used to Gloria."

Toni fought the urge to run to her father and bury her face in his shirt. She wanted to weep with him for the loss of their common ground. She wanted to display her newfound joy in their past. "Dad?"

"Yeah?"

"Will you ever want to talk about Idaho and the cherry blossoms?"

Anthony clenched his jaw. "No."

Toni nodded quietly as her father shut the door. Her memories then were truly orphaned.

Quietly, she listened to the sounds of her father and Gloria walking down the stairs. The front door quietly opened and closed. Soon the rental car sprang into life. Toni rose and went to her window. She could see her father backing out of the driveway, his torso turned to look out the rear window. Gloria was fiddling with a make-up compact.

When the car was in the street, Toni watched as Anthony put it in gear. He gave the house a lingering look. Toni saw him gazing at her window. Tentatively, she waved. Anthony waved back. He was running. Toni knew it. Quietly, she watched as he put the car in gear. It didn't take long for the taillights to be swallowed by the gray, dismal fog.

When the phone rang at eight-thirty, Toni was sure it was the realtor. Instead, it was Tye.

"Hey, Toni. I've been thinking of you. How are things going

with your dad?" Tye asked in a whisper.

"He left this morning."

"Oh, Toni, I'm so sorry." Tye paused. "I think I'm sorry. How do you feel about his early departure?"

"I don't know what I feel," Toni said honestly. "He's going to put the house up for sale."

Tye sucked in her breath. "Oh, my. That must've been a shock."

"Yeah."

"What are you going to do?"

"Wait until it sells and then find an apartment, I guess."

"Did you like his new wife?" Tye asked tentatively.

"She's okay, I guess," Toni said. "She tried real hard."

"Do you know when you'll be seeing him again?"

"No. I don't think he'll be coming here again. He mentioned the possibility of me going to Texas after they buy a house, but I can't see myself going to Texas anytime soon."

"What about Idaho?"

Toni was quiet. She hadn't been home in years. Home. Was Idaho home? It had been home years ago. It was the home of her memories.

"I'm sorry," Tye said. "I shouldn't be prying. I've just been thinking of you and—"

"No. You're not prying. I've been thinking a lot about Idaho lately, but hadn't thought of physically going back." Toni became thoughtful. "I haven't seen my mother in years."

A new and wary thought crept into Toni's mind. What about her mother? She was a part of those memories. They would recognize her. Would they reach out for her like they had reached out for her dad? Would her mother embrace them or turn them away? Toni closed her eyes. It had been close to six months since she had even talked to her mother on the phone. Toni couldn't deny that her mother had tried. Jolene Chandler had written letters and phoned faithfully once a month. But Toni let the answering machine pick up her mother's calls and she never responded to the letters. She blamed her mother for the divorce. Then there were all those humiliating Sundays where Jolene half-dragged, half-jerked Toni out of church if she happened to see Anthony. Toni had never forgiven her. But what about the other days? What about the cherry cobblers and homemade ice cream? If she closed her eyes and tried hard enough, she could still hear her mother's strong, clear voice echoing through the cherry trees as she called for Toni to come home. She could still see her plumpish figure wearing light summer dresses that billowed with the wind and whipped around her knees. The lines around her brown eyes that crinkled whenever she laughed.

"Listen, Toni, why don't you come over for dinner tonight? It's Friday and we're going to rent some movies and eat pizza. We're inviting some friends from Institute. What do you say?"

Toni jerked out of her thoughts. "Yeah. That sounds good," she said. "What time?"

"Oh, around seven."

"Okay." After saying a quick goodbye, Toni placed the receiver in the cradle. Idaho, with its dry summer heat, deep blue skies, and green fields. The cherry blossoms would be at their peak right now. Suddenly, Toni felt an overwhelming desire to pack her bags and head towards those cherry blossoms. She shook her head. No, that would never do. She was in college. She had responsibilities. Quietly, she walked to the bathroom, still deep in thought, and turned on the faucet. She needed to minimize the swelling in her face before she went to school. She glanced at the clock. She had a ten o'clock class and Toni was sure it would take the next hour to reduce the swelling around her eyes. She splashed the cold water onto her face, but her thoughts were thinking about home.

Chapter Twenty-Nine

The following morning, a jangling phone awakened Tye with a start. She grabbed the receiver. "Hello?"

"Tye? This is Sister Kohler. Sister Sutton is...I'm...we're at the hospital."

Tye propped herself on one elbow, fully awake. She glanced at the clock. Six-twelve A.M.

"I'm sorry to wake you and I know it's a Saturday, but Sister Sutton told me to call you early before you went to the barn. Sister Sutton had a very bad allergic reaction an hour or so ago and we had to come into the emergency room. They want to admit her for observation."

"I'll be right there," Tye replied.

"Thank you, Tye. I'm so worried and she is insisting that I go out to meet our appointments today. She doesn't want anyone to miss their lessons because of this. Sister Humphries from the other ward said she could meet me for splits. I can't leave Sister Sutton here alone. Could you just sit with her?"

"Of course. As soon as I'm showered and cleaned up I'll come on in. What time is your first appointment?

"I'm supposed to meet Sister Humphries here at the hospital at about seven-thirty. She's going to take me to the apartment so I can get cleaned up. Then we'll head out for splits. You've got plenty of time. I just didn't want to miss you. I apologize for the early call."

"I don't mind at all. I'll be there soon."

"Thanks."

Tye could hear the relief in Sister Kohler's voice.

As soon as she hung up, she threw the covers back and swung her legs around. The phone rang again and Tye jumped. "Hello?"

"Tye. This is Kyle. Ready for another show?"

"Umm. Kyle, I, um, I've already made plans." Tye wished she could buy some time to think. "What happened?"

"Jen's horse is still lame."

"He was fine last night."

"Yeah, well his knees stiffened up after a little exercise. I told Jen that might happen and that she should talk to you about riding in her place. I mean, her horse just had his stitches removed for heaven's sake, but she was determined to go to today's show. Now it looks like she's not going to be able to ride. What do you mean you have other plans?"

"One of the missionaries just called and was admitted to the hospital with an allergic reaction. I promised I'd go sit with her so her companion could go out on splits."

"What are splits?" Kyle asked. "Is somebody dying?"

"No. According to Sister Kohler, the doctors just want to admit her for observation."

"Look, I don't know who this Sister Kohler is, or what she's allergic to, but it sounds like if she's just being admitted for observation, she'll be fine. We need you to ride! This is what being the alternate is all about. You knew that if you were called you were going to have to drop everything and take care of business."

"I can't leave the sister missionaries hanging. I made a promise."

"Yeah. You also promised Katie you would be here for the team. Tye, we don't have a lot of time. We need to leave as soon as you get here. I can get your tack all set up and Trapper loaded. But, please hurry!"

"Kyle, you don't understand! Sister Sutton can't be left alone. It's the rules."

"What rules?"

"Mission rules."

"Tye, I don't know what you're talking about. But we can't leave until you get here. Everyone is waiting."

Silence hung on the line.

Tye swallowed hard. "Go without me," Tye said. "CarrieAnne can ride."

"Tye, do you realize what you're saying? How can you tell me this after the way CarrieAnne treated you the other night? She's going to think you're caving and she'll be unbearable. Are you going to let her have her way?"

"How can you ask me such a thing, Kyle? This is not about CarrieAnne. This is about Sister Sutton, who is sick in the hospital."

"Go visit her when you get home this afternoon. Look, Tye, I'm the captain of the team, and I am asking you to ride for the team."

Tye's mouth went dry. "I can't, Kyle. I've made a promise to the missionaries. They need me."

"Katie isn't going to be very happy about this."

Tye closed her eyes. She hadn't even thought of Katie. "No, I imagine not. But I can't ride today. Call me when you have more time and I'll explain."

"Oh, you'll be explaining all right, but it won't be to me."

"I understand," Tye replied.

"Okay," Kyle said before he hung up.

Tye sat on the edge of her bed. What happened? She had just turned over a riding opportunity to CarrieAnne. She could hardly believe it. And yet she had promised to sit with Sister Sutton. That promise had to come first—before any other commitment. But why? Surely Sister Kohler could get someone else to sit with Sister Sutton. It didn't matter. She had promised.

Tye swallowed again, moving into the bathroom. She turned on the water in the sink and stared at her toothbrush. Somehow, the two major pieces of her life had just collided. Was she giving in to CarrieAnne's relenting pressure? No, the thought hadn't even crossed her mind until Kyle had mentioned it.

Katie wasn't going to be very happy. Kyle obviously wasn't happy. CarrieAnne would be thrilled. Tye turned off the water and looked in the mirror as a small voice asked if she was happy with her decision. She blinked at her reflection. Yes, she was pleased. The sisters had called first. She had done the right thing by sticking with her original promise. It wasn't easy and there would be some fallout. Katie would probably reprimand her. Would Kyle understand?

Later, Tye walked into Sister Sutton's hospital room. Sister Kohler was dozing in a bedside chair. She sat up. "Oh, Tye, I'm so glad you could make it," she whispered. "Sister Sutton is sleeping."

"So were you," Tye smiled.

"It's been a long morning and it's only seven-thirty." She yawned.

Tye glanced at Sister Sutton. She had oxygen tubes in her nose.

Sister Kohler took Tye's elbow and led her out into the hall. "She was stung by a hornet and had some kind of reaction, which triggered her asthma."

"A hornet? This time of year?"

Sister Kohler shrugged. "I know it sounds bizarre, but since the weather has been warming up I've seen a few stray bees and wasps around our place. One must've gotten inside our apartment. Sister Sutton has never been stung before so we didn't know she was allergic. The sting woke her up, and then she immediately started wheezing. It was horrible. Thank goodness we only live a couple blocks from the hospital. I drove her here and the doctors and nurses literally started working on her in the car."

"Where was she stung?"

"On the arm. I think she rolled over on it." Sister Kohler continued, "The medications they gave her are supposed to make her sleepy. Plus, I think she was just exhausted from the whole episode. Sister Jorgenson, it was so hard to watch her try to breathe." Sister Kohler's voice wavered. "I was so scared. She could've died."

Tye nodded quietly. "But she didn't die, Sister Kohler. She's going to live."

Tears came into Sister Kohler's eyes as she let out a long sigh. She wiped her eyes.

Tye asked, "Are there any after-effects? What about when she wakes up? Will she be able to breathe?"

"The doctor said she should be completely normal, but probably a little tired. He told her she could expect to be a little sore from being so tense. He said she can go to church tomorrow, but no big social events. And he asked that we take it kind of easy on Monday, but by Tuesday she should be fine. He expects her to sleep most of the day so she won't even be able converse with you."

"That's okay. She needs her rest. I'll just sit here with her until you get back."

Sister Kohler gave her a wan smile. "I'm glad you brought your scriptures. It'll give you something to read."

Sister Humphries joined the two women. "How is our patient?"

she asked.

"Sleeping," Sister Kohler responded. All three women walked back into the hospital room and Sister Humphries, who was obviously a nurse, checked Sister Sutton's wrist and took her pulse.

"It's a habit," she muttered as she began counting. Placing Sister Sutton's arm next to her body, Sister Humphries said, "Her pulse is good and strong. She'll be okay."

Sister Kohler grabbed her purse. "Okay, Sister Jorgenson. We're off to take care of the Lord's work. It's what Sister Sutton wanted. I appreciate you taking care of her so we can do this."

The barn seemed far away as Tye looked at the tired but grateful face of Sister Kohler and then to her sleeping companion. Yes, she had done the right thing by coming here. Here, by Sister Sutton's bedside, in spite of the anxiety surrounding her ordeal, there was no restlessness or fear. When she was doing the Lord's work, the restless feeling disappeared, leaving in its place solid footing and a surety of her actions. How could she ever explain that to Kyle? She had tried the night they were interrupted by CarrieAnne, but it was so new to her that it had been hard to put the feelings into words. Maybe it was time for another attempt.

Hurrying to the phone, she called Kyle's number and left a message on his machine, asking him to phone back when he got home from the show.

Chapter Thirty

Later that afternoon, as Tye was drying her hair, Meggie came to her with the phone. She put her hand over the mouthpiece. "It's Kyle," she whispered.

Tye nodded as she took the phone. "Hello?"

"I got your message," Kyle said stiffly.

"Oh, good. Hey, I was wondering if we could meet for dinner. There's something I need to discuss with you."

"Don't you even want to know how the show went?" he asked.

"Well, yes, but I thought you would tell me about it over teriyaki chicken."

"Okay," he replied. "Teriyaki chicken. I'll pick you up in fifteen minutes."

~

Sitting in Kyle's truck, Tye suddenly felt at a loss for words. All afternoon she had waited for this opportunity to talk with Kyle about her decision to stay with the sisters and her desire to do missionary work. Now her carefully worded explanations and thoughtful prose abandoned her.

"So, tell me about the show," she said.

"It was uneventful. We came in first, but barely. Katie wasn't too happy about it."

"Did she say anything about my decision not to ride?"

"Not to me, but I imagine she'll have plenty to say to you."

They pulled into the restaurant parking lot in silence. A few minutes later the hostess showed them to a table.

"I really wish I understood the decision you made this morning, Tye. But I have to admit, I can't even begin to fathom it."

Tye put her menu aside. "Kyle, do you remember a couple of weeks ago when we were talking about what brought me the most satisfaction, and I told you it was my missionary work?"

He nodded.

"Well, those women who aid me in that work called me this morning. They're the full-time missionaries. One of them was very sick and they needed me. They called before you did and by then I had already promised I would look after the one who was sick, allowing the healthy missionary to keep her appointments."

"What are these mission rules you were talking about?"

"Missionaries go out in pairs. They're never allowed to be without a companion," she paused. "In the Bible, when Jesus sent His disciples out to teach, He sent them out in pairs. We follow that same admonition."

Kyle was thoughtful. "I think I understand, Tye. I don't know if I agree with it, but I understand."

"Good, because there's more."

The waiter came poised to take their order. Tye hurriedly picked up her menu and ran her finger down the list of entrées. She chose the teriyaki chicken with fried rice. Kyle ordered scallops in pan-fried noodles.

"What do you mean, there's more?" Kyle asked after the waiter left.

"I'm considering going on a full-time mission."

Kyle blinked. "What? What's a full-time mission? Does it have something to do with the women you met this morning?"

"Yes, in a way. You see, they're full-time missionaries."

"What exactly does that mean, Tye? Would you be able to stay here? Excuse my ignorance. I've never heard of full-time missions. How does it work?"

"I wouldn't be staying here," she said. "I would have to submit some papers stating my intentions, and then the Church would send me where they think I'd be needed."

Kyle looked at Tye uncomprehendingly. "I don't understand. Isn't this just something you can do while you're going to school? I mean, you say you're working with these women right now. Why can't you continue to work with these women, here, in Corvallis, while you're going to school?"

"Right now I only work about four to eight hours a week within the Corvallis area. A full-time mission requires full-time dedication for eighteen months."

"Eighteen months? What about Trapper? What about your career? Have you talked to Katie? She won't hold your scholarship, Tye."

Tye could feel Kyle's panic. "I know," Tye said calmly. "I wouldn't expect her to hold it."

Kyle was leaning on the table. "Do you know what you're saying? You're willing to give up a full scholarship to one of the best equine programs in the west to do what?"

"I know it's hard to understand, Kyle. I'm not even sure I

understand it myself. All I know is that when I'm engaged in this work, I feel whole, complete. The restlessness is gone."

Kyle was silent for a moment. Then he asked, "Does this have anything to do with CarrieAnne? She was really hard on you, and I know you have fears about Trapper being in danger."

"I understand how it could *look* like CarrieAnne has scared me off, but this doesn't have anything to do with CarrieAnne. It's really between me and the Lord."

"Don't you think it should have something to do with me? What about *us*, Tye? Can you just walk away from what we've created? Or maybe you're running."

The waiter returned with their meals and discreetly left. Tye barely noticed. Her appetite had diminished and the food was unappetizing.

"I'm not running," she stated.

"But you're willing to pack your bags and leave me for eighteen months. Doesn't that mean anything to you?"

Tye became flustered. "I have to admit that I hadn't thought that far ahead."

"Tye, what we have is so unique. But what if we made it even better? I'll become a Mormon, if it will help. I think I know how important that is to you," Kyle offered quietly.

Tye looked at Kyle incredulously. He had never even mentioned the Book of Mormon she had given him weeks ago. How could he even consider joining the Church? Would it make a difference? All those years Tye had wanted her mother to join the Church for her. Now Kyle was offering to do that very thing. It left her alone and sad. The only conversion that really mattered came through the Holy Ghost and an honest conviction that the church was true and the gospel was the good news. Tears stung her eyes. "It would be for all the wrong reasons, Kyle."

"You would be my reason. I don't see that as wrong." He continued, "Tye, you're one of the few women I've dated who really understands me." He pushed his plate out of the way and leaned his elbows on the table. "Look. We've got plenty of time. We don't need to be making any decisions right now. Why don't we just take our time? I can study Mormonism and I'm sure I could grow to love it. It's such a big part of you, and I love you. I'm sure we could work this out."

Tears escaped Tye as she put her hand over her mouth to keep from choking on the sob that was rising in her throat. Words tumbled inside of her in a jumbled heap, but she couldn't speak for fear of crying.

Kyle continued, "I know I said that I'd be leaving right after graduation, but I've been thinking that maybe I could stay here and work for a couple of years. Maybe I could even get on at the barn as an assistant trainer to Katie. Then after you graduate, we could move back east together."

Tye bit the inside of her cheek to chase away the sobs. "The Olympics have never been my goal, Kyle. It's yours."

"But it could be ours. Don't you see? We could work for it together. You can't deny that we make a great team, Tye. Let me study Mormonism and make that a team effort too."

"Becoming a member of the Church is a very personal thing."

"Yes, I can see how it would be," Kyle replied. He paused. "What do missionaries do?"

"They teach the gospel full-time."

"Teach me, Tye. Let me be your mission."

Silence hung in the air. It wasn't supposed to be this hard. The full brunt of her departure wasn't supposed to be filled with such agony and heartache. To this point it had felt like a quick weekend trip out-of-town where she could come back and everything would be the same. But as she looked at Kyle she knew that nothing would be the same. "I-I can't, Kyle. Don't you see? It wouldn't be right. The only reason you're even offering to listen about the Church is because I've told you I'm leaving for a while. What would happen if I stayed? It would only be a matter of time before you would resent me for what could very easily feel like a trap. It would ruin everything. You wouldn't be joining for the right reasons, Kyle."

"You could teach me the right reasons. Besides, I love you, Tye. Isn't that reason enough?"

Tears came to her eyes. She wished it was enough. She wished his love could secure their future. She wished her love could secure the future of her family, but it wasn't her decision to make.

Tye slowly shook her head. "Our love isn't enough. The reason has to come from inside," Tye placed her hand over her heart. "And I know this may sound strange to you, but it has to be completely independent of me."

"I don't understand, Tye," Kyle whispered.

"I know. I'm sorry, Kyle."

They both became silent. Tye picked at her food.

"Have you thought about Trapper?" Kyle asked.

Tye kept her eyes on her plate. Trapper. How could she possibly leave him for eighteen months? He was her friend, her partner, her companion. She swallowed. "I'll lease him out while I'm gone."

Kyle sat back in his chair. "Good luck."

"What's that supposed to mean?"

"We both know how difficult it can be to lease a horse of Trapper's caliber. You don't want some novice climbing on his back and ruining everything you've worked so hard to build. Most riders of your ability have their own horse or are training a string they can choose from. Trying to find the right rider for Trapper isn't going to be easy."

Tye closed her eyes. Kyle was right. Everything had to be just perfect for Trapper or Tye could never leave him. "It'll work out," she said quietly.

"How?"

"I don't know. I haven't even tried yet. Someone will come along."

"I don't think you've thought this through," he said

Tye agreed. "I haven't, but I will."

A strong, vacuumed silence developed. Tye didn't even hear the other conversations from other patrons.

Kyle spoke quietly. "I guess this means we won't be seeing each other anymore. I mean what's the point if you're heading off to heaven knows where?"

"Kyle, in my church people go on missions all the time."

"Do they just put their relationships on hold?"

"Many people do."

"Does that work out in the end? Do the two people who are committed to each other before the mission end up together after the mission?"

"Sometimes."

Kyle sighed. "I don't know if I can do that, Tye."

Tye covered Kyle's hand with her own. "Earlier you said that we had some time and you're right. We do have some time. I haven't even turned in my papers. It'll be summer before I'm called to my mission. Let's spend that time just getting to know each other."

Kyle shook his head. "I'm not sure I can keep seeing you knowing that in a few months you're going to be gone. Maybe we could put the relationship on hold, but we're both going to be very different people in eighteen months. Don't you understand how painful that would be? The fact is we're both going to grow and change, but we won't be together during that process. Besides, I don't think I could store up enough memories to last eighteen months. I was already worried about the unknown future. I would be back east, and you would still be here in the Northwest. I was thinking of how difficult that long-distance relationship would be so I was willing to consider a compromise. I would stay in the Northwest for one year, until you graduated. Can't you compromise this mission idea for the sake of our relationship? For Trapper's sake?"

Tye spoke slowly. "I appreciate the fact that you're willing to put your dream off for a year, Kyle. I know how hard that would be for you. But there's a big difference between what you're willing to compromise, and what you're asking me to give up. You're asking me to completely abandon the idea of a mission. I'm not so sure I can do that. It would be like me asking you to forego your Olympic dreams."

Kyle paused. "I don't see it that way at all. I've been planning on the Olympics since I was a child. Your idea to go on a mission seems fairly sudden to me. I just don't want you to make a mistake you may regret later."

"I know it seems fairly sudden, but I think I've been coming to this resolution for a long time now. I tried to talk about it with you when we were at the barn, but we were interrupted by CarrieAnne."

Kyle nodded slowly. "Yes, I remember," he said quietly.

Silence filled the space between them. Tye looked at her meal without interest, then pushed the plate away.

Kyle finally spoke quietly. "I'm going to need some time away from this, Tye. After that I just don't know."

The waiter came to the table. "Is everything all right?" he asked, obviously concerned with the uneaten meals.

"Yes, fine. Thank you," Kyle said. "May we have a check please?"

"Of course." The waiter produced the bill and Kyle paid him. Then he looked at Tye. "Are you finished?"

"Yes."

"Then I'll take you home."

As if on automatic, Tye rose from her chair and followed Kyle out into the parking lot. The breeze was fitful but it promised warmth.

The short drive to the apartment was silent. Kyle walked Tye up the steps to her apartment.

"Do you want to come in?" she asked.

Kyle shook his head. "No." He backed away. "I hope you find what you're looking for, Tye."

Then suddenly, before Tye could answer, Kyle turned and hurried down the stairs, leaving Tye to stare after him. She listened to his truck purr into life, but she still didn't go inside.

She had been right to discourage him from joining the Church for all the wrong reasons. So why did it hurt? What was this strange mixture of pain and sorrow mingling with her earlier joy? It didn't make any sense. But as Tye let herself into the apartment, she noticed one feeling was definitely absent. The unnamed restlessness was gone. In spite of the hurt, she didn't feel the vague shifting of sands in her soul. The wind of uncertainty had quit howling. Finally, the inner struggle was settled.

Chapter Thirty-One

Tye placed the phone to her ear and dialed her home number. She was about to hang up when she heard her father. He sounded breathless.

"Dad? Are you okay? You sound like you've been running a marathon."

"Oh, Tye. Hello. We're just planting our garden and it's hard to hear the phone."

"I was about to hang up. You need to get an answering machine," Tye said, already knowing her father would reject the idea.

"No. We don't need one of those. We've got the cellular phones in case someone has an emergency. That's all we need."

Tye's news was bursting from her. "Dad? Can I talk to you about something?"

Rex caught his breath. "You're getting married," he whispered breathlessly. "You're marrying that Kyle fellow."

A shock wave of pain and surprise rode through Tye. "No. Oh, no. It's nothing like that," she said quickly. Tye could hear her father relaxing. "I'm thinking about going on a mission." Tye heard a chair scrape against the kitchen linoleum.

"What's this?" Rex asked. "We've never talked about a mission before. What made you consider a mission?"

"Lots of things, really." She paused. "I guess I need to start at the beginning." Slowly Tye told her father about the restlessness that became urgent. She spoke about the joy and satisfaction that came from teaching Toni the gospel. "It made me realize how important sharing the gospel is to me," Tye concluded. "Once I started thinking about this, the restlessness has left me and I feel completely at peace."

"Completely at peace?" Rex asked.

"Well, maybe not quite." She told him about the conversation she and Kyle had shared earlier in the evening. "I guess I feel at peace because the restlessness has left me," Tye said. "I still have lots of things that need my care."

"What about Trapper?"

Tye's heart skipped a beat. "I'm not sure," she said slowly. "That's another part of the equation I can't work out."

"There's something else too," Rex said. "How will we pay for this? I hate to bring this up, Tye, but I'm concerned. If it weren't for your scholarship, I'd doubt we would have been able to afford to send you to college. I just don't see how we can come up with the extra funds for a mission."

"That's where Trapper comes in, Dad. I'm hoping to find someone who's willing to lease him by paying for his care and then sending me two hundred dollars a month. That would probably take care of some of my mission expenses. Also, I'm going to approach Meggie's parents about working as their receptionist until I leave."

"Yes. That would help. Do you think you can find someone willing to lease Trapper under those conditions? Most lease options only require the horse's care."

"I know, but Trapper's special."

"Well, there's no doubt about that."

Tye could hear her father's worries coming through the line. The tension broke. "Here's your mom, Tye. Why don't you tell her the good news."

A sudden rush of doubt broke over Tye like an ocean wave. What would her mother think? She understood the mission program and had always been kind to the missionaries, but would she support her own daughter in such an endeavor?

"What's this good news?" Trudy asked.

"Mom, do you remember when we talked about the different things I could do, and you said you'd support me in whatever I chose?"

"Yes, honey, I remember. Are you changing your major?"

"No. I'm thinking about a mission," Tye announced quietly.

Tye heard her mother suck in her breath. "A full-time mission?" Trudy asked.

"Yes, Mom."

She told her mother the same things she had told her father.

"Well, I guess I can see what could lead you to the desire to serve. You were always so keen on the young men and women who came to our home."

"And you'll support me in this?"

Trudy's voice became shaky. "Yes, Tye. I support you. I always will. I'll help you pick out your clothes and pray that the Lord will send you to some safe place," Trudy said quietly. "I'll miss you. I don't want to think about you leaving for eighteen months. But if this is what you want, then I'm behind you."

Tye began to understand the sacrifice her parents were making. This would be a leap of faith for all of them. They might not be able to financially invest in Tye's mission, but they would certainly be emotionally invested in her decision to serve. But then they had always been emotionally invested. They never had the money to attend the horse shows, but they made sure she had her registration fee and a packed lunch before sending her off with her trainer. They would greet her with a hug and a hot meal when she came home and then listen with interest for hours as she explained each detail of the show. When it was time for bed, her mother would always hug her close and whisper her gratitude for Tye's safety. It was almost like a prayer. How many hours had her mother spent sitting at home, worrying over Tye's safety and well-being? Everyone knew about the dangers of the sport. It wasn't a secret. And yet her folks never forbid her to explore and venture into the dangerous territory. They only tried to keep her educated and well-informed about the sport of her choice. There were many talks about safety and the importance of wearing a helmet. And during the conferences with her trainer the main concern was always about safety and the condition of Tye's equipment. But there was never any attempt to keep her away from her beloved Trapper.

"You've always supported me, haven't you, Mom?"

"Why, yes, honey. It's my job."

"No, it isn't. You don't have to support me." Tears came to Tye's eyes as she realized that she hadn't always been supportive of her mother. "Mom, I haven't always been good to you." A sob caught in her throat.

"You've done the best you could, Tye. We all do the best we can."

"No, Mom, I haven't done my best. Riding is like smoking, isn't it?"

"Well, now, I don't quite see the connection."

"Think about it. Riding is dangerous, yet I willfully participate and you've never stopped me. Smoking is dangerous too, and yet I've constantly nagged you about it. And not always because of your health, but because it made me feel different from the kids at church." The confession overwhelmed Tye. Tears came to her eyes.

"Just a minute, Tye. I think we need to make a very important difference between your decision to ride and my decision to smoke. Yes, they are both dangerous, but smoking is against the Word of Wisdom and you hold that dear. Nowhere in the scriptures does it say to stay away from horses."

"I've even been selfish in my desire to have you join the Church," Tye said through her tears. "I wanted you to do it because I wanted it. So I would feel like I belonged. So I could be sealed to my family. I never thought about you."

"Tye, the decision to join the Church is a very personal one."

Tye was silent for a moment. Isn't that what she had just said to Kyle? "Yes. I think I understand."

"I'm proud of you and your decision to go on a mission. I'm grateful for the Church and for how it has guided your father and me in raising you. I'm glad you want to give something back."

"It goes beyond that, Mom."

"Yes, I'm sure it does. But those are my reasons for being supportive."

Tye fought the urge to badger her mom. It had been her most common tool whenever they talked about the church. But this time, she was grateful. Grateful that her mother saw the value in her decision. "Thanks, Mom," Tye said quietly.

"I love you, Tye. You're my daughter." Trudy laughed. "Whether you like it or not."

Tye smiled. "I wouldn't trade you for anyone, Mom."

"Thanks, sweetie. Now, you keep me posted on this mission process. I want to hear everything and so does your father."

"Okay."

"And Tye? Be careful. Promise me you'll be careful."

"I'll be careful, Mom."

"I love you, Tye. Here's your father."

"I love you too, Mom."

Tye said a quick goodbye to her father, promising to keep him informed about the financial situation before she hung up the phone. She lay back on her bed and closed her eyes. Tears leaked through her lashes, and Tye allowed them to run into her hair unchecked. She was exhausted. Yet the most difficult discussion was ahead of her.

Chapter Thirty-Two

Sitting in Katie's office, Tye rubbed her palms against her pants. Katie was on the phone, and she glanced at Tye and motioned with her hand that the conversation was almost over. Tye wished it would go on forever.

Finally, Katie hung up. "What's up?" she asked.

"I've got something I need to tell you and I don't think you're going to like it."

Katie sighed. "Yes. I know about you and Kyle. That's between the two of you. I also know about CarrieAnne and her inappropriate behavior. I plan on having a word with her later this afternoon. If Trapper comes up with so much as an eyelash out of place I'll turn her over to the authorities. I'll also see to it that she never works in a barn in the United States, Canada or Europe. I don't put up with bad behavior in my barn."

Tye swallowed. "This isn't about CarrieAnne," she said softly. "It's not about Kyle either." She took a deep breath. "I won't be coming back next fall."

Katie lost her relaxed composure and looked hard at Tye. "What gives?"

Tye's mouth went dry. "I'm going to serve a mission for my church."

"Excuse me?"

"I'll probably be leaving sometime this summer."

"Wait just a minute," Katie said. Then she looked at the open door. She pushed her chair back and shut the door hard. "I think I deserve an explanation. If this has got something to do with Carrie-Anne, then we can take care of that right now."

"No. It's not CarrieAnne. I can understand why you would think that her threats would cause me to want to leave, but she really hasn't entered into the equation. And I'm not running from the break-up with Kyle, either. In fact, this is the reason why we broke up. I won't be gone for long—only eighteen months."

"It might as well be eighteen years. Tye, when I grant these scholarships, I hope my students will stay with me for the full four years. I realize there's no obligation on your part, but this isn't right. You should've told me about this possibility when you applied."

"I didn't know it was a possibility then," Tye said. "Please, Katie, don't be angry. This is just something I've got to do."

"And what about your teammates?"

"You can find someone to replace me." Tye waved her hand at the stack of applications. "There are at least a hundred people who would love to have my position."

"Yes and I chose you over all of them. What about Trapper?"

"I was hoping you could take him. I know he'd thrive under your care."

Katie shook her head. "I've already got two horses of my own. I don't need another one. I couldn't afford it anyway."

Tye's heart sank.

"I don't like this," Katie said. "I don't like it one bit. I'll put someone else in your spot, but it'll mess up the continuity of the team. You're sacrificing a lot of people for this."

Tye slowly nodded.

"I also hope you realize that you're not going to be able to waltz back in here after being gone a year-and-a-half and get your scholarship back."

"I know."

Katie blinked at Tye. "This is the most amazing thing I've ever heard. You're going to walk out of one of the best equestrian programs in the west, one that has offered you a full scholarship, including board for your horse to do what?"

"To serve a mission for The Church of Jesus Christ of Latter-day Saints."

"Don't expect my blessing," Katie said. "And I'll have to replace you as the alternate for the competition team. There's no sense in having you go to the shows if you're not going to be here next year."

Tye held her breath. That would make Kyle happy. At least they wouldn't be bumping into each other while at the shows.

"I'd throw you out right now if I could, but I'd have a fight on my hands with the academic committee." Katie sank back into her chair. "I'm really disappointed in you, Tye."

Tye remained silent.

Katie waved her hand towards the door. "You can go."

Tye stood. She wished she could think of something profound to say. Something that would help Katie understand. But her mind was blank. Instead, she slipped out through the door, closing it behind her. When she looked at CarrieAnne's smug look, she knew the conversation had been heard beyond the closed door.

Ignoring her quiet teammates, Tye walked towards Trapper's stall and let herself in. She stroked his neck, and he softly nickered.

What was she going to do without him? What was she going to do with him? Katie had been her best hope. She thought about asking her teammates if someone would be interested in taking him, but after the news of her defection got around, she doubted that any of them would be very sympathetic. She would have to advertise. A cold dread washed over Tye. Advertising would mean fielding a lot of calls and having to make a judgment on someone she didn't know. Putting her arms around Trapper's neck, Tye breathed a silent prayer.

Chapter Thirty-Three

Toni stared at the phone and swallowed. She picked up the receiver and then placed it back in its cradle. She hadn't called her mother in years. Their last telephone conversation had been six months ago but felt like six years ago.

Toni picked up the phone and dialed the number from her address book. Her palms began to perspire.

A familiar yet distant voice answered.

"Mom?"

Silence.

Finally, the voice spoke, "Toni?"

"Yeah. Hi, Mom."

"Toni girl?"

"Yeah, it's me."

"Is everything all right?"

Tears came to her eyes. No. Nothing was right, but how could she possibly explain? "Yeah, I'm fine. I just called to say hello."

"Well, I'm so glad you did. How's school?"

Toni closed her eyes. She **was** grateful for her mother's quick recovery. It made the conversation easier. "Good. My math classes are hard, but I think my grades will be okay."

Jolene laughed. "I remember my college math classes. They were hard. Your dad was always good at math."

"Yeah, well, he's not around much."

"Yes, I know. He's in Texas. It must be hard for you to be without him."

The awkward silence came creeping into the line.

"He got married, you know."

Jolene sucked in her breath before answering. "No, I didn't hear."

"He's in Texas for good now."

"I see."

"Mom, do you remember picking cherries?"

Jolene laughed. "Heavens, yes. We had more cherries than we knew what to do with. Do you remember that church service project?"

Toni grinned. She immediately felt better. "Yes, I remember winning the cherry picking contest and the bishop gave me a big, paper blue ribbon."

Jolene continued to laugh. "Oh, my yes. You wore that until it faded and turned purple."

Memories clamored around Toni now—each one looking for a voice. "Do you remember calling for me each evening?"

Jolene's voice became soft. "You'd go out into the cherry orchard and climb one of those big old trees to watch the sunset. Sometimes I thought you'd spend the night in the cherry orchard if I didn't call you."

"Oh, I'd never miss dessert."

"Your father had a sweet tooth as well. Why, if I didn't have some homemade treat, he'd keep after me until I'd make him something. He loved my cherry cobbler."

"Mom, why did you make fun of him in front of others?"

Jolene let out a long, sad sigh. "You remember that, do you?"

"Yes."

"I'm sorry about that."

"Sorry that I remember?"

"No. Sorry I was so unkind and thoughtless. I wrote a letter to your father and told him that very thing about five years ago. Didn't he tell you?"

"No."

"It took me awhile to take my share of the responsibility when it came to the failure of our marriage. For the longest time it was just easier to blame him. But gradually I began to understand my role. I was in therapy for a while, and I visited the bishop, too. Even though I wasn't going to church regularly, he encouraged me to come in for appointments. After a while I realized how terribly I had demeaned your father. That was part of what pushed him away." She sighed again. "Some things can't be fixed, Toni. By the time I realized what I had done, it was too late for us to ever reconcile. We didn't love each other anymore. But I knew I had to try to make things better as best I could, so I wrote him a letter and explained. He never wrote back so I don't know if he understood."

"He never told me."

"I suppose he didn't want to upset you."

"Maybe."

"Do you have good memories, Toni?"

The question took Toni by surprise. Tears came to her eyes. "Oh, Mom, I have these wonderful memories."

"That's good. I've worried that you would only remember the ugly things."

The tears were spilling onto Toni's cheeks. "No. It's the happy times that won't leave me alone."

"I'm glad for that, Toni. It means you won't grow bitter."

Toni swallowed her tears. "Mom, I've been thinking about coming to Idaho for a visit. I wouldn't stay long," Toni rushed. "Maybe just a few days."

"You can come and stay as long as you'd like, Toni girl. We can talk about old times and maybe pick some new cherries."

"I'd like that," Toni said.

"How about if I call you in a few days with my work schedule? I've turned the farm over to your Uncle Chad, and I work in Boise. I've got two weeks' vacation coming this summer. It would be nice if I didn't work while you were here."

"Okay."

After saying a brief goodbye, Toni hung up. Fatigue washed through her, but so did a new and hopeful feeling. Maybe her memories weren't orphaned after all.

The following Wednesday, Toni smiled wide when she greeted Sister Sutton and Tye at the door. She watched as each woman's gaze turned into a wide smile.

"Toni! You cut your hair!" Tye exclaimed.

"And dyed it too. It looks great," Sister Sutton said.

Toni ran her fingers through her shortened locks. "Thanks. It was time for a change," she said. "That bleached blonde look just didn't suit me anymore. I dyed it to match my original color. I'm going to grow it out."

She threw the door open wide and allowed the two missionaries entrance. They sat in the now familiar living room.

"Have you ever had long hair?" Sister Sutton asked.

"Oh, yes. When I was a girl, my hair hung to my hips. It was as long as Tye's."

Tye put her hand on her hair. "Your hair is so thick, I bet it looked beautiful."

"It was long, thick, and very healthy. My Primary teacher used to braid it for me." Toni laughed. "You know, I realize that was years ago, but it seems like yesterday."

"Memories are like that," Sister Sutton said. "If we're good to them, they'll shine bright all our lives."

"I've got some other news too. I'm going to Idaho to spend some time with my mom." Toni became sober. "I miss my home. I miss the cherry orchards and the warm, blue Idahoan sky. I haven't seen my mom in years, and I think it's time we did some exploring together."

"Do you feel ready for that?" Sister Sutton asked.

"Yes. I've been running all of my life," Toni said. "It's time I stopped and faced the past. Not all of it is good, but I've been blessed with some wonderful moments. I can't deny them any longer. They're crying out for me and I have to go." She sighed. "Besides, Dad is going to sell the house so I'm going to have to find an apartment and get on with my own life. It's time for me to put these things in their proper places. I need to figure out what's important so I can hang on to it."

"Where does the gospel fit in all of this?" Sister Sutton asked.

"It's one of the important things," Toni replied.

"Is your mom active?"

Toni shook her head. "No, I don't believe so, but she'll support me in my decision to go to church."

Toni turned to Tye. "I've been thinking that I should start looking for a roommate. I was wondering if you and Meggie would mind a third wheel."

Tye and Sister Sutton exchanged glances.

"I won't be coming back next fall," Tye said. "I'm turning in my papers for a mission."

Toni's eyes grew large. "You're going on a mission?"

"If they'll have me."

"Of course they'll have you! Oh, Tye, this is wonderful news. You'll make the greatest missionary."

Sister Sutton grinned. "Sister Kohler and I told her that very thing."

"Maybe you and Meggie could room while I'm away," Tye said. "I think the two of you could become great friends."

"We'll have to talk about that," Toni said.

Sister Sutton pulled out her scriptures. "Are you ready for the last discussion?" she asked.

Toni settled in her seat. "Yes," she said with confidence.

Later in the evening, after closing the door behind Tye and Sister Sutton, Toni allowed the silence of the house to envelope her. It no longer screamed, but rather wrapped around her like the cherry orchards in full bloom. It was hard to see the sky then, but the blossoms brought a softness to the air that felt tranquil and quiet. The feelings of peace were new and tender, and Toni pulled them close as the drumming anxiety began to fade. But the wonderful memories didn't fade. They were as bright as ever—beaming and full of life and joy. They weren't fighting for a place anymore. Through accepting them, Toni had given her orphaned past a home.

Chapter Thirty-Four

Tye hurried to the answering machine and scanned it for any sign of a message. Nothing. She sighed. Trapper had been advertised in the local three-day-event newsletter and the paper. For two weeks now she had been fielding calls from excited twelve- and thirteen-year-olds who were convinced they could guide Trapper to new heights. Three girls weren't even taking lessons and were just looking for horses to jump over obstacles they had set up in their home pastures. One young girl was just starting and wanted a horse that could be a teacher. She appreciated the young girls' enthusiasm, yet she just couldn't turn Trapper over to a novice. She didn't want him to be used as a training horse, an animal who would teach younger riders how to learn. Often those riders made drastic mistakes over and over—sawing on the reins and hardening the tender mouth of a horse—shifting around in their saddle so that the messages that came from the rider were so confusing that even the best-trained animal would eventually be worthless. None of the interested parties would be in Trapper's best interest.

Each time the phone would ring, Tye's heart would race and then plummet into disappointment when she realized that the caller would not be suitable for Trapper. Kyle was right. It would be hard to find someone who could lease him.

Life at the barn had been tense and subdued. Overnight Tye had become an outcast. No one understood her decision to walk away from the equestrian team. No one even tried. Not even fun-loving Janna could overcome her disappointment and her face showed her sadness. The rest of the members of the sophomore team were divided. Kim was glad Tye was leaving. She had a friend who had sent in an application and Kim was hoping for her appointment. Jim was angry with Tye for risking everyone and everything for which the sophomore team members had been working. He rarely looked at Tye and never spoke.

Tye never saw Kyle and no one spoke of him. If she hadn't glanced into Ben's stall periodically to see whether the duo were still at Oregon State, she would've been convinced he was gone. His disappearance from her life was complete. Graduation was coming soon. She wondered if he had been accepted at any of the barns back east, but there was no one she could ask.

Trapper sensed Tye's anxiety and didn't work well. Tye tried to maintain an easy-going attitude that would help ease Trapper's obvious anxiety, but she didn't pull it off very well and Trapper was sensitive. She tried to fit in quiet morning walks, but with finals around the corner, she found herself being pulled away from Trapper at the very time they needed each other the most.

Tye glanced at the clock. It was after 9:00 P.M. Pulling on her jacket, she hurried to the truck and drove to the barn. Killing the engine, Tye stepped out of the truck and listened to the beginnings of a spring symphony. Crickets were singing with the accompaniment of croaking frogs and the occasional yip of a coyote. The spring evening held a soft chill, causing Tye to pull her jacket close as she walked inside the barn. The warm earthy aroma of horses and hay greeted her and Tye smiled at their familiarity. She found it hard to believe that she would go eighteen months without stepping inside a place she considered a second home. Slowly moving down the aisle,

Tye came to Trapper's stall. He looked at her with sleepy disinterest.

Feelings of doubt crowded Tye. But she couldn't deny that ever since she had made her decision to go on a mission, the restlessness had completely left her. She felt satisfaction—deep and true satisfaction. But that didn't change her current dilemma regarding Trapper.

Tye leaned against Trapper and placed her cheek against his warm, soft neck.

"Tye?"

Tye startled and turned around. Kyle was looking at her.

Her knees went weak. "What are you doing here so late?" she asked, trying to recover.

"I was restless. I thought I'd stop by and take a look at Ben."

Tye gave him a doubting look. Ben was on the other side of the arena.

"I saw your truck in the parking lot. Besides, I also came to see Trapper," Kyle confessed.

Tye stood by her horse's side, keeping her hand on his neck. "Why?"

"I wanted to look him over. Have you found someone to lease him?"

Tye's heart sank even lower. "No." She resisted the urge to spill her heart to Kyle. She wanted to tell him that she was afraid she was just being picky and that her inability to find anyone good enough might keep her from leaving on her mission.

"Then I want him," Kyle said.

Tye's thoughts were jerked away from her worries and she sucked in her breath. "What? Kyle—"

"Hear me out, Tye. I have a plan." Kyle continued, "Willoughby Stables in Pennsylvania has taken me on as a trainer. Because I'll be working there I can have two stalls and feed for two horses. They only wanted to give me one, but I told them about Trapper and they're willing to let me keep him."

Tye's heart began to unravel in her chest. Turn Trapper over to Kyle? Move Trapper back east? It seemed like the perfect solution. Or was it just a bad idea? She trusted Kyle. Trapper would be in the best possible hands. He would be competing and training with the best the country had to offer. It was all she wished for him. But did she want Kyle to meet those hopes?

"I know what you're up against, Tye. Trapper is a fine animal and you don't want to see him misused. I'm not saying that people would hurt him on purpose. I'm just saying that if you get someone young and inexperienced, it could end up doing a lot of damage that you might not be able to undo. If he's with me, you know that won't happen."

Tye remained silent. Kyle had reached into her soul and revealed her biggest worry for her friend and partner of seven years.

"Why would you want to do this for me, Kyle? You don't want me to go on my mission. Why do you want to help me now?"

"I'm going to be completely honest with you, Tye. There are two reasons why I think this is the best thing. First, it would be best for Trapper. I know you feel that no one can take care of him as well as you and you're right about that, but if you're not around then we both know that I'm next in line." Kyle was quiet for a moment. "I know we have our misunderstandings Tye, but as far as Trapper's concerned, I believe you trust me."

"I do."

"My second reason is for both you and me. If I take Trapper, I hope you will be able to serve the best mission possible. You will never have to worry about him. I hope that will free you to teach people about your church in a way that will keep that restlessness away and allow you to come home feeling that you did your very best. I know how important it is for you to feel good about the job you do. It's the only way I know to support you." Kyle continued, "I'm also excited to take him because it allows me to add a great horse to my resume." Kyle's voice became softer. "But there's another reason. I guess I'm also hoping that you would want to see me when you come home. I was wrong when I said I couldn't store enough memories to last eighteen months. I think I already have enough memories. If I have Trapper, in some ways I will feel like I didn't have to completely let you go." He paused. "I won't wait for you, Tye. I can't offer you that kind of support. It's so foreign to everything I know. When two people love each other they should be together. Nothing should stand in their way. I was willing to sacrifice a job back east to stay here and wait for you to graduate. I guess it hurts to realize that you're not willing to sacrifice this mission to stay with me. But what I can do is take your horse and take it one day at a time."

Tye nodded. Kyle would be the best thing for Trapper.

Kyle continued. "If you come home from your mission and we decide we don't want to see each other, then I'll see that Trapper gets the best transportation home. I would only ask that you share that expense with me, since we both know it can cost well over a thousand dollars to send a horse from coast to coast."

Tye leaned against Trapper, trying to absorb Kyle's offer.

The silence echoed in the barn. Finally Kyle spoke again, "I know a lot has happened between us, Tye. But I also know that deep down we respect one another. And I know that you respect my work with Ben and know I'll look after Trapper. You *know* it."

"You're right, Kyle. I do respect you, and I know that Trapper would thrive in your care."

"Then let me take him—for the sake of all of us."

Tye nodded. "I need to think about it, Kyle."

Their eyes locked through the bars of Trapper's stall. Tye felt so separate from him, but part of her longed to reach out and touch him, to feel his warmth as she had on that first day when they had brought Gypsy into the world.

"Okay. I can understand," he said. "But you'll have to let me know soon. I'm scheduled to leave the day after commencement. I've got to plan my trip before I go. I need to make reservations with hotels that have barns, and I'll need to tell them how many horses I'll have with me."

"I understand."

Kyle nodded briefly before walking away.

Tye could hear his footsteps echoing on the cement floor. She listened as he opened Ben's door and then she sank into the soft sawdust on the floor of Trapper's stall. Closing her eyes, she whispered a fervent prayer but no answer came. Her mind was thick with the problem.

She sat for several minutes. She heard Kyle leave the barn and the familiar sound of his truck as he pulled out of the parking lot. She was alone once again. Anxiety pulled and tugged at her heart until her nerves began to jump. She briefly considered saddling Trapper up for a late night ride, but she wasn't dressed properly and she could only imagine his confusion if his routine was disturbed at ten o'clock in the evening.

She thought of Meggie and realized she hadn't left a note telling her where she was going. Meggie would probably be worried.

Climbing to her feet, Tye brushed off the sawdust. She gave Trapper his apple and with one last gentle pat she stepped out of his stall.

Chapter Thirty-Five

Tye stared at the open suitcase she had on her bed. Already she had packed all of Trapper's gear, and arrangements had been made for Kyle to take him back east. It had not been a difficult decision to make.

After Kyle made his offer, the phone remained eerily silent. Tye had called her trainer back home, but Thelma politely refused the offer. She was bringing along a new horse and wouldn't have any time for Trapper. With that final phone call, Tye ran out of ideas. She called Kyle and discussed the details of the lease. Tye promised to have the papers in the mail within the next few days. As she placed the phone receiver in the cradle she breathed a huge sigh of relief. She had done the right thing for Trapper, herself, and Kyle. Trapper would be leaving with Kyle in two weeks.

A knock on the door interrupted Tye's busy work.

"Come in."

Meggie appeared. "I heard you bumping around in here and thought maybe you'd taken up aerobics. Why are you packing now? We won't be leaving for home for another three weeks."

"It's never too early. Besides, I'm finished with these winter clothes." Tye jerked a thumb in the direction of three boxes that stood by the closet.

Meggie sat on the bed. "Want to talk about it?" she asked.

Tye let out a huge breath and sat down on the bed, her energy dissipating. "I'm turning Trapper over to Kyle."

Meggie nodded. "I see. How do you feel about that?"

"I know it's the right thing, but it's hard for me to imagine my life without Trapper. We've been together seven years. I can't imagine waking up in the morning without the responsibility of my barn duties."

Meggie smiled. "Oh, I think your mission duties will keep you plenty busy. You'll barely have time to think about anything else."

"I hope so," Tye replied.

Meggie grinned. "Now, tell me. Where are you hoping to go on your mission?"

Tye grew wistful. "I haven't given it much thought."

"Well, think about it."

Tye shook her head. "No. It's better that I don't. Sometimes I hope to serve a foreign mission. Other times I hope to stay stateside. When I'm really scared I hope I end up on Temple Square in Salt Lake City, but I'll go where Heavenly Father wants me to go."

"Isn't there a hymn about that?"

"Yes, and I'm trying to adopt that attitude. I'll go where the Lord wants me to go."

Meggie became silent for a moment. "I'm going to miss you, Tye. Eighteen months is a long time. I know I'll enjoy Toni as a roommate, but we'll both know someone is missing."

Tye smiled. "I'm so glad you and Toni are going to be rooming together."

Meggie nodded. "Toni and I will get along fine, but it won't be the same without you. We both agree."

"I know what you mean," Tye replied. "I'm looking forward to meeting new companions, but you'll always be my best friend, Meggie." She sighed. "It's hard to imagine that just four months ago, I didn't even know Toni Chandler. Now I can't imagine life without her."

Meggie climbed off the bed. "C'mon," she said. "Let's not sit around here in a glum mood. Let's pick Toni up and go get some ice cream." She reached her hand out to Tye.

Chapter Thirty-Six

Meggie sat at the picnic table on the grounds of her apartment building, soaking up the gentle springtime warmth the sun offered. Leaning against Neil, she raised her face to the sun. Reacting, Neil pulled Meggie closer.

"You smell good," he whispered in her ear.

Meggie giggled. "It's the sun."

"No, it's your shampoo," Neil replied.

Meggie giggled again.

"Are you ready to go to work at the bed and breakfast?" Neil asked.

Meggie sat up and turned to face him. "I'm ready," she said seriously. "I'm also anxious, nervous, and scared." Meggie changed the subject. "What about you? Do you have any plans when you get home?"

Neil looked down and changed the subject. "I brought the letters from Sammi Rae," he said. "Do you still want to see them?"

Meggie held her breath and nodded slowly. Neil handed her four letters. A new one. This one was addressed to Neil at Corvallis. So, he had given Sammi his address.

"How long have you been writing back?" Meggie asked.

"I wrote her for the first time last week and this letter came in reply." He pointed to the latest correspondence.

"Maybe I should start at the beginning," Meggie said as she reverently and more than a bit fearfully opened the first letter. Sam's writing was decorative with loops and a strong right-handed slant. The contents were mostly newsy about Brigham Young University's activities. She talked a lot about skiing and how she had learned to snowboard.

Her next letter requested a reply. She wanted Neil to know that she was no longer seeing Joshua. That relationship had been a big mistake, and she was sorry for the pain she had caused Neil and herself. She had continued to see Joshua for a few weeks after Neil left, but she didn't love him and wasn't interested in loving him. She missed Neil and realized it the minute he walked out of her life. Again, she apologized and asked for Neil to write back.

The third letter told Neil that Sammi was moving back home for the summer and that she would love it if he would direct his letters to her home in California. It was a short note just making reference to the upcoming move.

Meggie lingered over the fourth letter. Sammi thanked Neil for writing back and told him that she hoped for the chance to be able to see him. She missed him terribly. She had spent the last year trying to forget him, but she couldn't. She realized she had no right to ask for his presence back in her life, but she hoped Neil would at least give her the opportunity to share with him her regret. She invited him to her home in California. He could stay as long as he wanted, and she hoped he would stay for a while so that they could get to know each other again. She spoke of the beauty of her Monterey, California, home and informed Neil that her parents were also hopeful for the visit and were graciously opening their home for as long as he wished to stay.

Meggie's mouth went dry as she read the final words of invitation. Tears filled her eyes and blurred her view of Sam's penmanship. She blinked away the tears and folded the letter, handing it back to Neil.

"Are you going?" she asked.

Neil slowly nodded. "I have to," he said quietly.

A cloud covered the sun and Meggie involuntarily shivered.

Meggie nodded. "Yes, I suppose you do. I don't know what to say, Neil. I—"

Neil placed his hand on Meggie's knee. "I hope you'll wait."

"What?" Meggie asked incredulously.

"I know it's a lot to ask, but I hope you'll be willing to allow me to sort this out."

A new and honest bitterness arose in Meggie. "You want to keep your bird in the hand. Is that it?" she asked.

"No. I just need to settle this thing with Sammi."

"And how do you plan on settling it? Are you going down to California to tell her that you're sorry she feels so bad, but that you don't love her anymore?"

"I won't know that until I get down there."

"I understand that, Neil. I understand better than you do. You've already chosen Sammi Rae. You did it the minute you put pen to paper and wrote to her." Tears began piling up and Meggie fought them. She would not cry in front of Neil.

"Don't do this, Meggie. I hate the thought of losing you."

"Of course you do, Neil," Meggie said gently. "You should." Meggie stood and caressed Neil's hair. "But I won't share you with Sammi. I won't share you with the memory of Sammi either. She has a hold on you I've never been able to explain. I've only been able to worry over it. I don't want to worry over it anymore. Second place doesn't suit me, Neil. It's taken me a while to figure that out. But I know that now."

Gently, she kissed him on the cheek. The sun came out from its hiding place, and Meggie concentrated on its warmth. Neil gathered her in his arms—the embrace lingered and the kiss was full of longing and loneliness. It mingled with tears that began Meggie's mourning. Then with a gentle touch to Neil's face, Meggie backed away. This would be the final snapshot of him for the scrapbook in her mind: his blond hair blowing in the spring breeze and his hand raised in a final goodbye. She did not look back.

Chapter Thirty-Seven

For the next two weeks Tye tried not to think about the inevitable parting from Trapper. She went through her lessons with the team with perfunctory precision. No one spoke to her, except when absolutely necessary. Her status as a social outcast was complete. No one at the barn asked about her mission or the decision to leave the team. They had already branded her as a traitor—someone who put her own desires before those of her team. Tye saw no point in trying to convince them otherwise.

CarrieAnne quit taunting Tye. The older teammate had gotten what she wanted, but Tye couldn't concentrate on that. Her decision had been separate from CarrieAnne's influence. Tye watched as CarrieAnne began to hang around Kyle during the team's practices.

As Tye felt the sting of her brand that came from her human teammates, she turned to Trapper. He still loved Tye. He would always love her.

The night of graduation, Tye didn't attend the commencement ceremonies. Instead, she saddled Trapper for their last walk together. The barn was unusually quiet for an early evening, for which Tye was grateful.

Lovingly, she stroked Trapper's neck, then she led him out into the pink dusk. They had about an hour of daylight.

Placing her foot in the stirrup, Tye swung herself into the saddle, like she had a thousand times before. But this time was different. This would be the last time she would settle in the comfortable leather and feel Trapper's weight support her.

For a long minute, she didn't move. She willed time to stand still so she might live in this moment forever. She threw her head back and looked at the deepening sky. A pink aura was settling onto the horizon as the sun went down.

Trapper fussed. He was anxious to get underway.

Tye gave him a pat on the neck as she realized that this moment, nor any other moment, would ever stand still. Like Trapper, time was anxious to move forward and present new challenges and new opportunities. Nudging Trapper with her leg, Tye guided him toward the meadow. Spring wildflowers were beginning to show themselves, dotting the meadow grasses with their bobbing petals of purple, blue, yellow and white.

"It's beautiful here, isn't it, Trapper? I'm sorry we won't be able to finish our school years like we had planned."

Trapper flicked his ears in her direction. Tye smiled. He was listening. He always listened. Now he would be hearing a different voice. Kyle's voice. Tears came to Tye's eyes as she thought about the future that would be unfolding for Trapper. It made perfect sense that Trapper should be with Kyle. It didn't make the parting any easier, but it helped to know that he would be with a man who would look after him as she would.

Tye patted Trapper on the neck. Maybe he would be the bridge that could bring her and Kyle to a new and lasting friendship.

Bringing Trapper to a halt, Tye threw her head back once again and looked at the deepening color of the sky. It was purple now. Stars were beginning to wink into place. It would be dark soon.

Slowly and deliberately, Tye turned Trapper towards home. She savored everything about the evening. The cool spring grass and the delicate aroma of wildflowers that only came out at night. She breathed deeply of the earthy scent of Trapper mingling with the smell of her own hair and skin. It was familiar and it was precious. And for twenty-two months, it would be the only part of Trapper she would claim—a memory.

The following morning Tye stood in the bright late spring sun, holding Trapper by a lead rope. The horse stood obediently beside her. Kyle was leading Ben up the ramp and into the trailer. Trapper would be next. Tye fought the tears. To Trapper this was just another journey. Tye tried to remain calm. She didn't want to upset him. But tears kept surfacing. How could she do this? How could she leave Trapper for twenty-two months? The fragile peace she had felt the night before evaporated in the morning light like dew, and the desire to serve a mission dimmed as she ran her hand over Trapper's silken neck. She wrapped her arms around him in spite of the rising heat. Trapper lowered his head.

Softly, she whispered in his ear. "You're going on to new adventures, my boy," she whispered gently. "I'm going on new adventures too. You'll have Ben and Kyle, and we'll both have the Lord. I'll pray for you every day. We'll be fine. Time will fly and soon we'll be riding through meadows of wildflowers—just like yesterday."

Trapper's ears flicked in her direction and he nudged her with his nose. Tye smiled through the tears. He was always looking for his apple. Tears spilled onto Trapper's groomed coat as Tye drew her arms tighter around him. "Promise me that you'll remember," she cried softly. "Promise that you won't forget me."

Softly she stroked Trapper's mane. The horse stepped back and sniffed her hair. Pulling in the scent of her into his eternal memory bank.

Tye heard Kyle come down the ramp. He didn't interrupt her as she pulled away from Trapper. She continued to stroke his neck.

"I'll look after him, Tye. I promise."

"I know." Tye sniffed. "I'm going to miss him."

"Of course you will. Sending him off like this is a big deal. Now you know how I feel when I think about you going off to some unknown place—without me."

Tye met Kyle's eyes. Yes. She could understand.

"Look. I shouldn't have said that. I'm sorry."

"It's okay. Maybe for the first time, I do understand how you must've felt when I broke my news to you."

Tye didn't want the moment to end. She wished she could continue to stand in the early morning sun and let it bathe her face in its rays. She wanted to continue to feel Trapper near and to reach out to Kyle with understanding and love.

"Well, I hate to do this, Tye, but I need to go. I have to make Boise by sundown, and with these two in the back it's going to be slow going."

"Yes, of course."

Quietly, she gave Trapper his apple before handing Kyle the lead rope. Their fingers touched briefly as she turned over her beloved Trapper. Kyle reached into the back pocket of his jeans. "These are the papers. I've signed them exactly as you drew them up. I'm to pay you two-hundred dollars a month, plus see to his board and training for the next twenty-two months."

Tye took the papers from Kyle's outstretched hand.

Then she stepped back.

Kyle led Trapper into the trailer. He went willingly. Kyle fastened the horse to the trailer and placed the feed bag at Trapper's nose. He immediately buried himself in the sweet-smelling hay.

Kyle closed up the trailer and then walked around, making sure all windows were open. Then he stood before Tye. "I guess that's it. You've given me your home number so I'll call and let you know when we get to Pennsylvania. I expect it'll take about five days. If I can find a decent place with a big paddock or pasture, I might give them a day off from the travel. I'll see to it that they get some exercise, too."

Tye nodded numbly. Tears filled her eyes. She looked down at the ground.

Kyle stepped closer and raised Tye's chin with his fingers, but he said nothing.

Tye lowered her eyes.

"Look at me, Tye," Kyle said softly.

Tye looked into Kyle's eyes.

Gently, Kyle wiped away her tears. His touch felt familiar and comfortable. It made her want to weep all the more. He cupped her chin in his hands and drew her near. Tye went to him and began to sob.

"I know," Kyle soothed. "We're all going to make it through this, Tye. It's going to be fine."

Tye clung to Kyle. She breathed in the smell of clean hay and horse that mingled with the scent of sunshine on Kyle's skin.

Then she pulled away and placed her hands on Kyle's chest. "Thank you," she murmured quietly. "Thank you for taking him. I know this isn't the typical lease arrangement. Most of the time board and care for the horse is all that's required. I appreciate your willingness to help me with this, Kyle."

"I guess I'd do just about anything for you, Tye," he said.

"You might not feel that way in a year," she said honestly.

"Then I guess I'd do just about anything for Trapper," Kyle replied.

Tye nodded her understanding. Kyle would never allow his personal struggles with their relationship come between him and Trapper.

With one last caress of her cheek, he turned and walked around the trailer.

Tye heard the cab door open and shut then the engine start. Slowly, the vehicle began to pull away. Tye fought the crushing desire to run after it. Clenching her teeth, she willed herself to stay rooted. Kyle was leaving and was taking Trapper with him. It was neatly prearranged. She had the papers to prove it. But nothing could have prepared her for the emotion of the moment as the truck stopped at the end of the driveway and then pulled on to the country road—out of sight. Tye stood and listened to the motor until she couldn't hear it any longer. So, it was over. The long goodbye that she and Kyle had been working towards from the moment they met was now finished.

Swallowing hard, Tye didn't know where she should go. Then, as if being piloted by some unknown force, Tye headed for the meadow. She crossed the little creek, muddying her boots just as she had muddied Trapper's legs. She scrambled up the little embankment, cleared the trees that followed the water, and then once again found herself bathed in the brilliant sunshine. She found the boulder in the corner of the field and fell to her knees. Invited by its warmth, Tye placed her folded arms on the surface of the gray stone, buried her head in her arms, and allowed herself to weep.

Chapter Thirty-Eight

Meggie climbed out of Tye's car and looked at the beautifully landscaped lawn. So, this is where Toni lived.

"I can't believe this school year is over and we're going to be heading home this afternoon," Meggie said as she closed the door.

Tye leaned on the car door and drank in the early summer sun as she thought of Trapper. Kyle had been kind enough to call her when he reached Boise to let her know that Trapper was traveling well. She had peppered him with questions. Was Trapper staying in a clean barn? Did Trapper seem depressed or genuinely interested in his surroundings? Was it too hot in the trailer? Kyle had answered her questions with patience and sincerity. The barn was clean. If Kyle wasn't pleased, then he wouldn't have stayed, opting to camp out in the truck. Trapper was eating and seemed to be paying attention to his new environment. Traveling seemed to wear on both of the animals, but for the rest of the journey Kyle would take a couple of breaks during the day and allow them time out of the trailer for a short walk. Hearing Kyle's gentle voice on the line had reassured Tye. She glanced at her watch. He should be in Kansas by now—maybe even further east.

"Are you okay?" Meggie asked.

Tye came back to the present. "Yeah. I was just thinking."

"Let me guess. Trapper?"

"Always," Tye replied.

"Well, c'mon, let's go greet Toni before she thinks we've lost our minds sitting out here in her driveway."

"Did she tell you why she wanted us to come over this morning?" Tye asked.

"Nope. She just asked if we'd have the time to come by before we left for home."

Walking to the front door, Tye's curiosity rose. She had planned to see Toni before leaving for home, but this had sounded almost formal.

Toni greeted them with a smile as she threw the door wide open. "Come in," she said.

Tye looked around the familiar living room. There weren't any boxes that would give the indication of a move. "Have you packed?" Tye asked.

"Yes. Everything is in the car. I'll be leaving as soon as we finish here. I'm not taking very much with me. Just my personal belongings. When the house sells, Dad will have to fly out and pack what he wants. I doubt I'll be coming back here," Toni said. "We've already had about a dozen people look at the house. No one has made an offer, but it won't last the summer."

"How do you feel about that?" Tye asked.

Toni shrugged. "It really bothered me at first, but if I can leave something important, I'll feel better about it."

"What do you mean?" Meggie asked.

Toni smiled. "Come into the backyard."

The girls followed Toni. It was a lovely yard with cool, green grass and a wooden fence. In the corner stood a new tree. The root ball was in a burlap bag. Pink blossoms hung from the branches.

Tears came to Toni's eyes. "This tree will be the part of me that will always be here," she said. "This cherry tree will be my gift to this house—to this place I called home. Will you help me plant it?"

Meggie and Tye nodded eagerly.

Toni disappeared into the garage for a moment and then returned with three shovels. She handed each girl a shovel. Carefully, they broke through the sod and dug a hole. Gently, Toni untied the burlap sack and placed the roots of the tree into the ground. The girls covered the roots with dirt, arranging the sod.

"Now that you're leaving, who will water it?" Tye asked with a worried expression.

"The realtor said she'd look after it. A dying tree on the property isn't a good selling point."

The three girls stepped back from their work. The blossoms caught the sunlight and gave off a pink translucent glow.

"A part of you will remain here too," Toni said. Then she placed her hand over her heart. "And here as well." She turned to Tye. "Do you remember the day when you told me that the gospel can't replace my family, but could show me a new path?"

Tye nodded slowly.

"Well, you were right. I've learned that the gospel will give me brothers and sisters, and you and Meggie have become my sisters."

Tears spilled onto Tye's cheeks. Toni had accepted the gospel. Kyle had not, at least not yet, but that didn't diminish Tye's joy over Toni's decision. Is that how her mission would be? Would she rejoice with others who would accept the gospel and mourn for those who turned away? Could her heart hold such a wild extreme of emotions? Tye's heart felt as if it would burst with such emotions. The sorrow of watching Trapper leave was still embedded into her heart and now she would mourn over her own departure from Toni. And yet, a budding hope emerged. Like the blossoms on the newly planted tree, Tye hoped that her choices would bear fruit.

Pulling Toni close in a fierce embrace, a feeling of deep satisfaction welled up inside of Tye like a bubbling fountain of clear, pristine water. Toni was right. They were sisters. Nothing could change that now.

Meggie joined the embrace and all three girls mingled their tears together as they said a farewell that would last almost two years.

The girls drew apart and Toni gingerly fingered one of the blossoms. She could leave now. She could go home to Idaho and know that a part of her past would remain here, even if she never returned to this spot. She looked at Tye and Meggie. Both girls had tears running down their cheeks. This goodbye was proving harder than Toni had imagined. Her whole life had been filled with goodbyes. She had left Idaho and her mother. Then her father had left her and Oregon. But this goodbye was different. Or was it? Maybe none of her farewells were permanent. After all, she would come back to Corvallis and room with Meggie. She was returning to Idaho and her past. Things would change, but with that change came the possibility of new greetings—new hope.

Toni wiped her eyes. Then she took her friends' hands and squeezed them gently. "In two years, when we're all back together, we'll have to ask the new owners if we can come back here and see how this tree has grown. It will be our reunion."

Both Tye and Meggie nodded, and with wet eyes and cherry blossoms a solemn promise was made.

If you enjoyed this book, please send your positive comments, along with your mailing address to: gift@shellyjohnsonchoong.com by May 30, 2002, and we will send you a free gift.